COLIN AND THE
CONCUBINE

COLIN AND THE
CONCUBINE

DOMHNALL O'DONOGHUE

MERCIER PRESS

MERCIER PRESS
Cork
www.mercierpress.ie

© Domhnall O'Donoghue, 2019

ISBN: 978 1 78117 686 3

10 9 8 7 6 5 4 3 2 1

A CIP record for this title is available from the British Library

All characters and events in this book are entirely fictional. Any resemblance to any person, living or dead, which may occur inadvertently is completely unintentional.

Printed and bound in the EU.

FOR ANGELA STEEN

PROLOGUE

2019

'The outlook is somewhat grim, I'm afraid.'

When Alfred 'Freddie' Saint James received the news that he'd just months to live due to insubordinate kidneys, the one-time local councillor immediately envisaged a day spent guzzling the very thing that had played a role in his undoing: alcohol. The last thing the sixty-seven-year-old foresaw was that he would instead be traipsing up the driveway of his former home to plead with his estranged sibling, Colin, for a lifeline.

Yet that is what transpired.

'A transplant is your best shot of survival,' Dr Collins had earlier advised, moments after dropping the bombshell.

Wearing jeans and an oversized polo shirt, Freddie debated the various ways he could ask Colin for the permanent loan of one of his vital organs. Twenty-five long years had passed since the warring brothers last spoke to each other and Freddie wondered if his brother had managed to forgive him.

Not that he deserved it.

Maybe I went a little over the top at times, he conceded, as his brother's various humiliations raced through his mind. *Although, in my defence, things seem to have worked out well for him in the end. How many fellas would have given their right arm to be married to the best-looking woman in the town?*

Not quite ready to call upon those two loathsome words – 'I'm sorry' – the dying man stopped outside the house and sat on the steps in between two of the four large columns that had always acted as the property's bodyguards. Behind him stood two front doors instead of the original one, thanks to Freddie's outrageous decision following their parents' death to divide the property down the centre. The money he'd received for his half – in addition to his substantial portion of the inheritance – had been nothing short of a godsend at the time. Outside of his brief stint as a councillor, the man had never subscribed to the concept of working for a living.

Throughout his early childhood years, Freddie had been certain that he lived in a palace. Boasting two storeys, the magnificent house had been inspired by the designs of Italian architect Andrea Palladio and was once one of the most photographed properties in the entire country, thanks to his matriarch's success in that blasted housewife competition. He wondered what all those envious plebs who used to stream past the iron gates daily would think of its current, unimpressive state.

He examined the garden, struck by how small and mediocre it now looked in comparison to its halcyon days. Its controversial centrepiece – the rather rude fountain – no longer released water into the basin through the boy's little member. Navan's more conservative brethren would be delighted to learn that, today, moss offered the marble statue some warmth and much-needed cover.

His critique of the property was cut short by a sharp pain on one side of his torso. He placed his unsteady hand over his rib. He was ashamed and embarrassed by how pathetic his kidneys had turned out to be – though, of course, he could admit that the abuse to which he'd subjected them had played no small part in their – and his – impending demise.

With a heavy sigh, Freddie returned to his feet and finally knocked on the door of his ancestral home. He knew Colin was inside. Not only could he smell the delicious home baking, a skill that his brother had inherited from their mother, but in the front room, behind the net curtains, he could also see the television screen airing a match that involved the Meath football team. Freddie had no idea if Colin was a football supporter or not; in truth, there was very little about his brother that he did know, other than that he was accomplished with a mixing bowl. He himself had little interest in the sport. He was never able to appreciate the value of watching a piece of leather being kicked around a field, or understand the sport's ability to reduce so many grown men to tears. In saying that, since entering the world sixty-seven years earlier, Alfred Saint James had never cried once, not so much as a droplet. The closest he came to blubbering had been following his younger brother's birth in 1958.

They would not have been tears of joy.

Aware of Colin's limited hearing, Freddie knocked for a second time, louder and longer. His earlier, rare feelings of vulnerability were waning, replaced with the rage that had long been associated with him.

'Open the bloody door, you deaf moron!'

And just like that, the former councillor's wishes were answered. Before him stood his little brother, whose soft, easy-going face quickly became hijacked by a look of concern when he realised who was at the door.

'Finally.'

Freddie noticed his sister-in-law, Azra, in the kitchen, busy setting the table. Despite her questionable career choices in the past, the fellow had to admit that the Turkish delight was most certainly a thing of beauty – and remained remarkably well-preserved.

Surely she must be over sixty now, he thought, as he watched her place knives and forks on either side of place mats.

'What are you doing here?' Colin asked, instinctively taking a step backwards.

'I don't suppose you have a minute to spare, do you?' Freddie replied, feigning politeness.

'Well, em, I'm … accounts. I'm, em, attending to accounts. So …'

This quivering uncertainty reminded the uninvited guest who had the power in this pairing. Without so much as an explanation, Freddie barged past him, leaving his only brother somewhat unnerved.

'Come on in,' Colin mumbled as he followed him into the kitchen. 'I'll, em, stick the kettle on, shall I?'

1958

ONE

'Smelly pig!'

Around the time his mother became pregnant with her second child, Freddie had developed a habit of calling anybody who annoyed him a 'smelly pig'. When it came to doling out this insult, the freckle-faced six-year-old never paid a blind bit of notice to the person's status in society; everyone from his classmates in school to esteemed members of the clergy became targets, much to his parents' embarrassment.

'Please ignore him, Father. You know what children at his age are like – always testing boundaries.'

The Saint James' doorbell had been exhausted by the volume of angry neighbours calling to the house to complain about Freddie's naughty ways – callers like Lena Gorey, who appeared at their door one day, her angry face the same colour as the new, pink-red lipstick she sported.

'He marched straight up to my four-month-old daughter in her pram and, bold as you like, snatched the hat from her head and threw it into a puddle, shouting, "Smelly pigs don't wear bonnets!" I mean, Mrs Saint James, the world is tough enough without being attacked by a little boy in dungarees! And besides, who uses the word "bonnet" these days?'

The exasperated couple convinced themselves that it was just a phase. Beguiled by the little lad's charms, they sometimes questioned if their neighbours were entirely honest with their version of events – maybe they were jealous or wanted to spice up their humdrum lives by causing a scene?

'I'm sure Alfred was only trying to be friendly. People can be so stiff these days,' Mrs Saint James said to her husband that night as she combed her long, dark hair in front of the vanity table. As the pair readied themselves for bed, they declared Freddie's innocence to each other, arguing that they had the best boy in all of Navan, one who would, in a few months' time, be the best older brother imaginable.

'He'll think all his birthdays have come at once – a younger sibling he can play with and take care of!' Mrs Saint James predicted as she exchanged her comb for the nail clippers and began tending to her husband's fingernails, a task she carried out twice a month. The handsome and well-groomed banker bossed hundreds of staff members about each day at work, so he enjoyed giving his wife full control over him at home.

'You're absolutely right, sweetheart. As always.'

'Let's tell him the good news tomorrow, shall we?' Her excitement was so great, she cut the tip of her dear man's index finger.

***

The following morning, complete with a bandaged finger, Mr Saint James whisked Freddie and his wife away to County Meath's golden Bettystown beach for a dollop of ice cream and a paddle in the nippy Irish Sea. It hadn't crossed the child's mind that there was more to his adoring parents' intentions than it originally seemed – after all, he had only broken one vase and two plates that week, so he was undoubtedly owed this little treat. Therefore, upon hearing the words 'We have a little surprise for you', as they sat on the beach, he assumed that he was going to receive something like a pair of fancy shorts or sandals. It would be just in time for the summer, too.

'What is it?' he demanded, his cheeks now as bright as the red syrup that spiralled around his half-eaten ice cream.

He could see that his parents were equally exhilarated – if not more so – leaving Freddie to wonder if this surprise would be even greater than expected. Perhaps, at long last, they were finally going to present him with the magic flying carpet that he had been requesting since time immemorial.

'Tell me!' he barked, his patience wearing wafer thin.

However, there was no announcement that he was soon set to soar across the seven seas like Aladdin; instead, much to his disgust, he received the cataclysmic news that some good-for-nothing stork was delivering a little brother or sister to the household in four months' time.

'Isn't that just marvellous, Freddie?' his father added, kneeling beside him in the sand. 'Aren't you just tickled pink?'

On the contrary, red was the colour the child identified with the most, and he made absolutely no bones about allowing his true feelings to be known.

'Noooooo!' he roared, tonsils trembling. Not knowing how else to express his discontent, he flung his ice cream at some unsuspecting 'smelly pig' septuagenarian, who was too distracted trying to decode four across in the morning's crossword to duck for cover.

'Tell the stork to give it to another house!' Freddie demanded.

The tantrum continued and for the following few minutes his parents' emotions vacillated between embarrassment and rage.

'You will still be the man of the house, son,' his mother promised.

'Stop screaming this very moment – everybody is looking at us!' his father shouted. 'And pull up your trousers, for heaven's sake!'

This only worsened Freddie's tantrum.

His mother rubbed his back, as if hoping that this would calm him. 'Daddy is sorry, he didn't mean to shout at you – come and give Mummy a hug.'

But the boy's meltdown appeared interminable until an angry seagull – possibly a friend of the offended stork, Freddie later suspected – delivered his own parcel right on top of his head.

'Arrgh!'

Left with no other choice, the distraught parents grabbed their poo-covered offspring and spirited him away. The tissues that Mrs Saint James always kept up her sleeve were put to good use, wiping her son's head clean as they left.

'If he were my son,' a judgemental passer-by commented to the crossword enthusiast, 'I'd place him over my knee and give him a good lashing. That would shut him up, the little devil!'

'That's it! Four across – "Horned tempter"!' the elderly man exclaimed as he scribbled the letters SATAN in the only blank spaces remaining in his puzzle. 'My marbles are not what they used to be. Many thanks!'

For him, at least, the day had suddenly gotten a whole lot better. For the Saint James clan, on the other hand, the day was going from bad to worse.

'He's probably just a little tired,' Mrs Saint James maintained as they placed him, still kicking and screaming, into the back of their black Morris Minor.

Mr Saint James nodded, his nerves frayed from the whole ordeal.

Yes, Freddie was tired – sick and tired of having his authority challenged by unruly feathered creatures like storks and seagulls. He was sure of one thing, anyway, as the Saint Jameses sped away from Bettystown beach: there was only room for three in his nest and he was prepared to go to any lengths to ensure that things remained the way they were.

But how would he protect the status quo?

And with that thought, the tantrum ended. The child had a plan to come up with – one that would require concentration.

Much to his parents' delight, calm was finally restored.

For the time being.

TWO

In Istanbul, some 2,300 miles to the south-east of Navan, Azra Demir was a little girl with big ambitions. There was only one thing in life that she loved more than her beauty, and that was when others complimented it. Even though she was just three years of age, the youngster had become used to people gathering around her, cooing over her thick, brown hair or praising her striking almond eyes. Her neighbours often noted that she was the mirror image of her late mother. Azra, however, was not in a position to agree or disagree – aside from a single, tatty photograph pinned to one of the cupboards, she had never seen the woman who, according to those who knew her, was 'the most beautiful and gentle woman in all of Turkey'.

'She held you in her arms for a short moment,' her only brother, Yusuf, often told her, 'kissed you on your tiny nose, then left to be with Allah in paradise.'

Rather than being comforted by Yusuf's memory of this brief encounter with her mother, young Azra was furious that she'd been cast aside in favour of this Allah person who everyone kept fussing over.

He could hardly be as beautiful as me! she thought.

Many of the people who lived alongside the Demir family in Istanbul's central and traffic-clogged Eminönü neighbourhood felt obligated to look after her, seeing as her *baba* had reneged on practically all of his parental responsibilities. Instead, he preferred spending his days getting into various scrapes around the city. Recently, Yusuf was also rarely around. The ten-year-old had been forced to abandon his childhood in favour of the workforce, to ensure that the bills delivered to their run-down house were paid and that at least some food was put on the table.

The care that these neighbours insisted on showing Azra

during her early years was extremely commendable, particularly given that she was quite a difficult girl. Declining to share was a common occurrence, as was refusing to leave her bed or part with her cracked mirror. They had first-hand experience of their own children thinking that they were the centre of the universe, but there was something different about Azra; she just didn't fit into her humble surroundings. Even though it was too early to tell, the women worried that Azra would take after her father when it came to morals.

'I pity the man who marries you,' her neighbours often joked.

In her defence, Azra felt that, aside from her beauty, there was little for which she should be thankful and so she had no problem expressing her frustrations out loud. What with her mother's death, a father who was never around, and her brother's round-the-clock work schedule, all the youngster had was a filthy hovel in which she was often forced to remain all alone.

Her only joy came when, each night, she drifted off into a deep slumber where she was whisked away from the noisy, always-under-construction Eminönü neighbourhood to be worshipped by knights and kings.

Someday, she vowed. *Someday*.

THREE

A ritual Freddie enjoyed more than anything was his daily bath.

With the tub positioned upstairs in the main bathroom overlooking the apple trees in the back garden, he had always found it an inspiring place to plot. A year earlier, while soaking in the enamelled tub, Freddie had concocted a plan to destroy the grand piano after overhearing a suggestion that he should start taking lessons. Shortly afterwards, it was from this bubbly kingdom that Freddie had resolved to do away with Lucy, the family dog, as a means of ending her insistence on barking throughout the night.

The solution to his latest pickle, however, was proving harder to reach. But, ever-confident in his abilities, Freddie trusted that it would come.

As his tired mother cleaned the dirt from beneath his finger-nails, the boy scoured the dark recesses of his mind to find the most suitable method by which to free the family from the unwanted and ever-growing burden inside his mother.

'You adore playing in the garden, don't you, my darling,' his mother remarked, finally clearing the last of the dirt from his nails. She was secretly dreading checking on the current state of her beautiful petunias. 'Imagine, you'll soon have a little brother or sister who I'm sure will only be delighted to join you on your little adventures outside! Why don't you put your hand on my belly and tell them where your favourite place in the gardens is? The orchard? The sundial? The labyrinth?'

Freddie pretended not to hear her request. By now, he was beyond exhausted by his parents' endless suggestions that he try to bond with his unborn sibling by talking to it or singing to it or similar nonsense. Despite the usually calming influence of the yellow rubber duck bobbing up and down on the water's surface, he was starting to feel agitated again. He had to take action before it was too late.

But how?

After so much success, was he, at long last, being forced to admit that his deviousness had limitations?

Fat chance.

'I hope you were kind to all your little friends on the patio this morning, my darling,' his mother continued. 'I don't want to find any more tortured snails and worms on the terrace furniture. We are all God's creatures, remember.'

Freddie smiled, remembering this morning's massacre across the grey paving slabs. Suddenly his whizzing mind had its 'Eureka' moment. It was inspired. He would take his lead from his favourite pastime: the squishing and squashing of the garden's insects – except, on this occasion, rather than his clenched fist, it would be his mother who would do the squishing!

'Thank you, Mummy.'

'For what?'

'Oh, nothing,' he replied, shoving the rubber duck underwater.

His mother smiled at his obvious happiness and couldn't resist giving her angelic child a big sloppy kiss on his wet cheeks. 'Who is the sweetest boy in all of Navan?' she cooed.

After a while, his mother lifted a wrinkled Freddie out of the bath and patted him down with his favourite fluffy towel. Freddie stood millimetres from the mirror – his dark, angular haircut contrasting with the gilt of the faux-antique frame. He released a broad, toothy smile.

'May I have some of the biscuits you just baked, Mummy?' he asked as she dressed him in his new, yellow pyjamas, knowing that she would be unable to resist giving in to her darling boy's demands. And after all his hard work planning, he felt he deserved a little treat.

FOUR

Azra, who was also eating a biscuit, sat perched in her *baba*'s strong, tattooed arms – enjoying one of the rare times that he had brought a treat to the house.

'I came into some money recently,' he explained as he carried her outside to enjoy the sunshine and watch the never-ending traffic speed past them.

His daughter was impressed that he hadn't fallen asleep on the kitchen floor or across the toilet seat as he usually did when he returned home. He'd even managed to shave his stubble for once – he looked so young! Better again, the disgusting smell of alcohol was also absent. She hated it when her father came home drunk; he had the manners of an animal when intoxicated – burping, hiccupping and, quite regularly, wetting himself. It was unforgivable.

Today, her feelings for her *baba* were altered. As he held her close to his warm, furry chest, basking in the hot weather, she truly believed that this man loved her – even if he had yet to compliment the red ribbon in her hair, a recent present from one of her neighbours. Such intimate moments between the pair were rare, granted, but when they came, Azra quickly forgot about those long days alone with nothing else to entertain her but her own imagination. How she wished this day would never end.

When five men and a woman initially began to approach them a few minutes later, Azra thought they were friends of her *baba* coming to visit. Surely *they* will praise her red ribbon, she predicted. Despite the crumbs on her ugly, hand-me-down dress, the girl was satisfied that she looked a picture. What's more, she had just learned a new song and decided that she would perform it for them – her beauty coupled with her angelic singing voice would, Azra was certain, melt the hearts of *baba*'s friends.

Maybe after I finish the biscuit, she mused.

Before she could enjoy another mouthful, however, a dark cloud covered the sun – foreboding what was about to come. Her first suspicion that things weren't as they seemed came when she realised that the faces of the approaching six were not awash with the usual smiles that she'd come to take for granted; instead, they appeared angry and aggressive, and unwilling to heap praise where it was obviously deserved.

The second oddity was the knives each revealed from their pockets. Perhaps they were planning to assist her *baba* in preparing some meat for dinner that evening? He could use the help, seeing as, according to Yusuf, he had never gotten the hang of cooking since taking over from their deceased *anne*.

The third and final clue that the gang who had now encircled them were not friends came when her *baba* held her out towards them, as if she were a shield – an act that led her to drop the remains of the biscuit onto the street. As she fought back the tears, Azra longed to be back in her house, looking into her cracked mirror and brushing her hair. '*Baba*, I want to go inside,' she pleaded, trying to squirm out of his arms.

Suddenly, one of the strange men roughly grabbed her and flung her into the lone bush that grew beside their front door.

Heaped in a ball, dazed, Azra couldn't open her eyes. She could just hear sounds – principally her father's voice yelling and roaring. His cries, she could tell, were different from what she and her brother had become used to. It was as if he were in pain.

I do hope he isn't hurting, Azra thought, as she drifted off into deep unconsciousness. *Well, maybe a little.* After all, he hadn't told her how pretty her red ribbon looked in her hair – and that was just rude!

FIVE

Sometimes described by bitter-lipped neighbours as garish and over-the-top, the extensive renovations made to modernise the Saint James' ancestral home had taken three long years to complete, such was the ambitious scale of their plans. The fact that the new lady of the house insisted on overseeing every minute detail of the design – inside and out – had not made the process any easier for the builders. It was a good job that halfway through its revamp, Mr Saint James had inherited a sizeable fortune from a spinster aunt; otherwise the project might never have been finished. Even though he received a more than generous salary at the bank – along with a downright scandalous end-of-year bonus – his wife had a special gift for making budgets multiply in size, so Aunt Tilda's untimely death truly had been a blessing. When the renovations had finally been completed – just a month shy of Freddie's arrival – the couple agreed that it had all been worth it.

There was only one problem that concerned Mrs Saint James, particularly when her pride and joy began walking: their beautiful home stood within spitting distance of a busy and dangerous road that carried plenty of speeding, Dublin-bound traffic. As the years passed, her anxiety grew, despite the addition of a twelve-foot boundary wall.

With a brother or sister to kill, Freddie decided to use his mother's Achilles heel to his advantage. He waited for an opportune moment before, one afternoon, escaping from the house and deftly scaling the steel gates like a squirrel and positioning himself on the other side. Part one of his sure-fire plan was complete.

Now for part two.

Freddie filled his lungs before releasing a roar that people typically saved for an All-Ireland final.

'Help, Mummy! Help!'

Inside, on the chaise longue, a somewhat groggy Mrs Saint James awoke from an unexpected afternoon nap. Hearing Freddie's cries, she became filled with confusion and alarm.

'Freddie, my darling! Where are you? What is the matter?'

She shuffled to the sitting-room window where the sight in front of her rendered her heart on the verge of an attack.

'Freddie! Get back in here this very minute!' she roared, her life – and his – flashing before her eyes. Petrified that Freddie was on the threshold of meeting his ruin at the hands of some unforgiving Ford Anglia, her protective instinct got the better of her and she raced outside. Barefooted, she bolted down the driveway, her desperate state leaving her oblivious to the thin wire that Freddie had discreetly fastened between the base of the fountain on which the weak-bladdered statue stood and one of the oak trees lining the driveway.

Please let it work, please let it work, Freddie thought, watching the scene unfold.

As she closed in on the wire, he hoped that it was securely tied – and invisible; the last thing he wanted was for her to see it and jump over it like a hurdler in the Olympic Games. However, his concerns were unnecessary: in her panic, the poor woman never saw a thing and came crashing down, landing slap bang on the bothersome bump.

Squish, squash. Just like the garden insects.

A devilish grin spread from ear to ear. While the sight of his near-unconscious mother was somewhat disagreeable to witness, Freddie reminded himself that he had been left with no other option and so put to bed any remorse.

He climbed the gate again and, as he gallantly came to her rescue, he could not help but become transfixed by the tiny stream of blood that leaked from his unfortunate victim. It reminded him of the colourful spinning top he had seen in the shop window of

Tierney's Newsagent's a few days earlier. Maybe if he was extra good between now and his upcoming seventh birthday, a mere six and a half weeks away, he might receive such a gift?

I'll tell Mummy to get it for me when she wakes up.

SIX

It took Azra the best part of a week to wake up following the brutal attack on her father. When she finally opened her eyes, the youngster was surprised to discover that she was not on her own lumpy bed, but a far more comfortable alternative. In fact, her bed was just one of many crammed into a long, narrow room. All the others also had children lying on them, most of whom wore bandages or had tubes attached to their arms or noses.

'You've decided to join us once again.'

Azra tried to turn her head to see who was speaking to her but it hurt too much.

'Don't make any sudden movements, angel,' the voice, which belonged to a nurse, advised. 'You've been badly injured, so it's important that you rest as much as possible.'

As she spoke, the nurse – who had now moved into Azra's line of sight – scribbled something on a piece of paper attached to a clipboard that hung from the bottom of the bed. After she finished writing, the nurse placed an object that resembled a thin glass pen into her mouth.

'Fantastic,' she nodded after removing the glass pen and stepping closer to Azra. 'You'll be back to your cheeky self in no time!'

After she adjusted the pillows, the nurse delicately squeezed the young patient's hand. 'There's somebody here who'd like to see you, but I'll only let him in if you promise not to move or talk too much, okay?'

'I promise,' Azra agreed, her heart lifting at the thought of seeing her *baba* again. She had a sudden flashback to the altercation and felt a massive pang of guilt for wishing him ill for not complimenting her ribbon. She needed to be more patient with those who didn't immediately shower her with praise.

I will say sorry when he's here, Azra resolved.

But it was not her father who sat down beside her. It was Yusuf. His usually upbeat demeanour had vanished, replaced by a look that made him appear twenty years old rather than the ten years he'd currently lived.

'Where's *baba*?' she demanded, looking expectantly towards the entrance.

'That bastard?' her sibling muttered, eyes averted.

'Yusuf!' Why was her brother calling him such horrible names?

'You're too young to understand, Azra, but, one day you will realise that it's for the best that he is out of our lives.'

Yes, she had received a wallop to the head, but despite this, Azra was sure in her heart that she would never agree with what her brother was suggesting. Nobody knew more than she did that he was bestial most of the time and that it was unlikely he would feature on any 'Father of the Year' lists in the near future, but she couldn't understand why her brother suddenly wanted to turn them into orphans. Maybe he had also suffered some trauma to the head and wasn't thinking correctly? Should she call that kind nurse back and get her to place that glass thingy into Yusuf's mouth?

'I want to see him,' she ordered, looking expectantly over his shoulder towards the door.

'Azra, you don't understand; *baba* is dead.'

As her brother talked about how it was 'just the two of us now' and promised to look after her and protect her, Azra attempted to process what she had just been told. Without thinking, she closed her tear-filled eyes and did what everyone else seemed to do in these situations.

She prayed to Allah.

The young supplicant begged that her brother's claims were nothing more than a tall tale and that when she opened her eyes again, her *baba* would be standing beside them, holding a delicious slice of *baklava* and telling Azra that she was the most beautiful princess in all the world. On second thoughts, she decided that there was no need for any treats or compliments: she just wanted her family to be together again.

Please, Allah, please.

Much to her dismay, when she opened her eyes, she saw that it was still just her brother by her side. Her prayers had gone unanswered.

First Allah had stolen her *anne*, and now He had taken her *baba*. She turned away from Yusuf, sobbing, and as she drifted off to sleep she thought: *I hate you, Allah. You have no heart.*

It would take several years before Azra managed to piece back together her own, broken one.

SEVEN

Mrs Saint James did not want to know the particulars of her unborn child's condition. There was a beating heart within and, for her, that was enough.

There was still hope.

'Your baby has experienced a severe trauma – you must prepare yourself for the fact that it might have a disability,' the soft-spoken Dr Higgins informed her shortly after she awoke in the Rotunda Hospital the morning after her fall.

'And we'll love him all the more,' the expectant mother vowed.

Since the horrific events, her only wish was that her second son – for she had always known it to be another boy – would survive the accident. Anything else, she and her husband would 'embrace with courage and fortitude'.

The medical team decided that Mrs Saint James should remain in hospital until the birth, an arrangement that allowed her plenty of time to reflect upon the accident. Initially, the facts of what happened were hazy. The only thing that had stood out in her mind was a sense that her feet had hit something as she raced down the driveway. A thin, horizontal, red mark near the bottom of her shin backed up her claims. Her husband suggested that, in her panic, she'd probably tripped on her shoelaces, but once she recalled that she hadn't been wearing shoes at the time, she demanded that he search the area. She had a terrible hunch that the whole affair might not have been an accident after all.

Could it be that her darling son, the light of her life, had caused the accident? While children deal with crisis situations in a variety of ways, he did seem unusually thrilled by her current state in hospital and kept enquiring whether the nursery could now be turned into a games room, seeing as no baby was going to be using it.

Please let me be mistaken. Please, please, please! she begged.

Unfortunately, the wire, which Mr Saint James later discovered hidden under Freddie's bed, confirmed her suspicions.

'He tried to kill his unborn brother,' she said out loud, unaware that one of the nurses was within earshot. (A note was soon made by the concerned nurse to up this patient's dose of medication.)

Like any mother, at first, she tried desperately to justify his actions.

He probably stills bears the trauma of his birth when the umbilical cord was wrapped around his neck.

She even attempted to hold herself accountable.

Why didn't I listen to his teacher when she advised us to seek professional assistance for his temper? And all those warnings from the neighbours! How could I have been so foolish and naive?

However, as the hours passed, she kept returning to one conclusion: Freddie was wicked – nothing more, nothing less. For the first time in her near seven years as a parent, she felt something that shocked her to the core.

Hatred for her son.

If he has caused harm to this baby …

It turned out that she did not have to wait much longer to discover the ramifications of the fall for, three weeks later, Mrs Saint James gave birth to a seemingly healthy boy, despite his being two months premature. Other than the fact that his early arrival meant that his weight was somewhat on the lean side – just shy of six pounds – miraculously, everything else appeared to be fine and dandy.

'You have a resilient child here,' Dr Higgins informed the proud parents after giving the new arrival an examination.

Before the mother and child were discharged, however, one final test was administered: a newborn hearing screening. This didn't go quite as well as Dr Higgins had hoped. 'There seems to be a little damage to the nerves of his inner ears, I'm afraid,' he informed them.

'He's not deaf, is he?' Mr Saint James asked.

'Not completely, and it's tough to tell at this early stage, but it's likely that he'll be quite hard of hearing.'

As the men discussed the ins and outs of the prognosis, Mrs Saint James just cradled the latest addition to their family.

'While you might not be able to hear as well as everyone else, my darling,' she whispered, forgetting that her words were falling on somewhat deaf ears, 'I promise you we will provide you with everything that you lack.'

At that moment, she announced that she would be calling the boy Colin – a name that she knew was a derivative of Nicholas, meaning 'Victory of the People'. She was determined that, despite his shaky start, her tiny combatant would eventually emerge triumphant.

'He's going to be a winner, that much I know,' she pledged.

We'll see about that, Smelly Pig, Freddie thought, as he sat alone in the corner of the private room, livid that his master plan had – like his mother a few weeks earlier – fallen flat.

But he knew there would be plenty of time to rectify that.

1967

EIGHT

'I couldn't be prouder of *both* my sons.'

Colin had thought long and hard about what he wanted for his ninth birthday. However, not even in his wildest dreams did he imagine that his wish would come true.

That his brother would be his friend.

But, as Leslie, a cheery interviewer from *Woman's Way* magazine, probed his mother – the recently crowned winner of the inaugural Housewife of the Year competition – about the secrets to a successful home, the boy was ecstatic to learn that Freddie was joining him and their parents. Not only that, but his mother, who had rarely spoken a kind word about his older sibling before entering the competition, was now gushing with praise. He even noticed that Freddie was, for once, smiling, clearly uplifted by the kind sentiments their mother was sharing.

'They are different, my boys, but I love them equally. And aren't they so handsome, dressed in their chinos and shirts!'

Birthday wishes really do come true, Colin thought, as he exchanged a smile with his brother.

With the sun shining down on them, they sat around a cast-iron table in the middle of their patio in the back garden, chatting away about Mrs Saint James' success in the competition, which had grabbed the attention of the entire country. Sponsored by McDonnells, ESB and the aforementioned magazine, the prestigious event had seen hundreds upon hundreds of housewives pitted against each other in regional heats across every county in Ireland, before culminating in a tense, televised final in Dublin's swanky Shelbourne hotel.

On the night, the six finalists had been tasked with wowing the judges with their culinary and conversational skills, and as a testament to the standard in the competition, two winners had emerged – Navan's own Mary Saint James and Kay Johnson from

Limerick. While the two winners walked away with a generous £500 cheque and a split-level cooker each, the real prize was the immediate fame that they were both afforded. This magazine interview and subsequent family photoshoot were just the tips of the iceberg. The winning duo had already charmed the country on *The Late Late Show*, RTÉ's top-rated chat show.

There had also been radio slots, gala parties and book deals. Since the victory a month earlier, the housewives had come to enjoy a celebrity status on a par with All-Ireland winners. Each day, proud neighbours and strangers called to the Saint James' house, eager to shake the hands of the victorious housewife. (Mrs Brady, who had been pipped at the post by Mrs Saint James in the Meath heats, couldn't understand what the fuss was about. She was adamant that her own soufflé had been far superior to that made by her one-time friend.) Colin adored his mother but never more so than these past few weeks – and, apart from the mean-spirited Mrs Brady, the entire nation felt the same.

'I think it's time someone blew out their candles, don't you?' Leslie teased when she saw Mr Saint James emerge from the kitchen carrying a strawberry-covered Victoria sponge. 'Is this one of your creations, Mrs Saint James?'

Mrs Saint James smiled and turned to Colin. 'It's *his* creation, isn't that right, Colin? As God is my witness, Leslie, this little man is even teaching me things in the kitchen these days.' She elbowed her husband as he placed the masterpiece on the table. 'Isn't that right, Daddy?'

He nodded vigorously. 'It sure is! I'd better watch the waistline with you two about!'

Colin loved seeing how proud his father was of his mother; in fact, it was he who had entered her in the competition in the first place – much to her mock annoyance. If anyone knew how talented she was around the kitchen, it was Colin's father.

'Don't forget to make a wish, my darling,' his mother reminded him.

Without further delay, the young baker eyed up the candle-lit cake in front of him, took a deep breath and blew the nine candles out as the others clapped in encouragement. After the cheering subsided, a photographer herded everyone to the front of the house and instructed the proud parents, the 'man-of-the-hour' and his older brother to stand beside the fountain in the front garden.

When it came to his looks, Colin had received Mrs Saint James' piercing blue eyes and dark hair, and his father's delicate nose. This combination meant that, rather fortuitously, Colin had been gifted his parents' best features while avoiding their less winning ones – his father's unsightly rosacea, for instance.

'Say cheese!' the photographer ordered. As he furiously clicked his camera, he couldn't help but envy the Saint James family.

They have it all – including a cheeky fountain!

'Right,' Leslie eventually said to the photographer, 'Colin's friends are going to be arriving any minute, so I think we should let him go and enjoy his special day.'

As Mr Saint James led the pair towards their car, Colin spotted his father discreetly handing his brother some money. Maybe Freddie was planning to organise some birthday treat or other?

This day is getting better and better!

Colin's mother pulled him close. 'On the day you were born, my darling,' she loudly said into his ear, 'I promised that you would be a winner. But, often, I think that it was me who God has made victorious since that day – and I'm not talking about the Housewife of the Year competition – I'm talking about the fact that He has given me the greatest son imaginable.'

'Sons,' Colin corrected.

'Yes,' Freddie teased, walking past them in the direction of the house, 'don't forget about me, Mummy.'

Their mother didn't even attempt to keep up the pretence from the interview now that Leslie was gone; her public façade slipped entirely away. She simply ignored Freddie's statement, as if he had said nothing. As if he wasn't even present.

Instead, her attention remained on her favoured son. 'Colin, I can't believe you made this cake all by yourself – it looks absolutely scrumptious, you talented little fellow,' she praised. 'What did you wish for?'

'It has already come true.'

'Are you going to share your secret with me?'

Colin turned towards Freddie but was disappointed to see that he had already disappeared into the house. Knowing that it was bad luck to reveal the particulars of his request, the birthday boy remained tight-lipped. Still, he couldn't help but steal a glance towards Freddie's bedroom window, where the sullen fifteen-year-old now stood, lighting a cigarette.

That my brother will be my friend – not just today but forever and always.

For his eighth birthday, Colin had wished for proper hearing like everyone else, and when he received a new, more advanced aid a week later, his hearing – while far from perfect – had vastly improved, thereby making him realise that birthday wishes could actually come true. As a result, expectations were sky high this year.

People were now starting to arrive for his party. Using the distraction of Mrs Brady informing his mother of the (recently invented) dietary requirements for her son, Raymond, Colin rushed into the house and climbed towards his brother's bedroom, a slice of cake now in hand. His gentle knocking went unanswered, but just as he was about to admit defeat and return outside to his guests, Freddie finally opened the door.

'Is that for me?' Freddie asked, examining the cake.

'Yes! I thought you might like some!'

'Oh, I would.'

'I could bake you something if you want. Just tell me what your favourite cake or pastry is!'

'Aw, aren't you sweet, lil bro,' he enthused, popping a strawberry from the slice of cake into his mouth.

'Colin!' his mother roared from the hallway below them, clearly annoyed. 'Your friends have all arrived! Come down at once.' She only ever used that high-pitched tone with him when Colin attempted to befriend his older sibling.

'Coming, Mummy!' he answered reluctantly.

Freddie sneered. 'You better not get on the wrong side of her, especially seeing as she's had a few sherries.'

'Has she?'

'And you know what happened that other time she was three sheets to the wind.'

'What happened?'

'Let's just say you wouldn't have suffered problems with your hearing if she'd opted for the Ballygowan!'

Colin was totally confused by what his brother was charging her with – *he must have gotten the story mixed up?* – but, ever the optimist, he decided to focus on the fact that this exchange was lasting longer than anything he had experienced in the past.

'Colin!' their mother roared again, her voice becoming increasingly vexed.

'Let me take a quick mouthful before you run off,' Freddie whispered, reaching for the slice of cake.

Just as Colin was about to look skyward and thank whomever had answered his birthday wish, he felt a whack to his face. Eyes covered, he only worked out what had happened when he felt the sponge falling from the tip of his nose onto his freshly polished shoes.

'Not quite to my liking, I'm afraid. See you the next time she wants to pretend to the world that she's the perfect mother,' Freddie quipped as he slammed the door shut.

Stunned, Colin remained rooted to the spot until the sound of his mother calling him again finally woke him from his stupor.

'I'll be down in a minute,' he answered, voice breaking, before disappearing into the bathroom.

In the end it was closer to twenty minutes – the length of time it took for him to clear the cake from his face and for his tears to subside.

NINE

Surrounded by many friends and admirers, Azra sashayed into her teenage years safe in the knowledge that she was growing more beautiful by the day. Not that she had much time to reflect on the fact as, at thirteen, she joined the workforce in one of Istanbul's most exclusive establishments – the Pera Palace Hotel.

'I've had to call in many favours to get you this job, Azra; don't let me down,' Yusuf warned her as they walked towards the hotel on her first day. Thanks to the generosity of some manager called Mustafa Bey, he had already been in employment there for a couple of years.

'Yes, *kardeş* – we have discussed this a thousand times!'

Since the hotel hired him, she had noticed that her sibling had adopted a voice that was far different from everyone else's in their neighbourhood. He now structured his sentences in a funny, formalised fashion. She had not teased him for this new practice because, secretly, she found it quite enchanting.

At long last, I'm no longer the only member of this community with some ambition! she thought.

As she crossed the threshold of the staff's entrance at the back of the hotel, Azra was rendered speechless by the refined world into which she entered. Amidst great pomp and ceremony, the luxurious property had held a grand opening ball to welcome its first guests over seventy years earlier, many of whom were the glamorous passengers of the Orient Express. Literary sleuth Agatha Christie, for example, had been a long-term resident in the establishment and she, like everyone else who crossed its threshold, praised the blend of neoclassical, art nouveau and oriental design found throughout the premises. Now, years later, its reputation was not just celebrated in Turkey; it was revered around the globe. And this was where the teenager would begin her working life.

Azra's enthusiasm for her new job quickly faded, however, when she discovered that her duties would simply consist of throwing the remains of the guests' meals into the bins outside before passing the plates to the kitchen porter for the first of three washes. She was further disappointed when she discovered that she was not allowed to talk to the stylish and elegant women with their lovely frocks. Where was the fun in that?

It could be much, much worse, she reminded herself every day as she flung leftover *dolma* or untouched *kayisi tatlisi* into the bins. *One day, someone will be cleaning my gold-plated dishes – maybe even that cretin, Mustafa Bey. Actually, I wouldn't want his greasy, spotty skin anywhere near my beautiful tableware!*

Her brother might have waxed lyrical about the hotel manager, but she could not see anything pleasant or good-natured about him. He had an extremely disagreeable way of breathing, almost as if his pinched nose housed a selection of wild animals eager to escape. Worst of all was the way that he continuously hovered around her brother with a sickening grin etched across his repulsive face. If she were in Yusuf's position, she would have told him to hightail it a long time ago. Fortunately for the siblings, Yusuf was far more patient and accommodating.

Nonetheless, despite her misgivings about the boss, the teenager kept her counsel and, every night, when they left the hotel, Yusuf was relieved to discover that his self-involved sister had managed to stay out of trouble.

However, her good behaviour, like the Ottoman Empire, was not to last.

TEN

Mr Saint James' domestic empire had collapsed entirely. In between the glitz and glamour of social engagements and media commitments, he often caught his wife – the country's premier housewife – staring at the oak tree in the front garden. The wire used by Freddie for his horrific deed all those years ago had left not just a figurative mark on the family's life, but also a literal one around the bark.

'Why do you keep looking at the tree?' he asked her one evening; he would have assumed that a constant reminder was the last thing she wanted.

'Because I don't want to forget what he did,' she tartly replied. 'If I forget, then I will forgive – and that must never happen.'

This singular and uncompassionate mindset was taking a significant toll on their relationship. He had naively entered her into the housewife competition in an effort to unite his clan when he'd realised that her views of Freddie were worsening. It was obvious to the blind that her inclusion of Freddie in the various interviews was simply a way for his wife to present an image of domestic harmony to the country – yet he had hoped that, eventually, these interactions would yield dividends.

Put simply, they had not.

Freddie had played along, of course – though this was mainly due to the many financial bribes Mr Saint James had offered him – but the banker could see that the relationship between mother and elder son had, if anything, only worsened. As a result, he worried for Freddie. He could see that the teenager was suffering because of her rejection. He'd lost count of the number of donations he'd been forced to make to his son's boarding school as a way of smoothing over the various scrapes the teenager had gotten himself into practically every other day. Mr Saint James wrote to Freddie often and told his own lies, like how '*everyone* is thinking of you'. The sad truth was that Mr Saint James knew that his life partner would not change her mind about their eldest son – she had always been unyielding in her views once they were set. Ironically, it was one of the reasons he had fallen in love with her in the first place. However, the love he once had for that stunning, headstrong young woman – whose father had first introduced them to each other at the Meath Banker's Christmas Ball twenty years earlier – was now on life support.

***

Without knowing what else to do, a month after Colin's birthday Mr Saint James invited the family doctor to the house for supper, hoping that – in between the cocktails and the *hors-d'oeuvres* – the physician might be able to have a quiet word with his wife about the whole situation.

'If you'll allow me to offer you a little advice, Mary,' Dr Cassells said as they enjoyed the warm September air on the terrace on the evening of the soirée, 'write a letter to Freddie. You don't have to give it to him – it is simply a way to free yourself of the anger and resentment that you still clearly harbour for him. If you don't mind me saying, it will be Colin who'll lose out in the long run.'

Always the perfect housewife and hostess, Mrs Saint James smiled, at the same time making a mental note to stay clear of the Martinis that night lest she found herself telling Dr Cassells – and her blabber-mouth husband – what she really thought of them.

'You are always on the clock, Richard!' she joked, with perfect passive-aggressive condescension. 'Now, let's go in and have some of my delicious prawn cocktail. It's a new recipe!'

That night, however, sleep would not come for Mrs Saint James – and it had nothing to do with the shellfish whirling around in her stomach. As she tossed and turned, Dr Cassells' warning about

Colin losing out kept spinning around in her mind. Consumed with guilt, she eventually crept out of the bedroom and made her way to the kitchen.

For the sake of my darling Colin alone.

Pen in hand, she started pouring years and years of bitterness onto the page in front of her. In extraordinary detail, she described the horrific events surrounding her 'accident' and how foolish she had felt for thinking that her firstborn could challenge Jesus in terms of piousness.

And while you deprived your brother of his full faculties, it was you who played the martyr, even having the audacity to call him a 'smelly pig' while he slept soundly in his crib, one line read.

As the ink flowed from the pen, so too did the sweat from her brow. Rather than freeing herself from the shackles of the past, the Housewife of the Year found herself feeling even more appalled than ever. If anything, seeing Freddie's deeds writ large on the page made his actions all the more real and unforgivable.

It's the most unnatural thing in the world for a mother to say these three words to their son, but it's how I feel: I hate you.

Shocked at the venom that was escaping from her every pore, Mrs Saint James flung the pen from her hand and shoved the letter into a crack at the back of one of the presses.

I'm sorry, Colin, she thought moments later, as she sipped on a restorative brandy. *I know how much you want to bond with your brother, but it's just something that I cannot encourage.*

And, as Mr Saint James could attest, she was sure to never renege on her word.

ELEVEN

Azra had to renege on her word.

She had been employed at the hotel for a couple of months, and the teenager prided herself on her ability to adhere to all the rules that her brother had set out – as tricky as she often found it.

However, today was an emergency.

She had been experiencing terrible cramps for the past few days – a sure-fire sign that her period was due, an experience that was still new to her. Based on the severity of the pain on that Wednesday evening, she had imagined that it was hell-bent on coming with as much fanfare as the Pera Palace Hotel witnessed all those decades ago when its first Orient Express visitors had arrived. She desperately needed to flee the building and return home to lie down, but this was something she was reluctant to do without the blessing of her brother. She wouldn't want anyone to accuse her of abandoning her duties – as deserving as they were of abandonment.

It was only when she decided to track her brother down that the teenager realised she had no idea where he was. Azra knew that he served as one of the hotel's many doormen, but when she peeked through the door window from the staff-only hallway and into the reception area, she could not see him at his usual posting.

Maybe he's on a break? she thought, although that would have been unusual, seeing as they both started their shift just an hour earlier.

She returned to the kitchen to ask the other staff members if they knew of his whereabouts. The clear majority of the kitchen staff were men, and most of them had made little effort to engage with her on any level since she'd joined the fold – other than shoving dirty plates into her hands.

'Excuse me, Onur, could you tell me where I might find Yusuf? He's not in his usual spot at the door.'

'That's not his *usual* place, little woman,' he spat out in a manner so scornful that Azra wished she had kept her mouth shut – cramps suddenly seemed the least of her concerns now. Onur liked to think of himself as a kindred spirit to Elvis Presley – in truth, his ridiculous black quiff was the only similarity this talentless, charmless man shared with The King. 'Do you want to know where his "usual" place is? And the reason that you, a little scrounger with your family history, have obtained employment in this refined establishment?'

'Stop, Onur,' one of his colleagues urged. 'She's only a child.'

'I don't care anymore,' Azra interrupted, trying not to get angry that they were using her upbringing against her. From the corner of her eye, she could see that the dirty plates that she was expected to clear had now developed into quite a substantial pile. For the first time since starting work at the Pera Palace Hotel, she longed to be knee-deep in grime.

'Don't care? Well, aren't you a selfish sister?' Onur attacked, now lowering himself so that his face was in line with hers. 'You don't care about all the sacrifices your brother has made so that he, and now you, can work here? You don't care that at least twice a week, your brother has to call to Mustafa Bey's office to keep him happy? You don't care that, as a result, your brother can barely walk?'

'That's enough, Onur,' the head chef ordered. 'Get back to work – you as well, Azra.'

She had never spoken to the head chef in her short time there but, at that moment, she wanted to hug and thank him for saving her from all this unpleasantness.

As she returned to her workstation, she reminded herself to have a conversation with Yusuf that night; if he was having difficulties walking, as Onur implied, he must be more careful lifting all those suitcases – they could cause him a serious injury.

Once back at her station, Azra realised that her monthlies had made an appearance during her confrontation with that ogre. As finely tailored as her apron was, it hadn't the ability to conceal her bloodied embarrassment.

Discreetly, she reached for one of the plates and spilt the remnants of a bowl of soup down her apron.

Now it looked as if she were a girl who was guilty of clumsiness and not of nature.

TWELVE

Colin's classroom, the walls of which were decorated with impressive projects about the Boyne River and the Hill of Tara, enjoyed a lofty status amongst teachers and pupils alike owing to it being the largest room in St Enda's Primary School – a school Colin was not supposed to have attended.

It had originally been assumed that he would follow in the footsteps of his older brother – and indeed those of his father and grandfather – by enrolling in St Finian's Boarding School in Westmeath. However, the thought of only seeing her darling child every second Sunday had sent Mrs Saint James into a frenzy, so to keep the peace it was decided that he would be educated locally instead.

Colin had ended up being more than happy with this arrangement, particularly as it was in St Enda's, three years earlier, that the youngster had first laid eyes on the prettiest girl he was sure had ever existed: Mamie May Mooney. She was the only pupil who remembered to speak to him slowly and loudly to ensure that he could understand what was being said. From the get-go, Colin knew that he wanted to spend his life with this ethereal redhead.

Not everyone held Mamie May in the same high regard, unfortunately – particularly their kind but exasperated teacher, Master Cantwell. Extremely impressionable, not even the most generous of souls would have described Mamie May as bright.

In any case, it wasn't her brain that appealed to Colin; it was her heart.

The classroom also had access to a storeroom, a place where the principal stocked all that was important to the school, including the often-discussed boxes of biscuits and sweets, delicacies that were saved for auspicious occasions like communions or confirmations. Under no circumstances was anyone allowed to enter the storeroom without authorisation from the principal.

One crisp October morning, news reached the school that Master Cantwell had been the victim of a bout of pneumonia (due to his reluctance to wear scarves and gloves, Mrs Saint James asserted, while she force-fed Colin chicken soup later that afternoon). Nothing excited the children more than when Master Cantwell found himself in a convalescent state. While the cat's away ...

That morning, as Colin, Mamie May and the rest of the nine-year-olds waited to be divided amongst the other years, excitement and mischievousness got the better of classmate Raymond Brady. An out-and-out brat, he, like his mother, also harboured resentment – in his case, it was towards Mamie May. He told himself that it was because she had received a bigger slice of Colin's Victoria sponge a couple of months earlier. The fact that his mammy was still in the throes of a depression following her defeat to Mrs Saint James at the regional heats of the Housewife of the Year competition afforded his menacing nature *carte blanche*.

'Principal Hilliard just asked me to tell ye to go into the storeroom,' he informed Mamie May with so much conviction that even Paul Newman would have been impressed.

'Really?' she replied, delighted to have been selected for such a momentous undertaking.

Raymond informed her that she'd been tasked with bringing a box of biscuits from the storeroom to Principal Hilliard; apparently, he expected the school inspector that morning and wanted to sweeten him up with a few treats.

'He said to bring the ones that aren't stale,' Raymond added.

'How will I know which ones the stale ones are?' Mamie May asked, her initial delight quickly making way for a sense of panic that she might mess up the task.

'He said you should test some to make sure!' he informed her.

'Okay,' Mamie May said, her initial excitement returning. It did not dawn on her to check the expiration date on the box, or to question whether Raymond was simply pulling her leg – even though he had a notorious reputation in the school for doing so.

She stood on her chair, unbolted the stiff lock on the storeroom door and went in.

'Try that box there first – the one on the top shelf. Eat as many as ye like,' Raymond encouraged, struggling to contain his glee. 'Better to make sure there aren't any stale ones hiding in the bottom!' On the shelf, the young girl could see a box that had a fancy golden ribbon tied around it. She lugged her chair with her, placed it in front of the shelves and set to work.

As she devoured the biscuits, Mamie May couldn't believe her luck – usually, the principal charged them with picking up litter in the yard or running to the nearby postbox with letters; this was, by far, the best mission she had ever received.

'It tastes good to me!' she shouted as she cleaned the crumbs from her mouth.

'Try another just to be sure!'

'Okay!'

Getting carried away, she sampled three more.

Just as she was about to try a fifth one, Principal Hilliard stormed in. 'You disgusting, gluttonous urchin!' he roared, dragging her from the chair by the scruff of her neck. 'Who in the hell do you think you are – Elizabeth Taylor?'

He screamed and shouted with such venom that one might have been forgiven for thinking that the nine-year-old had been in the middle of swiping the contents of the Last Supper.

'Put out your grubby hands this very minute!' he ordered.

When she reluctantly obeyed, he unleashed four lashes with his ruler, one for each biscuit she had devoured.

As the girl fought back the tears, she looked over at Raymond, expecting him to explain the confusion to Principal Hilliard.

When she saw him stifling a laugh instead, the proverbial penny finally dropped.

After she was permitted to return to her seat, Mamie May decided that she wasn't going to hold it against Raymond. She concluded that it was no one's fault but her own for not being able to decipher between those telling her the truth and those setting her up for a fall.

Naturally, it distressed Colin to see his best friend being humiliated, particularly seeing as the challenges he faced with his hearing meant that he was not always aware of the things that were happening to her until it was too late. And yet, today, like the other occasions when her classmates got the better of her, Mamie May never played the victim – a trait that Colin admired in her so much.

Oh, how he wished his older brother wasn't living in that stuffy boarding school so that he could run home and regale him with the dramatic events of the day and share his praise for his stoical sweetheart! Not that it mattered where his brother was – deep down, Colin knew that even if his older brother had been at home and available for his take on the day's events, it would only have been met with a cruel silence or an embarrassment of profanities (terms that had admirably progressed from his 'smelly pig' days). Colin's poor hearing, thankfully, filtered out many of the unkind insults. However, when Freddie punctuated them with the slamming of his bedroom door, Colin always received the message.

It may not have been loud, but it was most definitely clear.

THIRTEEN

Azra wanted to slam the staff hallway door, such was her anger towards it. She conceded that it was a pretty, well-constructed structure, but how she longed to wrench it from its hinges and hurl it into the Bosphorous Strait. That way, she would have enjoyed a clear view of all the glamorous comings and goings within the hotel.

The teenager had been cautioned time and time again that the many wealthy and elite guests did not want to see signs of poverty during their stay at the Pera Palace Hotel, and that unless she and her 'dirty face' remained out of sight in the kitchen, she would find herself out of a job.

'Don't think I haven't noticed you peeping out through the doors, Azra,' Mustafa Bey told her one morning, unimpressed. 'Step one foot outside and that will be the end of your employment here, do you understand?'

No, I don't understand, you weasel! is what the teenager wanted to shout, but, remembering her brother's stern words, she decided it was best to hold her tongue.

'Yes, Mustafa Bey. I understand.'

Unfortunately, as most young people would attest, remaining true to your word can often be quite the undertaking.

When Azra heard a loud cacophony of laughter in the foyer one afternoon, she couldn't resist creeping down the hallway that linked the kitchen and the foyer to steal a glance at the magical scene. Despite the risky nature of the act, the sight in front of her made it worthwhile.

Standing amongst a small swarm of elegant guests was the most stylish bride Azra had ever laid eyes on. What an outfit! Having made a habit of retrieving and devouring the magazines that the guests discarded, Azra had become quite the expert in all things sartorial. She knew straight away that the lady's bell-sleeved dress was currently a staple in the world of bridal fashion. The built-in cape was a flourish that exactly mirrored what she had seen in the pages of one of the magazine's spreads earlier in the week. Azra admired the colourful bouquet of flowers that she held in her hands – the perfect accessory to complement the outfit. How she longed to touch the ensemble just for a moment!

The newlyweds moved towards the lounge area – and even though she knew she was committing a hanging offence – Azra boldly followed.

As she passed across the foyer and through the doors of the lounge area, the youngster saw that the guests had now bunched together beside a sweet-sounding piano. Even though the wedding party had formed a protective shield around the chic fashionista, Azra was determined to place her hand on the fabulous, white frock.

Avoiding the many lit cigars that hovered menacingly above her face, Azra got down on her hands and knees and, thanks to her petite size, made her way through the forest of long legs, the bright white colour of the dress obligingly playing the role of guide. As she closed in on her target, the naughty trespasser promised herself that she would only stroke the fabric for a brief moment before returning to the kitchen.

Except, her ill-conceived plan was soon thwarted.

One of the men, who was animatedly arguing the merits of the never-ending Vietnam War, stood on Azra's foot. This led him to lose his balance, trip over Azra and push one of the other, older guests to the ground. On his way southwards, the ageing gentleman released his flute of champagne, the contents of which rained down on the root of all this bother: the wedding dress.

Within seconds, Mustafa Bey and a battalion of staff had fished the culprit out from the crowd.

'I knew it was a mistake agreeing to give you a job, you little bitch!' Mustafa Bey roared, much to the shock of the others. Such was the man's anger that he forgot the hotel's protocol forbidding such tongue-lashings in front of the guests. 'You are your *baba*'s daughter – that much we can all agree upon!' he declared, his hand strangling her wrist.

Azra was at a loss as to why he had randomly introduced her deceased father into his scolding. She had spent years trying to find out information about him, but every time she had broached the subject a stony silence greeted her. Her brother, especially, became quite flustered and nervous when quizzed.

'He's dead, that's all there is to it,' Yusuf would bark.

She always knew that her mother had died on the day of her birth, but she suspected that her father's demise was more compli-cated than that. Though she'd been present for his end, her tender age and subsequent bang to the head meant she'd no memory of it. All she had was a vague recollection of a hospital – and there had been something about a large biscuit – but that was the height of it. Which was why, amid the furore, she focused on the fact that, once and for all, she might learn something about her father and his passing.

'You knew my *baba*?'

Mustafa Bey scoffed. 'Everyone knew him, the thieving bastard!'

'Don't, Mustafa Bey!' Yusuf shouted, dashing into the scene, having just learned of his sister's transgression. That the top button of his trousers was open – usually a serious crime – did not concern anyone at that moment. 'I am sorry for what has just happened. We will both leave now, but there is no need to say anything further, please.'

'I want to know!' shouted Azra, on the verge of a full-blown tantrum.

'Yes, we all want to know,' one of the curious bridesmaids interjected.

'You want to know about one of the most loathsome men Istanbul has ever produced?' Mustafa Bey asked.

'No,' Yusuf begged, 'I thought we had a … an agreement.'

'A man who gambled away every lira he could get his grubby hands on?' Mustafa Bey continued. 'A man who owed almost every person in the city money? A man who should have thrown himself into the Bosphorus Strait but, instead, decided to rob a children's charity of every single lira they had in their safe – money that should have gone to help the sick children of Istanbul. Do you know how many young lives could have been saved?'

A chorus of gasps followed, although not a single sound escaped Azra's open mouth.

'When the police could not get enough evidence, a noble group of citizens thought it best to take action themselves and, with the help of their knives, they got their justice, one stab at a time.'

Azra initially thought the charges against her father were Mustafa Bey's sick way of punishing her for ruining the bride's dress, but when her older brother did not attempt to deny the allegations, she realised that what their manager had said was true.

'Come on, Azra; let's go,' Yusuf ordered, before leading her away, leaving a roomful of guests who were disgusted and trans-fixed in equal measures.

That is, save for the one person who should have been most outraged by the ugly scene – the bride. Beneath the make-up, her soft face was hijacked by compassion and empathy.

'Wait!'

Before the siblings reached the door of the hotel, the bride ran over to them. If possible, she now looked even more beautiful as she handed Azra the bouquet and gave her a warm embrace.

'Never give up,' she whispered into the teenager's ear in an accent that was just as coarse as her own.

How on earth … ?

After her initial surprise, Azra couldn't help but notice the bride's stunning ring – it was the most beautiful object she had ever seen in her short life.

'And do exactly what I've done,' the bride added with a glint in her eyes. 'Marry rich!'

As she watched the bride return to the bar, Azra decided there and then that she would take the lady's advice and would never give up.

And marry rich, she vowed, holding the flowers tight. *Rich*.

FOURTEEN

Colin always liked to tease things out. If he received an Easter egg, he would leave it, untouched, under his bed until the summer. If he got an ice-cream cone, he would be the last person in the family to finish it, savouring every melting mouthful. And when it came to the opening of his birthday presents, he applied the exact same approach.

It took Colin two long months to tear off the wrapping paper covering the various gifts, and now that he had finally completed the task, the shelves in his bedroom were almost collapsing under the weight of the various toys. If forced to select his favourite, he would have chosen the red toy train that Mamie May had given him. In fairness, she could have gifted him a kidney bean and he would have cherished it. His love for the train was so great that he gave it pride of place on his bedside locker.

So, of course, his brother smashed it to smithereens.

When Colin discovered what had happened, he didn't breathe a word to his parents; he didn't want Freddie to hate him even more than he already did. Instead, he decided to bring the remaining presents into school – out of harm's way, as it were. If he thought that his presents would find sanctuary in the classroom, however, he was mistaken.

Whether Raymond had any genuine desire to play with Colin's bowling pins was up for debate; what was certain was his desire to prevent Mamie May from using them. There was just something about her that brought out his worst side. Not only did her stupidity annoy him, but he also hated how she robbed all of Colin's attention. Raymond could see how smitten Colin was with her, hanging on her every word, even though everything that came out of her mouth, he felt, was on a par with what was uttered in Baby Infants.

He was not properly aware of it at the time, but Raymond had something of a crush on Colin and he couldn't understand why these feelings weren't being reciprocated.

I did nothing but be nice to him. Why didn't he choose me to do the wheelbarrow race with him during P.E. last week? I'm stronger than Mamie May. Way stronger.

And by way of proving his point, he marched straight up to the pair of sickly lovebirds and demanded that she hand him the bowling pins.

'Give them to me now!'

'Ye can play with us if ye like,' Mamie May suggested.

The bully noticed Colin rewarding her attempts at inclusivity with the type of puppy-eyed look that Raymond longed for himself. Having no control over his jealousy and not knowing what else to do, the youngster grabbed a bowling pin from Mamie May's hand and belted her over the head with it. While fighting others wasn't an act that was alien to him, hitting girls was and, yes, he was well aware that it was an awful thing to do. But he couldn't help himself. He raised his arm again and dealt her another blow.

And another.

As he was on the verge of his fourth wallop, he felt a bang to the face; such was its force that he soon found himself lying flat on the ground, blood pouring from his nose. Seconds after he began processing what had just happened, he realised that it might have been Mamie May – a girl – who had delivered the convincing thump.

Please let it have been a boy who done it! I'll never do anything like that again if You make sure it was a boy who boxed me. Please! he begged the Almighty.

Even though he was not deserving of having prayers answered, it soon emerged that it wasn't Mamie May or any of her female counterparts who had delivered the blow; it was the sweetest and gentlest boy who had ever walked the earth.

Colin.

'Don't you ever touch her again, do you hear me, Raymond?' he warned, standing over him.

Ashamed, Raymond started bawling crying and didn't stop until Colin hugged him and Mamie May forgave him. That afternoon proved that only one person would ever be the object of Colin's affection: Mamie May Mooney.

Raymond would just have to settle for being his best friend instead.

FIFTEEN

Freddie had gotten it all wrong.

Ever since Colin's arrival on the scene, he had convinced himself that his brother's disability was the only reason the 'smelly pig' had been the primary object of his mother's affections. He had been confident that following a measure of time, when the excitement and novelty had fizzled out, his parents would reinstate him to his lofty position within the family. Now, all these years later, it was finally clear that this would never happen; his disgustingly sweet sibling had usurped all of their mother's attention – had turned her against him, even – and she was not a woman for changing.

To make matters worse, following the stupid Housewife of the Year competition, he had been reduced to nothing more than a prop in the endless photographs – *the bitch puts on a good show, I'll give her that* – and the troubled teenager had to fight every urge not to follow in the footsteps of Charles Manson and put an end to this charade once and for all.

His hatred for her and Colin was multiplying day by day.

He had tried to find solace elsewhere. Cigarettes and alcohol had emerged as his new family, and the office of money-loving Principal Cullen became something of a home from home. ('You are lucky your father is such a generous man, Alfred!')

Freddie's angry and aggressive demeanour, combined with his handsome and chiselled features, meant that he had developed quite the reputation around Meath. Such a lifestyle came at a price, unfortunately, and even though his father – his only ally – secretly gave him a generous amount of weekly pocket money, it wasn't long before said pockets were empty again.

Days before Christmas, the sixteen-year-old broke into *The Meath Chronicle* and, after relieving the paper of many of its prized contents, such as the kitty for the Christmas party, the hooligan had the audacity to make himself a pot of tea and use the paper's fancy equipment. As he sipped on his cuppa, he produced official-looking fundraising cards on behalf of the newly invented Navan Society for the Deaf – a highly lucrative scam that saw him collect north of ten pounds over the festive season.

'Aren't you such a loyal, loving brother,' one of his unsuspecting victims praised him. 'Mrs Saint James doesn't know how lucky she is – sure it's no wonder she walked away with the top prize at the competition!'

'Her skills as a mother have no limits, Mr O'Dwyer. I'll be sure to pass on your kind words,' Freddie assured him.

Yes, some of the town's older residents were clueless about the hellraiser's loose morals, but its younger residents were not. Boys wanted to be like him; girls wanted to kiss him – everyone wanted to be around him, but none more so than Colin, who could not for the life of him understand why his older brother dismissed him at every turn, as well as saying such unkind things to him.

'You know your hearing is banjaxed because Mummy was on the sauce during your pregnancy,' Freddie told Colin as they washed the dinner plates together after the Christmas feast. 'Don't tell her I told you …'

Aside from sewing some seeds about their mother's non-existent alcoholism, Freddie firmly believed that it would only be a matter of time before he stumbled upon the ideal manner of getting his ultimate revenge on Colin for usurping his rightful place in the family hierarchy.

In the end, it would take another few years for this opportunity for revenge to arrive.

The wait, however, would be worth it.

1977

SIXTEEN

'Will you, Mamie May Mooney, make an honest woman out of me? No, man! I mean man!' Colin leaned against the mirror, exasperated. *You better not mess it up.*

While he was busy impressing lecturers with his culinary masterpieces in college every day, Colin had decided that the only thing he really wanted to make was a wife out of his redheaded beauty, Mamie May.

That was why the besotted eighteen-year-old put on his new suit and led her all the way up to the lantern-like summit of the Tower of Lloyd on the outskirts of Kells. The hundred-foot lighthouse folly offered stunning views of the surrounding countryside – even as far as the Mourne Mountains in County Down on a bright day. Except, that March afternoon, Leinster suddenly found itself besieged by the type of storm that was usually saved for biblical passages. As thunder and lightning created chaos outside, and with the threat of the windows crashing in on them growing every second, Colin cursed himself for his bad timing even as he popped the question.

Mamie May, on the other hand, was in her element and gladly shouted, 'Yes, yes, yes!'

When Mamie May looked at the ring he placed on her finger, she thought it was heavenly. What she didn't realise was that, if sold, the brilliant, pear-shaped diamond could have fed a hungry village for a year. Originally bequeathed to Colin's family by the same late aunt whose generosity had paid for much of their home's refurbishment, the ring had created conflict between Mr Saint James and his relatives – not because the others wanted 'a keepsake to be reminded of dear Aunt Tilda' as they insisted at the time, but on account of its value. No one knew for certain where the deceased spinster had originally acquired the jewel but, whatever its origins, it was quietly decided – largely by Mrs Saint James – that the sparkling ring would be given to her darling youngest child when the time arrived for him to propose.

She had not foreseen this day arriving so soon.

'People are getting married in their forties and fifties now,' she pointed out to Colin when he revealed his intentions to his parents. Ill-prepared to play the role of 'Second Lady' in her darling son's life, Mrs Saint James agreed to support the proposal only on condition that the newlyweds moved into the family home straight after the ceremony.

'There's so much space,' she argued, 'we'd hardly see each other! And don't even think that I'm going to let you stop going to college!'

There was only one thing that would make Colin's upcoming wedding even more magical: having his brother by his side. But, as anticipated, his initial request for Freddie to be his best man received an RSVP of the blue variety. Ever the optimist, Colin held out hope that Freddie would have a change of heart.

You don't have to give me your decision straight away, he advised in a note that he dropped off at his brother's pokey flat above the pharmacy on Brew's Hill. *Maybe you could think about it? It would mean the absolute world to Mamie May and me. How handsome you would look, dressed in an elegant, three-piece suit. We will pay for that, naturally! Also, I'm going to bake the cake and plan to include a tier of chocolate biscuit. Your favourite.*

A reply never came.

SEVENTEEN

The incident at the Pera Palace Hotel had a lasting effect on Azra – not the public humiliation she had received, but something else. In fact, she'd bounced back from her dismissal and dressing-down quite quickly, helped by the news that Yusuf's successor hadn't been as accommodating as her brother when it came to Mustafa Bey's advances – far from it. (She doubted the creep received many visitors during his three-month stint in hospital.) What stayed in her memory from the incident instead was the beautiful bride and her matter-of-fact advice to 'marry rich'. The bouquet she had gifted her had long since wilted away, but the image of the lady's dazzling wedding ring remained vivid in her mind – and offered her a great distraction every time blasted pangs of hunger demanded her attention.

Azra realised that despite the ongoing changes around the globe, she still lived very much in a man's world. They ruled banks and mosques and governments and countries. She often felt that the dogs on the street enjoyed more rights than the majority of the female population. And while her education was certainly limited, she was worldly enough to know that there was one place where she and her female counterparts boasted more power than men.

In the bedroom.

Hell-bent on using this to her advantage, Azra vowed to go to any lengths to accomplish her mission of escaping the poverty to which she had become accustomed; somehow, she would find a way of upgrading her life.

Azra knew the city housed many rich and well-connected men, always on the look-out for a beautiful lady to take to galas or on business trips.

But where were they?

Deep down, the now twenty-one-year-old felt that when it came to looks, she was on a par with Farrah Fawcett or Faye Dunaway. Yet, much to her surprise and frustration, no rich man had ever had dignified designs on her. But she would be damned if she was going to remain impoverished by settling for some drunken sailor or smelly fisherman.

Every day, Azra, complete with a basket of soon-to-expire flowers, walked from the banks of the Bosphorus Strait towards the bustling and vibrant Grand Bazaar, eyes peeled. When she'd first begun flogging tulips in the 1960s, inspired by the bouquet she had received from the bride, the hippy, flower-power movement had arrived in Istanbul and provided her with a buoyant business. Now, a decade later, demand had waned. With Yusuf hardly ever around thanks to his job on a cruise ship (as much as he tried, he'd been unable to secure his sister a position on board), Azra knew that she would soon have to make good on that vow she had made to herself if she didn't want to starve. But where was her blasted knight in shining armour?

As Azra wandered between the coffee and the spices in the Grand Bazaar, she thought, *You're too poor, that's the problem. Unless …*

In that moment Azra finally realised that if she was going to prove appealing to wealthy and affluent men, she would need to convince them that she, too, was wealthy and affluent. To make it, first she would have to fake it.

EIGHTEEN

At first, it had not been Freddie's intention to break his brother's heart, but a month before the nuptials were due to take place, the cad set in place a plan that would succeed in doing just that.

Upon hearing the news that Mamie May had been the recipient of the family's much-envied pear-shaped diamond ring, he momentarily cast aside his anger at the loss of what he deemed his inheritance. With Colin set to leave for a life of marital bliss, he instead entertained the idea that he might now be afforded the role of prodigal son and invited to return to the family home, having been exiled since his expulsion from school all those years earlier. But when his mother walked straight past him in the shopping centre shortly after the announcement of the engagement, he'd finally accepted once and for all that those glorious, halcyon days when he had ruled the roost were irretrievably lost to the past.

What else did you expect, you fool? That bitch has barely said more than a 'hello' to you in almost nineteen years; why would it be any different just because that insufferable bastard is getting married?

That didn't mean he was going to sit back and do nothing.

They can marry in Westminster for all I care – but they're not getting Aunt Tilda's ring. That's mine.

A couple of weeks after Easter Sunday, Freddie spotted his future sister-in-law walking towards him as he sat on the River Boyne railway bridge, which offered breathtaking views across the picturesque town. Here, he was enjoying a few cans and finding strange pleasure in the unpleasant weather – being overly fond of the hooch left his body constantly hot and clammy, so he was one of the few people in Ireland who welcomed the country's lousy weather.

He cast his beverage aside and raced over to Mamie May, but before he could even say hello, she was blurting out that her neighbour, Mrs Vaughan, one of the nearby secondary school's science teachers, had forgotten to bring home a stack of copybooks and the eighteen-year-old had offered to oblige her. However, Mamie May being Mamie May, she had failed to notice that she'd retrieved Mrs Nugent's first-year English copies instead. Regardless of the contents within, there was a strong breeze that day and she was clearly in need of a little assistance. Which is where the duplicitous lout came in.

'Can I offer you a hand, Mamie May?' he asked with an innocence that would have put an altar boy to shame.

As soon as the words passed his lips, a bright glint appeared in Mamie May's eyes. This twinkle did not appear because she was surprised that he had uttered his first words to her. It was not because she saw herself possibly becoming the healing force between the two estranged siblings.

It appeared, Freddie knew, because she desired him.

If further proof was needed, the giddy manner in which she fidgeted with the pear-shaped diamond on her finger suggested that the rock was the only thing that was solid in her relationship with his brother.

Sod the ring, Freddie thought, he was going to steal her heart as well. *How about that for revenge!* Besides, he hadn't realised until that moment what a cute little redhead she was.

'Thank you,' she eventually replied, turning her face in the direction of the oncoming breeze (in the hope that it would cool her blushing cheeks, he suspected). Never one to miss a golden opportunity, Freddie used the short walk to her car to fill her innocent ears with a sob story so dramatic that it would have been worthy of the Abbey Theatre's stage. He discussed how broken he was as a result of being made an outcast by his family, particularly his mother. If only he had someone in his life who would introduce a 'dash of light into the darkness'.

'My only hope is that it's not too late for me,' he informed her, 'and that, someday, I will find somebody who will see past my flaws and faults. Does that make any sense, Molly May?'

'Mamie May, and it does. Absolutely.'

'A woman who might allow me to create a new life with her,' he continued, 'and who will rear children with me and help guide our sons and daughters away from all the shadows that I have found myself in over the years.'

Even Freddie was surprised by how authentic and convincing his babble sounded.

'You will, I am certain of it, Freddie,' she assured him.

As Freddie described her as a 'lone star in the constellation', Mamie May accidentally tripped over a rogue stone, requiring her to catch hold of Freddie's arm. Mrs Nugent's copybooks went flying.

'Oh, heaven's above!' she cried, mortified.

As they dashed about, trying to rescue the first-year students' copybooks, they ended up crouched behind a discreet grove of trees. Such was their proximity, the nuns from the nearby Order of Saint Aloysius would have been left clutching their rosary beads for dear life should they have witnessed the scene. Freddie hoped that the smell of his afternoon's alcoholic indulgences or the perspiration dripping from his forehead would not sully the moment.

'Mamie May, you –'

'I, em, have to get going,' a flustered Mamie May said, breaking away and forgetting the majority of the copybooks in the process.

While he may not have sealed the deal with the all-important kiss, in that moment Freddie knew that he had successfully coaxed out Mamie May's true colours – revealing traits that might have been described by the judgemental contingency as 'fickle' and 'disloyal'. A little more work and he was certain that he could persuade her to change horses.

One of Mrs Nugent's essays that still lay bunched in a pile by Freddie's feet was entitled, *Was Brutus an Honourable Hero in Julius Caesar?* One did not need to be a soothsayer to deduce on which side of the knife Colin was soon going to find himself.

NINETEEN

Azra returned to the Pera Palace Hotel one spring evening – but she had no intention of wearing an apron and disappearing into a mound of leftover food. Instead, donning a simple red skirt and cream blouse that she had recently inherited from a deceased neighbour, the young lady sat in the Kubbeli Saloon Tea Lounge.

'I think I might have some rose hip,' she said to a waiter. (*My knight had better come along soon*, she thought as she scanned the prices on the menu. The attempt to emulate that bride's success was proving expensive – this beverage alone was set to cost her almost a week's income.)

As she looked around for suitable bachelors, she observed how the light flooded the space thanks to the six sky-lit domes above. As well as sunlight, she hoped that luck would shine upon her today.

She had read a notice in one of the newspapers that she'd used to wrap her flowers about a convention taking place that weekend in the hotel for vintage automobile vendors from all over Turkey – surely, she would be the perfect accessory for any Rolls Royce or Aston Martin.

'I think we can do better than tea.'

Azra turned around. Standing before her was a young, handsome man whose soft skin suggested that he was of a similar age to her. He held aloft a pair of Martinis.

'*Teşekkür ederim*,' she thanked him, adopting the poshest voice she could conjure.

'You're more than welcome.'

Not only was Azra thrilled that she didn't have to part with her hard-earned money, she was also delighted that her plan was seemingly falling into place with ease.

Why didn't you have the wisdom to do this a couple of years ago?

The hours you would have saved traipsing across the city selling sickly flowers for next to nothing!

'What's a beautiful woman like you doing sitting here all alone?'

'I have been stood up! By my own brother! And it wouldn't be the first time – he works in shipping – cruises – and you know how unreliable that business is!'

'Well, lucky for me that he was too busy to meet you. Do you like cars?' the man, who introduced himself as Kemal, asked as he pulled his chair closer to her. 'I bet you are a lady with great taste.'

'I most certainly am,' she replied, stifling a cough after taking her first sip, the strength of the Martini proving a little overwhelming. 'So, you sell cars?'

Kemal nodded. 'My family does – Jaguars, Cadillacs, Chevrolets – you name it, we sell it.'

Azra hoped that she wouldn't be called upon to actually name any additional makes of cars, seeing as her knowledge about motors was modest to say the very least.

'And you, Miss …?'

'Call me Azra.'

'What is it you do, Azra?'

'I am a florist,' she replied with impressive confidence. 'The business is currently expanding.'

'I would imagine that many of your customers confuse you for the flowers you sell because you have the beauty of a rose and the elegance of an orchid.'

Having spent nearly an eternity surrounded by men who spat, scratched and swore, Azra was relishing every moment of this enchanting encounter with an erudite and flattering young man.

Before she had an opportunity to reply, a group of cheery vendors entered and monopolised the entire bar.

'Shall we go somewhere a little … quieter?' Kemal suggested.

The next thing she knew, Azra was walking under the foyer's

magnificent chandeliers and making her way to Kemal's bedroom with the assistance of the hotel's famed elevator, which had once been the only one of its kind in the entire city. Thanks to her inability to remain in the kitchen when employed by the hotel, much of the building was familiar to her: the velvet curtains; the marble pillars; the decorative tiles. What wasn't familiar was being in the hotel as a guest, *and not a slave*, she thought.

If only Mustafa Bey could see me now!

However, the only person who laid his eyes on her – on *all* of her – was Kemal.

When, minutes later, Azra gripped the bed in ecstasy, she wasn't certain if these strong feelings were on account of this man's love-making skills, or the prospect that she was well on her way to becoming a millionaire's wife. She looked around the bright and beautifully furnished bedroom and, in between the huffing and puffing, she visualised herself getting ready for her Big Day here, brushing her hair and applying her make-up in front of the vanity table.

What will we have for the reception meal? she wondered as Kemal reached his climax.

Such fantasies were short-lived, unfortunately.

'Okay, you have to leave now,' he ordered as he rolled off her, satisfied. 'My wife will be back any minute.'

He disappeared into the bathroom, turning on the shower.

As she fought back tears, Azra quickly dressed and exited the hotel room, making her way back to the world she knew only too well.

Not the hotel's delightful tea rooms, but the streets.

TWENTY

On the verge of sabotaging his brother's seemingly rock-solid relationship, Freddie's quest for justice was in full swing. For the first time in a long time, he felt vital once again. He would have been the first to admit that since Colin's unwelcome arrival into the world, he had lost some of his pluck and self-confidence. Even though alcohol and the odd recreational drug or two had rather pleasant forget-my-woes effects, nothing made him quite as giddy or as high as having the power to destroy other people's lives – especially those who were responsible for those woes.

'I haven't been able to stop thinking about you,' he informed Mamie May as they trudged along the leafy Boyne ramparts walk for the fourteenth time in as many days – as much as he loathed hanging out with this extraordinarily dim woman, he was sure that his sacrifice would eventually be worth it. The hats and scarves that they were obliged to wear on account of the day's weather conditions proved to be an excellent means of remaining incognito. 'Every time I see you, my feelings grow stronger and stronger,' he lied. 'I don't suppose you have been thinking about me by any chance?'

'I've not slept a wink in two weeks!' Mamie May admitted. 'What does that mean?'

'That you love me,' Freddie stated with certainty.

'Really? I thought it was because I was feeling –'

'Which is a good job,' he interrupted, uninterested in hearing about her guilt, 'because I love you, too.'

He placed a hand on her face and gently guided it towards his.

'I hope you don't mind if I …' He then kissed her soft yet trembling lips.

Freddie had always hoped that his moment for revenge would arrive, and now that it was upon him, it was better than he had ever imagined. And this was only the beginning; soon it would be time to go nuclear and implement his own personal Hiroshima.

But not quite yet – first, he was going to leave Mamie May to savour their delicate embrace. While he didn't want to brag about his kissing abilities, he knew that if sleep had eluded her for two weeks, it most certainly wasn't going to make a reappearance now.

Confident of how everything was progressing, he said his goodbyes. He had some familial obligations to fulfil that evening – it was his kid brother's stag party in Smyth's. Wouldn't it be just wicked if he didn't make an appearance!

TWENTY-ONE

Azra could have written a book about the amount of times she was left disappointed by the men of Istanbul. Why was she finding it so difficult to convince the city's eligible wealthy bachelors that she was a social equal, and why were follow-up dates never forthcoming? Despite her beauty, it was becoming obvious to her that these lusty males were never going to shower her with gifts and jewellery and save her from the filthy streets. In terms of her achieving her goal, this was problematic.

Then one summer's day, Azra caught sight of a party of wealthy, immaculately turned out tourists strutting towards Topkapi Palace. Even though this one-time residence of the Ottoman sultans had been transformed into a museum, Azra had yet to visit. It wasn't the high admission price alone that prevented her from venturing in; instead, she had always felt that it was a place for those wealthier than she – wealthier and better.

However, as the elegant ladies sauntered past her, something within her was roused. *If you believe in yourself inwardly, they will believe in you outwardly*, she told herself, tying her greasy hair into a ponytail with a tatty handkerchief. With the help of a nearby fountain, she then cleaned the dirt from her hands and face. Complete with a newfound determination, Azra cast aside her self-doubt (along with her sickly basket of flowers) and, full of gung-ho, marched through the lofty Imperial Gates and hid herself amongst the large group. How she hoped that one of them would find her so irresistible that he would save her from her grim reality. Or even provide her with a hot meal – not that she'd be able to recognise one if it was served in front of her; that's how long it had been since she'd last enjoyed something other than nuts or bruised fruit.

Little did she realise that the following thirty minutes would involve an introduction that would change the trajectory of her life forever.

Not to a person, but to a pear-shaped diamond.

***

'Ladies and gents, I hope you've enjoyed the tour so far, but I'm confident that you will all agree that what I am going to show you next is the palace's *pièce de résistance,*' the tour guide announced to the group of rich Americans (and one poor Turk) about an hour into the tour. 'Yes, these courtyards and gardens that we're currently walking through are special, but they pale in comparison to the next item on our itinerary. It is the eighty-six carat, pear-shaped diamond – one of the biggest in the world – located over there in the Imperial Treasury, which I will take you to next. Follow me, please.'

As they walked through the doors and into the room, they bypassed all the other magnificent objects on display, such as bejewelled Korans, dessert sets, pendants, chains and rings, and walked straight towards the enormous jewel that hung in a glass case. The size of a lemon, Azra decided, it rendered her completely speechless; in that moment, she was convinced that every single star in the sky had grouped to form this brilliant object.

'It is … glorious,' she whispered.

While her gaze remained fixed on the jewel, Azra listened attentively to the guide as he told them how the diamond was unearthed.

'Legend has it that a poor fisherman near Yenikapi was wandering along the shore when he noticed a shiny stone,' he revealed. 'Curiosity got the better of him, and he picked it up and popped it in his pocket. When he showed it to a jeweller a couple of days later, the fisherman was left devastated when told that it was just a piece of glass!'

'How could anyone confuse this remarkable diamond with a piece of glass? Good grief!' one of the ladies interjected, dumbfounded.

'Well, this jeweller may not have claimed the best eyesight in Constantinople, but he had a big heart and, feeling sorry for the disappointed fisherman, he offered him three spoons for it, an offer which was readily accepted. Can you imagine it?'

'Spoons!' the same flabbergasted lady cried out.

'Hard to believe, that's for sure.'

'And how did it end up here in the palace?' another member of the assembly asked.

'Well, later the diamond was bought by an official on behalf of the sultan, but its unique name is a tip of the hat to its unlikely discovery and the unlucky fisherman – the Spoonmaker's Diamond. There's a lesson there, I suppose – always keep a keen eye out for opportunities to transform your life.'

'Yes, but a greater lesson is not to foolishly squander a potential fortune by giving it to some blind jeweller,' another lady retorted.

Husband or no husband, I don't care how I get it, Azra thought. *One day, I will have a jewel as glorious and as glittering as the Spoonmaker's Diamond dangling from around my neck or proudly sitting on my finger.*

And, as luck would have it, the next stop on the guide's itinerary revealed the exact manner by which Azra would ultimately succeed in her ambitious quest.

TWENTY-TWO

Two weeks before the I Dos were due to take place, Colin finally accepted that on this occasion, no news on the Freddie front was not, in fact, good news.

'Some people are not very confident standing up in front of friends and family, Colin,' his father mentioned by way of comfort.

Not even a gun pointed straight between his eyes would leave Freddie frightened, Colin reflected. No, he simply had to accept that while he had received many blessings in life – devoted parents and a darling wife-to-be – a loving brother was not one of them.

Having thrown in the towel, Colin decided that at his stag party in Smyth's on the Square that night, he would ask his old school pal, Raymond Brady, to take on the role. Surrounded by friends and a battalion of Mamie May's lively brothers, Colin was on the verge of making the request when he felt a tap on the shoulder.

'Hey, kiddo,' Freddie shouted, his clean-shaven face now hijacked by something very few had witnessed in years – a smile.

'Hi, how are … I didn't know you were … What are you having to drink?' Colin mumbled, the sight of his brother leaving him completely tongue-tied.

'Save your money, lil bro – you're gonna need all the pennies you can get now that you're about to start a family.'

Freddie then led him to the bar, free from Mamie May's boisterous family, for he wanted to be certain that his hard-of-hearing sibling heard every word he was about to say.

'How's Mummy? Is she still …?' he mimed the action of drinking.

'I never –'

'You're right – this isn't the time to discuss such upsetting matters. All I'll say is that you're a bigger man than me. I don't know if I'd be so forgiving, particularly given what she did.'

'You're wrong, Freddie. Mummy said that she tripped over her shoelaces –'

Freddie leaned in towards his brother. 'Look, lil bro, I'm well aware that I've been a bit of a brute all these years and I know that I could have made things between us at home much easier if I'd been a little more ... civil. You know, we should have really stuck together, especially being the sons of a ...' He again mimed the drinking gesture, much to Colin's annoyance. He had never seen any evidence of his mother having a drinking problem.

Freddie continued, 'We're the lucky two who actually received a birth – God knows how many others ... Anyway, if it's not too late, I would like to try and make things better between us now – between all of us.'

If Colin hadn't been carefully reading his brother's lips he would have doubted that the words he was hearing were true.

Freddie smiled. 'So, if you'll have me, I'd be honoured to be your best man.'

When Mamie May had given him her positive response on top of the Tower of Lloyd a few months earlier, Colin never imagined that any other moment could have matched the elation he'd felt. Allegations about their mother's behaviour aside, this exchange was proving to be a contender.

'Nothing would make me happier,' the stag replied, fighting back the tears. 'Thank you.'

Before sentimentality ran amok, the duo decided that there was no need for any more words other than *sláinte*, so they ordered a couple of celebratory pints of Guinness.

Even if the five libations he enjoyed that evening had been alcohol-free, Colin would still have been left feeling as drunk as a skunk, such was his ecstasy. If he'd been aware of what his brother had been plotting over the past few weeks, however, his delight would have been short-lived.

TWENTY-THREE

Forget becoming a wife, I'm going to become a concubine! Azra thought as she continued on her tour of the Topkapi Palace.

'It is no secret that concubines played a pivotal role in Topkapi Palace over the centuries,' the guide explained as the group wandered from the blue, gold and terracotta harem and through the arches that lined the aptly named Courtyard of the Sultan's Consorts and the Concubines. 'You probably don't need me to tell you that Muslim women were forbidden from engaging in such activities, so white, Christian slaves – up to three hundred at any given time – were sourced instead.'

By now, Azra had forgotten that she'd gate-crashed this tour and stood to be reprimanded if discovered. She was so engrossed by the world she had just entered, she simply couldn't resist learning more about the life of a concubine.

'How did the sultan choose the concubines every night?' she asked in a faux-American accent.

The guide stepped closer. 'It was said that every night he would wave a handkerchief at his lady of choice. Of course, the sultans had their favourites, and these ladies had quite an influence in the palace and enjoyed plenty of luxury.'

Azra could hardly believe what was being said. It was almost as if the guide had heard the mission that she'd just set for herself, and he was now giving her information about how best to proceed.

'What did these concubines look like?' she quizzed.

'Oh, exquisite,' he answered, as he led the band through the various narrow walkways. 'In saying that, it appears that Sultan Ibrahim I, who died in 1648, had something of an eye for ladies who were …'

He stopped himself short, remembering that this particular party consisted of refined men and women whose sensibilities might be offended by such conversations.

'Who were …?' Azra probed, much to the delight of the others, who were battling both their blushes and curiosity in equal measure.

'Obese!' he whispered, startling Azra with the prospect of having to eat *sis kebab* until her belly ballooned.

'But his tastes are not to be taken as definitive,' the guide added, 'because it has also been rumoured that he ordered the drowning of the entire two hundred and eighty girls – on an impulse!'

'Given their weight, I'd say they made quite the splash,' one of the ladies quipped under her breath.

Obesity aside, Azra hoped that the guide would reveal further information to facilitate her quest to free herself from her sorry existence and become the owner of a jewel that would rival the Spoonmaker's Diamond!

'Something that a lot of people don't realise,' he continued, 'is that the concubines were all educated.'

He pointed towards a door.

'Inside there is the Teacher's Room. The concubines had to learn many things before they were ready to meet the sultan.'

Azra's face dropped – the only schooling she had ever received was from her neighbours, and that was only to afford her a basic standard of reading and writing. She had some knowledge of fashion stemming from her days surrounded by stylish women in the Pera Palace Hotel, and, thanks to her brother's insistence on speaking 'the language of the modern world' – both during their time at the Pera Palace and even now on his rare visits home from the cruise ship – she had developed a decent standard of English, idioms and the odd pronunciation aside. Other than that, Azra knew very little about anything.

There's scant chance that I'll ever be able to impress men with my non-existent knowledge of geography or mathematics.

She was left pondering her dilemma as the guide and the rest of the group sauntered off towards the apartments of the Queen Mother. Before they had disappeared through the doors, Azra's mind was already set.

If that's what it takes to get out of this life and own a pear-shaped diamond, then that's what it takes, she resolved, before vowing to read every single book she could get her hands on.

Firstly, she was going to have to brush up on her reading skills.

TWENTY-FOUR

'Maybe I'm reading things incorrectly but I'm positive that you love me and I love you,' Freddie whispered into Mamie May's ear. It was two nights before her planned wedding to Colin and the pair of clandestine lovers sat in Freddie's barely functioning car, which was parked down a country lane just outside Kells, some ten safe miles north of Navan.

'Yes, but –'

'And if you go through with this wedding, it will be the worst thing that you could do to Colin.'

'Do you think?'

'Why don't you tell him about our kiss and see what he'd say.'

Her expression fell at that suggestion; she looked on the verge of tears.

That will keep her quiet!

Now, he knew, was his *Enola Gay* moment. *Bombs away!*

'Listen, how's this for a plan,' he continued. 'There's no point in wasting a good wedding dress, so why don't we run away to Dublin and get hitched?'

Mamie May frowned. 'Really? You want to marry me?'

'I couldn't think of anything that would make me happier, sweetheart.'

'Okay so,' a hesitant Mamie May answered, turning away from him and staring out into the field.

'I think it would be best if I broke the news to Colin, don't you?' Freddie casually added. 'I'll tell him immediately.'

Of course, he had no intention of doing any such thing. Freddie was not content with merely stealing Mamie May and, of course, the magnificent ring; he wanted to bring as much pain as possible down upon his brother. The thought of the humiliation Colin would endure, waiting hopelessly in St Mary's Church in two days' time, provided Freddie with so much excitement that he knew it was the only course of action to take.

'Yes, if you say so.'

Now that the most crucial aspect of his plan was sorted, he turned on the engine and started the journey home. This chicanery was proving far too simple for Freddie: was this young woman the most easily manipulated person alive? So far, she was barely putting up much of a fight.

However, as they slowly made their way back to the main road along the muddy track, he noticed that she was toying with her ring – or *his* ring. He stopped the car on the verge of the road in front of an upturned tree that had been a victim of one of Ireland's many meteorological hissy-fits. When he looked at her, Freddie observed that she was smiling from ear to ear, but her eyes revealed a deep sadness that he knew he had to eliminate without delay.

'You're worried about hurting Colin, aren't you?'

She nodded, anxious to express her reservations.

'It would be surprising if you weren't.'

'Really?'

'Of course. Look, you are probably under the impression that my brother and I don't know too much about each other, but one thing I am certain of is that he is much stronger than people think. After all, there is a reason he was named Colin – it means "victory" or something.'

'It doesn't, does it? I wonder what "Mamie May" means?'

Freddie patted her knee. 'I wonder. Anyway, while he might be losing the most beautiful girl in the world,' he waffled, 'one day, he will emerge triumphant. That's what people called Colin do.'

As her long-suffering teacher, Master Crotty, would have attested ('No, Mamie May, the capital of England is not Navan, no matter how much you'd like it to be!'), this young lady was not only a few pendants short of a chandelier but also gullible beyond belief, and so she accepted the words of this silver-tongued rogue without question.

Freddie turned his attention back towards the road. 'One more thing – don't tell *anyone* about anything, okay? It's our little secret for now,' he added.

'Okay!' she nodded, full of excitement now that her guilt had been assuaged. 'I won't breathe a word!'

TWENTY-FIVE

Questioning the wisdom of her master plan, Azra lay on a mattress in a well-known brothel in the Karaköy area – one that was only delighted to welcome her, given the young lady's stunning beauty.

'You'll be a big hit with our customers,' Baris Remzi, the pock-faced, toothless owner of the establishment had promised during her initial interview as he pawed her with his dirty hands. 'We know that you are twenty-one but, if they ask, you can tell them that you are sixteen. They will like that.'

Azra had observed that even though her body had developed into one befitting her age, her face continued to resemble that of an adolescent, a quality that would surely stand her in good stead in the future. Despite her newbie status, she had already noticed that the brothel's other ladies would not look out of place in a graveyard; as a result, it didn't appear that customers were exactly banging down their doors.

As she made her way to her new room, she promised herself that she'd do whatever it took to maintain her youthful complexion. Unlike some of her new colleagues, she would not allow cigarettes or alcohol to pass her lips and, while she was yet to receive any reimbursement for her services, once she began earning she would invest every lira into her appearance. This, combined with vigorous exercise and a healthy lifestyle, would ensure that she'd become the most sought-after concubine in all of Turkey.

Her own Spoonmaker's Diamond would inevitably follow.

Even though it was her first night, her expectations for her new career were already being challenged and she found herself becoming increasingly stressed. As she moved her belongings into the property, she ignored the niggling doubts running amok within and instead focused on Remzi Bey's assurance that all of the city's wealthiest and most esteemed men frequented the establishment. Yet, the grotty room that Remzi Bey had allocated for her was the complete antithesis of the delightful and decorative harem in Topkapi Palace, a place she had been visiting on an almost daily basis over the past few months. Where was the chaise longue? The portraits on the wall? Could her employers not have sourced a beautiful gilded mirror somewhere? Some fresh flowers, perhaps? And as for the rancid odour, even the local fishermen who spent their days catching fish emanated a more pleasing fragrance. Surely her wealthy clients would expect something a little more ... glamorous? Unless her clients weren't, in fact, wealthy.

Oh no! I fear I have been incredibly naive about all this.

As if these distressing revelations weren't enough, when her debut customer arrived he did not ask her to discuss the contributions made to the world by Plato and Aristotle, or ask what the French is for 'I have one brother and no sisters'. Instead, he demanded that she insert her finger into somewhere she would rather not. And judging by his unkempt attire, it didn't seem likely that this particular 'gentleman' would be placing a fabulous diamond ring on it anytime soon, regardless of where she inserted it.

And to think of all those hours I spent in that library on the sug-gestion of that bloody tour guide! Why was I so stupid? Of course, men have only one thing on their mind. If I ever see that guide again, she threatened as the dirty man continued pointing towards a territory that none of her geography books had ever mentioned.

She looked towards the door – its rusty hinges meant that it had swung open.

So much for privacy.

It was then she noticed her name scrawled on a piece of paper that hung from the door and, despite her sorry state, she couldn't help but laugh.

I'm not sure my baba *foresaw this future for me when he called me Azra,* she thought, given the literal meaning of her name.

Virgin.

TWENTY-SIX

The history books confirm that great sporting events have often taken place on Saturday afternoons, but none of these events were as nail-biting and thrilling as what Freddie witnessed outside St Mary's Church on the day of his brother's planned wedding.

Perched on the bonnet of his father's Jaguar in the nearby Fair Green, and mostly concealed by a couple of large trees in the churchyard, Freddie enjoyed a VIP view of the glorious pandemonium thanks to the help of binoculars. While he was dressed in full wedding regalia – an outfit fit for a groom, though, rather than a best man – he was brazenly using his top hat as a makeshift ashtray. He only wished he had brought a few beers with him.

Fittingly, it has been reported that the architect of the church had fashioned the impressive interiors on a Parisian opera house and, by God, the drama about to unfold was akin to *Carmen* or *La Traviata*.

When the church bells heralded two o'clock, meaning that the bride-to-be was due any moment, the priest ushered everyone inside. In doing so, he had, in effect, blown the starting whistle.

Game on!

The first set of fireworks went off with the quick re-emergence of the frantic wedding party, trying to ascertain why the best man was a no-show, and why it had taken everybody until now to realise this fact. (Living with a partially deaf brother meant that Freddie had a teeny tiny bit of experience in the act of reading lips – which helped as he watched his family through the binoculars.)

'Where is he, Dad?' Colin asked, his cheeks flushed.

'I don't know – do you think something has happened to him?'

'Maybe he got the times mixed up.'

'I knew he should have gotten suited and booted with us this afternoon, Colin – why did we agree to just meet him here? What were we thinking?'

'He must be on his way,' Colin hoped.

'I said this was a big mistake, didn't I!' their mother said. 'You should have listened to me!'

'He wouldn't have changed his mind, would he, Mummy? He was so kind and loving that night in Smyth's – there's no way he would let me down like this.'

Freddie smirked, lighting another cigarette.

Following an indecipherable debate about how best to proceed, Freddie just about made out that Colin's pal Raymond would, after all, be charged with the role of best man, much to the delight of his mother, Mrs Brady – who, a fool for all things dramatic, was hovering in the background. 'Sure, isn't he only beautifully turned out anyway,' she praised.

'Yes, he's a topper, your fella,' Mr Saint James added. 'Although his father has yet to return that lawnmower I loaned him five years ago.'

'Not today, Andrew,' Mrs Saint James groaned, before dragging her husband and the others back into the church.

As Freddie stubbed out his twelfth cigarette of the day, he reflected on the woman he had married earlier that morning in a registry office, and who was now waiting for him in a pokey hotel room on Dublin's Gardiner Street, oblivious to the destruction her no-show was causing.

'You promise you told him?' she had asked repeatedly that morning.

'Of course I did – do you think I'm a monster? He completely understands!'

'And you rang my parents?'

'Sure,' he lied.

Freddie watched as his new in-laws sheepishly approached

the church, taking deep breaths before opening the doors and summoning the jilted groom-to-be and his parents outside to reveal the devastating news that Mamie May was nowhere to be found.

'We're so sorry, Colin. Her bedroom window was open – she must have snuck out sometime this morning. We were hoping she'd come back; we waited to the last possible minute, but there's been no sign of her. We're so sorry.'

Despite the fact that he detested his brother a thousand times over, Freddie had wondered whether he might experience a pang of guilt upon seeing Colin's robust and upright body unravel and crumble to the ground. The newly married man even prepared himself for the possibility of some tears escaping from his eyes when he caught sight of his mother, the one-time Housewife of the Year, throwing her arms skywards before collapsing to the ground with a wallop, sullying her beautiful teal jacket.

Nope.

As the events played out, Freddie realised that he didn't feel a single iota of emotion other than contentment and vindication. Thank goodness for that.

I didn't manage to kill you back in 1958, he thought, *but I most certainly succeeded today. And, as for you, Mummy – I hope you'll now have the decency to call* Woman's Way *and tell all their readers what a disappointment you've become.*

And with that, he hopped into his own banger of a car and sped away from the scene of the crime in the direction of Dublin – not to honeymoon with the new Missus Saint James, but, instead, to play poker with some Spanish sailors he had bumped into in the hotel the previous night.

Firstly, he just needed to swipe the family heirloom from his virgin bride – an object that would allow him to have a proper bit of fun at long last.

It's no more than I deserve.

1991

TWENTY-SEVEN

'Colin, have you got a pen to scribble down my order?' Trish shouted from the confines of the bedroom that used to belong to her late in-laws, a location she hadn't left in over ten days, occasional toilet breaks aside. Her voice's glass-shattering levels were not only to facilitate her husband's lifelong difficulties with hearing; they were on account of the fact that she was famished, an unpleasant sensation that she wanted to remedy post-haste.

'I'll remember,' Colin replied entering the bedroom – a rather ambitious promise considering the number of courses she was sure to demand.

'Well, you'll be marching all the way back to the China Garden if you forget so much as a prawn cracker, d'ye hear me?'

Colin managed a weak nod.

'Right, let's decide on your order first,' she continued, mindful that she needed to sign off on both of their choices without delay if she was to ensure that her husband and, more importantly, the food, would return home before the start of that night's episode of *Beverly Hills 90210*, her new favourite television series. 'I don't think you should get the spare ribs again; I felt they were a bit dry last week. What about duck spring rolls for starters and Sweet & Sour Chicken for mains?'

The thirty-three-year-old Colin answered by offering another feeble nod; today, if she had suggested sheep's eyes or dog's offal, he would also have agreed.

'And there's no point in getting you a banana split again; it melted into a sludge the last time, since you foolishly put it on top of all the hot food.'

'Sorry.'

'Besides, I left a sliver of that banoffee pie you baked earlier – that will do you. There's no need to be greedy, after all.'

'I suppose not.'

'I'm going to have …' Trish mused, scanning the menu in her mind, 'em … Well, I think I'll venture for something other than duck because I'll probably finish your spring rolls …'

As his wife weighed up the pros and cons of the various dishes, Colin's mind drifted away, once again focusing on the brief encounter he'd had with his older brother that afternoon – or, to be more accurate, his brother's image, which had been stuck to a telephone pole. Much to Colin's shock and disgust, it turned out that his sibling had decided to become a local councillor, and now his duplicitous face was gracing a seemingly endless series of posters across the town of Navan, brazenly mounted on every lamp post and traffic light in sight.

It was Alfred Saint James' image alone that was being used in the material for this out-of-nowhere political campaign; blessedly, the woman who'd left Colin never wanting to wake up again almost fourteen years earlier was nowhere to be seen. If he'd been forced to stare at her beautiful and delicate features from here until the day of the election, he'd have been more susceptible to a heart attack than his ten-meals-a-day wife.

Freddie had succeeded in leaving Colin unsettled and out of sorts every time they had met since that fateful day in 1977. Today had been no different, even if he had just locked eyes with a sorry-looking poster. In all the intervening years, absolutely nothing had helped Colin heal and move forward from that heart-breaking act of betrayal. His mother, when she'd still been alive, didn't do anything to improve the situation, banning Freddie and Mamie May from the estate, calling them names that he'd thought only sailors had in their vocabulary. Mr Saint James, whom Colin had often suspected was helping his estranged sibling and former fiancée financially following their banishment, attempted a reconciliation on numerous occasions, but his wife's responses were always of the 'over my dead body' variety. (By the time her body did actually die seven years later, it seemed that a tired Mr Saint James had given up the fight and pursued the reconciliation no further.)

With difficulty, Colin rescued his jacket from under Trish's beached form, placed it on his scrawny body and patted his breast pocket to ensure that there was enough money for the couple's large order. *Thank God for inheritances.*

'I'll be back soon,' he muttered.

Despite the fact that Trish had yet to give her final decision over whether to opt for a side portion of egg-fried rice or chips, Colin made his way out of the bedroom and down the stairs, ignoring his wife's admonishing cries to wait. As he traipsed down the stony driveway, Colin noticed his next-door neighbour, Oliver, tanned and laden down with duty-free purchases.

'Back from Turkey again?' Colin questioned, conjuring up as much feigned interest as possible. He was aware that this man, who Trish always claimed was a dead ringer for Bruce Willis, was employed by the Irish Embassy there, but had no idea what he did. 'Ankara, isn't it?'

'You got it in one, Colin – but the real fun is to be had in Istanbul,' Oliver replied theatrically, elongating the final 'l'. 'I'll never tire of it. Hagia Sophia, the Bosphorus Strait, Topkapi Palace. This is only a flying visit home – I'm actually heading back out there again in a couple of days. Just here to say a quick hello to my dogs.'

'I didn't realise you had dogs.'

'Well, I had to have them adopted a couple of years ago, you know, because of being in Turkey, but their new mammy and daddy are always happy for me to visit.'

Colin managed a half-hearted 'Isn't that nice' smile.

'Anyway,' Oliver continued, trying to plough through the awkward silence, 'you and Trish should think about popping over for a little trip sometime – they have this nutty, syrupy, pastry dessert that herself would only be crazy for!'

'Someday, Oliver, someday.'

Knowing that such a promise would probably never be fulfilled given the Saint James' near-reclusive state, the well-travelled explorer fished out a large bottle of rakı from one of his bags before handing it to a grateful Colin.

'Until you do, this will give you a taste of Turkey, so to speak.'

Following a seemingly endless series of 'Thank you ever so much' and a promise to bake the carrot cake that Oliver loved so much, Colin gave his neighbour a quick, courteous wave and dropped the rakı into the house before continuing on his way into town.

As he approached the gates, Colin couldn't help but think of how fortunate he had been that it was Oliver – a single, rarely seen civil servant – who had purchased his brother's half of the house after their father followed in their mother's footsteps and went the way of all flesh some years earlier.

The crude division of the house down the middle would not have found praise from even the most generous of architects and it was just one further example of the way that things Colin once cherished had been sabotaged. (How fortunate for Freddie that his father had shed his mortal coil two years after his mother, thereby affording the softie the opportunity to reinsert his eldest child into the will, having been erased from it completely by their mother following his attempts at fratricide.)

When the solicitor informed Colin in writing that his brother intended to split the property in two, his already barely functioning heart had taken another beating. It wasn't just because the family home he had once loved so much would be drastically reimagined with a vulgar partition down the centre of the property; it was because he had assumed that Freddie and Mamie May would inform him of their plans for the house in person, which he had hoped would lead to some apology or, at the very least, an explanation as to why they'd so cruelly betrayed him. Such words might have afforded him a sort of finality to the whole, unpleasant affair. But that was fanciful thinking, it soon emerged, and rather than receiving that much-needed closure, Colin was left with endless questions, an unhappy wife who was ballooning by the day, and a spirit that was floating aimlessly downstream.

The well-worn gates required only the lightest of touches to open, which suited Colin, seeing as he needed to conserve his strength for the many takeaway bags that he would soon be carrying.

As he made his way along the path that would ultimately lead him to Navan's town centre, he kept his gaze lowered in an attempt to avoid glimpsing the posters. But, because of this – compounded by his lifelong difficulties with hearing – as he crossed the road, Colin failed to notice a car racing in his direction. It was only when the white Lada crashed into a road sign to the side of Colin that he realised what had transpired.

While the poor driver had to contend with whiplash and a damaged bumper, the most unfavourable aspect of this accident from Colin's perspective was that the road sign was now bowing, and, despite his best intentions, he found himself facing his brother's blasted poster.

'Why weren't you looking where you were going? You can't just cross the road without looking, you stupid –' the driver shouted as he stumbled out of the vehicle, dazed and confused.

But at that moment Colin had little interest in taking responsibility for his actions; he was far too busy picking up a stone that lay on the road.

'One day, I'll do this to you in person, you treacherous cad!' Colin roared before hurling the stone at his brother's face.

Little did he realise that such an opportunity would rear its head in just over a year's time.

TWENTY-EIGHT

'Take off your trousers, please.'

Thankfully, Azra learned from her earlier naivety and, within a week, she had packed her bags, leaving a furious Remzi Bey in her wake, and moved to a second brothel in a more salubrious area along the Bosphorus Strait. The moment the determined social-climber passed through the gates of the plush apartment complex, she knew that this establishment would be much more suitable for her quest to escape from the poverty to which she had become accustomed.

Fourteen years later, her childhood dream of owning a Spoon-maker's Diamond continued to be her final thought as she drifted off to sleep each night.

While the world remained in shock because of the untimely demise of superstar Freddie Mercury to the horrid AIDS virus that had been storming the gay community since 1985, that winter Azra was about to have her own brush with death.

The now well-seasoned concubine had just ordered her fourth client of the day to remove his clothes and, initially, hadn't anticipated any issue. When the young and well-built man didn't attempt to prise open as much as a button, however, Azra realised that he was there for reasons other than fornication.

The knife that he then revealed quickly confirmed her suspicions.

'It is not too late to repent, my child,' the good Christian informed her, his voice delirious, his manner threatening. 'God loves even His most sinful children – even harlots like you.'

Surrounded by well-regarded businessmen and millionaires, the thirty-six-year-old had never felt unsafe in her chosen career – frustrated by her lack of diamonds and *Pretty Woman*-esque wedding proposals, yes, but never in danger. This brothel employed burly men who hovered about the hallways, always at hand to intervene during any hairy moments, if necessary. Secretly, and with the help of a Polaroid camera, she also took a cheeky photograph of each of her new clients as they undressed or were in the throes of ecstasy – not for any vulgar reasons like blackmailing them, but simply as a way of protecting herself. Just in case. Thankfully, she never had an occasion to do anything with them other than store them in a tin box.

That wasn't to say that all her encounters had been plain sailing.

She always remembered the engineer who had spent an immeasurable amount of time on the oil rigs in the Black Sea where his only companions were of the nose-picking, arse-scratching variety. The prospect of his dalliance with Azra proved so overwhelming that he succumbed to the grim reaper a few short moments after unbuckling his belt. (Dead or alive, the poor soul had to pay his dues argued her boss, Solak Bey, as he rifled through his pockets before the authorities were alerted to the sorry scene.)

This day, however, Azra knew that mishandling the situation facing her might see her following in the footsteps of that excitable oil-rigger – and that just wouldn't do. The lady still had much to accomplish – she had yet to get her hands on her Spoonmaker's Diamond, for crying out loud! She needed to act quickly and efficiently. As she commenced a series of deep inhalations, Azra concluded that the best course of action was to play along with the spiritual charade.

'Thank you, my friend, for your concerns about my theological well-being,' she replied beatifically. 'Would it be possible to leave me with the Bible so that I can study His teachings without delay? I'm sure I will find it extremely informative and enlightening.'

The man hesitated, unsure of himself for a moment. Something smelt fishy to him (although that was hardly surprising, he thought, given the fact that he was standing slap-bang in the middle of a brothel). No, the strumpet was trying to fob him off, he was sure of it.

She was messing with the wrong person.

'I'm supposed to believe you, am I? You are just like all the other women in the world – dirty, immoral and sinful. You will never change!'

Of course, women are always to blame! she thought but decided to keep her opinion on his flawed argument to herself for now. Hoping that one of the security men was close by, Azra slowly edged herself towards the door. As she was about to release a cry for help, the fanatic grabbed her by the neck and shoved her against the wall. The knife loomed close to her terrified face.

'You will never change! So there's only one option!'

Without her voice to call upon, Azra kicked and walloped him, but she just couldn't compete with his strength – or his remarkable capacity to withstand a jolt to his nether regions. With her ability to breathe severely compromised, she turned her energies to the room and, with her feet, knocked the few items of furniture that stood beside her to the floor. A lamp smashed, as did an empty glass. But, despite the commotion, no assistance came.

The two combatants locked eyes. Azra could see that the only satisfactory conclusion for her attacker was a bloodied body lying strewn across the floor. That outcome didn't suit Azra in the slightest so, not knowing what else to do, she started to lick her lips.

And wink.

And blow him kisses.

'Mwah!'

She contorted her face just as all the men had done in this very room over the years. Like them, she looked ridiculous.

'What on earth are you doing?' her attacker asked. 'Stop that this minute, you disgusting –'

Taking advantage of his confusion and repulsion, with the last remaining smidgeon of energy she had left Azra pushed the brute away. As he crashed to the floor, she let out a hoarse shout, and the door finally opened.

About time.

The person who raced in and grabbed the knife from her assailant, before forcing him into a headlock, wasn't one of the bouncers or Solak Bey, however. It was a dashing man who could easily be mistaken for Bruce Willis, and whose accent – an accent she'd encountered a couple of times throughout her career – revealed to her that he was from a country that was famed for its luck.

Ireland.

1992

TWENTY-NINE

County Meath was christened the 'Royal County' thanks to her wealth of magnificent jewels such as Newgrange passage tomb, the Book of Kells and the River Boyne. This river had witnessed many thrilling historical events, notably the seventeenth-century battle between a certain William of Orange and his father-in-law, James II – a bloody family quarrel that *almost* put all others in the shade. While the Hill of Tara – the site from where one hundred and forty-two kings were said to have reigned – was beloved by locals, it was another Tara that had proven most worthy of song and story.

Navan's Tara Mines.

Cited as the largest zinc and lead deposit in Europe, the enterprise had kept hundreds of men and women in shoes since first discovered in 1970. Located on the northern outskirts of the palindromical town, the scope of the mines could not be appreciated by the average passer-by, seeing as its true grandeur lay several hundred metres underground.

It had not taken long for this subterranean might to find admirers around the world, including a Finnish stainless-steel company that enjoyed the rather jolly name of Outokumpu. In fact, so impressed were these Nordic business people that in 1986 – the same year that saw God take up temporary residence in a certain Argentinian footballer's left hand – the company purchased a seventy-five per cent share in the mines, resulting in a small contingency of Finnish people descending upon the town.

Six years following their arrival, these Nordic shareholders received word from home that their fellow countrymen and women had just launched a quirky sporting contest. Feeling a little homesick, they thought it was high time that their adopted hometown of Navan experienced some of Finland's traditions, old and new, and so a committee was formed to organise a cross-culture event. Unbeknownst to them at the time, these celebrations – and one event in particular – would provide the backdrop to the next chapter of an ongoing sibling rivalry: the wife-carrying competition.

***

As Trish lay sprawled out on the bed watching the latest episode of *Melrose Place*, Colin flicked through the week's *Meath Chronicle* beside her. This had been his way of educating himself about what was happening in and around Navan ever since deciding upon a self-imposed exile from town life after his brother's victory in the local elections a year earlier. (Thank heavens for home deliveries!) Raymond, his loyal schoolfriend, now the editor at the paper, would pop a copy into the letter box every Wednesday with a note scrawled across the top: 'Here if you need me.'

As of yet, there had been no response to his kind offer.

Colin scanned an article reflecting on the continued disappointment felt by many that the county football team had been knocked out of the All-Ireland Football Championship in the first round. He then read with interest about the latest misdemeanours that were being presented before the judges at Trim's District Court. Vandalism appeared to be the current crime *du jour*, and while Colin was yet to put a foot on the wrong side of the law, he secretly envied those who'd smashed the windows of the Lyric Cinema or sprayed vulgarities across the side of the Post Office. While Colin had never let himself down by uttering language of the blue variety, he wondered if it would be advisable to park social etiquette and just let loose. How thrilling it would be, he imagined, to call his supposedly reformed brother a few choice expletives.

By God, how he deserved them.

Colin felt tiredness approach, so he folded the paper and placed it on the bedside locker before resting his head on the pillow. Not that sleep was an ally – it was frequently interrupted by nightmares, where duplicitous siblings and double-crossing fiancées were recurring characters. It seemed cruel to Colin that the duo wasn't content with dominating his daily life, but were determined to hijack his sleep as well.

He decided to go without his portion of the duvet, seeing as the majority of it was covered in crumbs from the chocolate-chip biscuits he had baked for his wife earlier that evening. Funnily enough, Colin hadn't much interest in duvets and blankets in recent times, primarily because he had been experiencing blasted night-time sweating – a condition that his doctor put down to anxiety.

'Are you sure you won't entertain the idea of taking a little medication, Colin? You are compromising your quality of life,' Dr Cassells had once tried to persuade him, with little success. Like so many others in Ireland, Colin foolishly felt that medication was only for illnesses like tonsillitis or arthritis and not anything related to the mind.

'I'm sure it will pass,' Colin had replied – a prediction that would have left Nosferatu doubled over with laughter.

Even though it was just 9.30 p.m., Colin had no difficulty drifting off, though his dreams soon turned troubled. His night-mares were always vivid – aside from the usual suspects, another recurring image his mind often stumbled upon was one that involved all of his teeth crumbling in his mouth. There was no explanation as to why they fell apart; he would just suddenly have a pile of yellowish-brown teeth bunched on top of his tongue. Often, he would wake up clutching his neck, convinced that he was swallowing his stained ivories. This night, however, the dental drama didn't plague him for too long as Trish rudely woke him by releasing a blood-curdling roar that could have competed with a hurricane. (Yes, Colin continued to have difficulties with his hearing, but despite his best efforts, he could never entirely drown out the sounds of his full-voiced wife.)

'You brazen hussy!' she cried before throwing an empty can of Cidona at some fictional female making a move on the fictional male on screen.

Struggling to return to the Land of Nod, Colin lay wide-eyed. Just as he was about to start counting sheep, he noticed the words 'Wife-Carrying Competition' emblazoned across the back page of the paper. Curiosity piqued, and unlikely to get much sleep seeing as his wife continued to writhe in anger beside him, he sat upright and retrieved *The Meath Chronicle* from the bedside table. The back page listed information on the party organised by Tara Mines' Finnish stakeholders. Colin had little interest in learning about the bouncy castle that would be available for the children on the day, or the various Nordic delicacies set to be on offer. The editorial documenting the particulars of the wife-carrying competition, the day's headline act, on the other hand, proved to be a riveting read:

Having just launched in Finland this year, the wife-carrying competition might appear humorous to us, but our Finnish friends are determined to wipe the smiles off our faces on the day, so be warned!

The objective is simple: in twos, husbands must race against each other across a tricky obstacle course, 253.5 metres in length, while simultaneously carrying their nearest and dearest, who must weigh at least 59 kilogrammes. According to Finnish rules, the wife must also be over the age of 17 but seeing as we Irish must wait until we are a ripe 18 before walking down the aisle, that requirement is a given. We hope! Anyway, the couple who completes the course in the shortest amount of time will be deemed victorious.

The manner by which our dear ladies are hoisted onto the men are threefold: piggyback, over-the-shoulder or hanging upside-down with the wife's legs around the husband's shoulders. In a nod to impartiality, the judges present on the day will be representatives of both countries, so any claims of favouritism will be given short shrift.

Sources reveal that our Finnish friends have already kicked off their training for the big event. So, people of Meath, put down those pints and get training!

The peculiar nature of the competition was not the reason why so many emotions were stirring within Colin. Instead, it was the small black-and-white picture of the recently elected local councillor that lay beside the editorial, along with the caption: 'I'm game. Are you?'

Colin realised that his brother was challenging him to a duel. He suddenly felt a fierce determination to live up to the victorious name his mother had given him. Maybe, after all, it was still possible for him to emerge triumphant – for once.

You can be sure that I'm game, Councillor Alfred Saint James. See you on the starting line!

THIRTY

When she'd first encountered Irish people, Azra was delighted to discover that they were cheery and high-spirited folk. If religious guilt got the better of them, as it often did with new clients, the Irish would ensure that they got bang for their buck by spending the remainder of the thirty-minute session talking with Azra about this, that and everything. This afforded her fantastic opportunities to improve her English and expand her limited knowledge of the world.

She struck up a couple of friendships with these sociable Irish customers – how could she resist their charm and the bright twinkle in their eyes? And, unlike many of the men she had to indulge, these Irish lads were refreshingly self-deprecating and thought nothing of putting themselves down. There were many aspects of their personalities that she enjoyed, but how she chuckled at their fondness for using the word 'yoke' to describe everything – except the inside of an egg, of course.

'We went to see these yokes last night twirling around in circles, wearing these funny costumes.'

'Our tour guide is an awful aul yoke.'

'I don't suppose you have that yoke that you put on your willy to stop ye having babies, do ye?'

She did, although sometimes she thought that earplugs would have been a more appropriate form of protection during such interactions.

However, one Irishman was different; he was someone to whom she could have listened all day and night.

Her knight in shining armour, Oliver Flood.

When he'd first visited the brothel a few months earlier and saved her life from the psychotic Bible basher, she could not have realised that she would soon fall head over heels in love with him.

But that is exactly what happened. Better yet, the more she got to know Oliver, the less interested she became in the status of his bank balance. Their connection was proving to be brighter than the Spoonmaker's Diamond – a realisation that proved both thrilling and terrifying in equal measure.

Please let him feel the same way, she hoped as she lay with him one rainy summer's evening in her small flat.

'*Táim i ngrá leat,*' Oliver whispered, lighting up a post-coital cigarette.

'What does that mean?' she asked as she traced the shape of a heart across his bare chest, relishing the fact there their recent encounters were no longer limited to the thirty minutes the brothel afforded its patrons.

'That's for me to know and you to find out!'

Much to her own amazement, earlier that evening Azra had confided in him that while she was surrounded by men day and night, she had recently become lonely.

'Especially every time you return to Ankara.'

Oliver suspected that, as much as Azra cherished her independence, she might like to start a relationship. Someone who had her back. An allegiance. In fact, he was confident that he fitted the bill perfectly.

'Come on, tell me what it means!' she demanded. '*Táim i ngrá leat.*'

'I didn't think it was possible, but you are even cuter when you speak in Irish – no matter how awful your pronunciation is!'

Oliver had told her a lot about himself, including how he lived in a thriving Norman town called Navan, a place about thirty miles north of Dublin.

'Can you credit it – it's spelt the same way backwards as it is forwards!' he had previously informed her about a hundred times.

As a senior staff member at the Irish Embassy in Ankara, he

visited Istanbul often, and when he was there, he always called upon Azra. He had become smitten with her – a feeling that he prayed was not unrequited.

'Oliver, apart from saving my beef a few months ago ...'

Bacon. He couldn't bring himself to correct her.

'... you have done something that nobody else has ever done: you make me laugh!'

Whether it was dancing in his ill-fitting underwear, singing out of tune or speaking in silly voices, she told him how grateful she was that he seemed entirely hell-bent on putting her in good humour – a rare quality amongst the men she encountered.

'There's another way I know to make you laugh,' he teased, climbing over her.

'Yes?'

'Yes, like this!' he announced before tickling her stomach.

While it was against house rules, for their past few encounters Oliver had been meeting Azra outside of office hours, as it were, for walks and talks, food and drink. As the weeks went on, they even started holding each other's hand. The pair would always chat about the day's current affairs – from weighty issues, such as the strengths and weaknesses of John Major as Prime Minister of the United Kingdom, to more casual fare, such as the strengths and weaknesses of *The Silence of the Lambs*.

'I thought it was about farmyard animals and brought my ten-year-old niece. How we made it past the ushers is beyond me!' he quipped the night before as they walked past the cone-capped, cylindrical Galata Tower. 'She cried for about two weeks after!'

Things between them were almost perfect. The only fly in the ointment, he revealed, after the tickles and laughter subsided, was the professional path she pursued in life.

'Would we have ever met if I had not worked here?' she reminded him.

Nonetheless, as much as she sidestepped the subject, it was clear that Oliver longed for her to change careers. He often wondered whether he would be able to teach an old dog new tricks (although if what he had just experienced was anything to go by, it was certain that she was a mistress of all the tricks).

If only I could find a way of taking her away from Istanbul – even for a short time, he thought as he stubbed out his cigarette. *Maybe then she might realise that, free from the sordid brothel and lecherous men, there are so many adventures waiting for her. If she was of the persuasion, she might even permit me to be her companion. I wonder would she like Ankara? Or Navan? I'm sure everyone would give her a fine welcome.*

And so, as he dressed himself, Oliver decided that the only cure for love was marriage.

'*Táim i ngrá leat,*' Azra repeated, still not having the foggiest idea what she was saying.

And I'm in love with you, too. I really am.

'Oliver, come on – are you still not going to tell me what it means?'

'Instead of telling you, beautiful lady, I'm going to show you,' he replied before disappearing into the city to buy a ring – one suitable for the most enchanting woman in Istanbul.

THIRTY-ONE

Freddie had no love for the people of Navan. The previous year, he had realised that the most effective way of channelling this feeling was to become a councillor and have them at his mercy.

As usual, the fellow had not adequately thought through his plan.

Since emerging triumphant in the elections, Councillor Alfred Saint James had been forced to allocate his Wednesday mornings to listening to the whims and complaints of his constituents before assuring them that he would move mountains to help them. It was about as enjoyable as sitting through a Good Friday liturgy delivered by an elderly and stammering priest, he often felt.

Seated in front of him in his bare and unwelcoming office, his constituents spoke at length, with complete disregard for the large notice that hung on the wall behind the councillor imploring people to be mindful of the clock. Councillor Saint James often felt that he deserved a Nobel Peace Prize for not reaching for the bread knife from the nearby kitchenette and channelling his inner Sweeney Todd.

The complaints were varied and many:

'Councillor, I've been on the housing list for almost three years, and I'm expecting another set of twins in November – come on, can you sort us out for God's sake?'

'Councillor, you know me, I'm not one to complain, but those potholes all the way up Railway Street are absolutely disgraceful! Wait for it to rain and you could open a selection of swimming pools! You've got to do something!'

'Me mam has been on one of them hospital trollies for four full days. And ye should see the schlop she's been served – I could do better meself, and I'm just about able to cook toast – and sure that's only burnt bread!'

It was evident to Councillor Alfred Saint James that many of his constituents held the belief that they housed stand-up comedians within and yearned for an Open Mic. Oh, how he longed to punch them on the kisser, silencing their stupid jokes.

On days like these, it didn't take much for the councillor to become distracted. As the townsfolk prattled on, he often found himself gazing out the window onto the busy Market Square and watching the world go by. This particular morning, as Norma Hegarty was describing – seemingly in real time – the unsociable hours her neighbours kept, Freddie saw something that gave him nothing short of a shock. In fact, he had to do a double-take.

His brother was running across the square in front of him, decked out in luminescent sporting gear, without a care in the world. To add insult to injury, his elephantine wife was trailing behind him.

'What the …?'

He jumped out of his seat and bolted out of the office, leaving poor Mrs Hegarty's story unfinished. Emerging onto the street, Freddie ignored pipe-smoking Mr Thompson, next in line to waste the councillor's time, and focused instead on the unlikely duo scuttling in the direction of Ludlow Street. Even when Trish stopped in front of Spicer's Bakery and started drooling over the beautiful pastries and cakes within, a simple call of encouragement from Colin was all it took to resume her jogging.

Don't tell me they are taking part in the race, are they?

How on earth had his brother managed to convince that notoriously lazy and unmotivated woman not only to sign up for the competition but, more surprisingly, to train for the event? Had he some incriminating evidence on her, perhaps? Had he placed a bomb on her person?

What's more, did he *really* believe that they stood a shot at winning?

Here was me thinking that today was going to be a bad day, he thought, laughing hysterically. When Freddie's party had browbeaten him into signing up for the juvenile wife-carrying competition, he hadn't even fleetingly entertained the notion that it might prove to be another opportunity to humiliate the brother. Seeing as the pilfering of Colin's one true love many moons earlier had already had the desired effect – rendering his sibling a shadow of his former self – Freddie had felt sure that the poor chap wouldn't even watch the competition from afar, let alone attempt to lug twenty-odd stone of solid fat across his shoulders and participate.

But, in this case, it seemed that he was wrong. For once, he was thrilled that he had misjudged the situation.

Game on, little brother. Game on.

THIRTY-TWO

Trish only ever had one dream in life, and that was to attend the Eurovision Song Contest. Ever since Ireland's first entry into this hugely popular celebration of music and culture on that March evening in 1965, when Butch Moore sang on an Italian stage about walking through the streets in the rain, eight-year-old Trish had vowed that she would do whatever it took to bag herself tickets for the front row.

She became captivated by the marvellous escapism that the event offered, not to mention the unabashed spectacle, glamour and nail-biting tension of the voting. As a bonus, thanks to the Eurovision, Trish could impressively list off every country in Europe *en Français* and count all the way up to *douze points* – despite barely showing up to a single French class when at school.

In fact, it had been her love for the show that dictated the trajectory of her life. In 1980, as heart-throb Johnny Logan was en route to the Hague to fly the Irish flag, the then twenty-two-year-old had been enjoying a ginger ale in Loughran's Bar with her inebriated parents. Boasting a healthier figure then, Trish caught the attention of a visiting salesman, armed with not only a van full of men's stockings and women's hosiery but also the most silver tongue in all of Leinster.

'I'm crazy about the Eurovision Song Contest,' she announced, seconds after their initial hellos. 'And I would do whatever it takes to be there.'

'Tell me, who has been your favourite Irish entrant so far?' he quizzed, having fallen for her childlike enthusiasm.

'It would have to be Dickie Rock – I love Dickie!'

'I bet you do, ye naughty girl,' he responded while surreptitiously removing his wedding ring. 'How would you feel if I could get you tickets for the final?'

Before he could say, 'Here are the votes from the Irish jury', she was lying flat in the back of the rogue's van, legs akimbo. (The performance, she would later reflect, would do well to score a mere *quatre points*.)

One didn't have to be equipped with the intellectual ability of Sherlock Holmes to deduce that the only production Trish was set to experience was of the *reproduction* variety. As soon as her father became aware of the mess in which his daughter had found herself, he declared that there were only three options:

1) Take the first ferry to England, not The Hague.
2) Hone her laundering skills with the Magdalene Sisters.
3) Or marry that rich, deaf guy they had befriended in Loughran's, where he had been drowning his sorrows ever since being jilted at the altar three years earlier.

After such a public humiliation, it would require little effort to swoop in and take advantage of his vulnerability, Mr Smith wagered. 'Sure, he's been going around the town like a ghost this past while – he needs a good woman to sort him out – and who better than our Trish?'

Mr Smith was surprised – and delighted – to learn that not only was Trish enthusiastic about the plan, but also that it didn't take his daughter much effort to persuade Colin of her charms, as they soon began dating. That she was with child did not matter one iota to him, nor to his overbearing, Housewife-of-the-Year mother. It appeared that the fellow was in such dire need of a lifeline that his parents would have agreed to any demands – but there was only one that Trish had in mind.

Marriage.

***

With her bump growing bigger every day, the last-minute wedding took place much sooner than anyone would normally have recommended – and on a Friday, as the more traditional Saturday was fully booked up in Navan and its environs. Colin was unable to provide Trish with the family heirloom, seeing as his wretched brother had gambled it away to supplement his hell-raising ways three years previously, but he did manage to acquire a ring befitting the occasion. It was decorated with rubies, which, he informed her, represented courage – a quality that they would soon have to call upon, even if they didn't know it at the time.

Even though their union had an unusual genesis, it was pointed out by the small congregation, including his best man, Raymond, that the two battered souls weren't such a bad match after all. There even stood something resembling a chance that they might have a happy future.

So, about an hour later, as the unlikely duo navigated their way through the downpour of confetti and out into the churchyard, they hoped that luck would *finally* be on their side.

However, anyone keen to embrace the good omens on a wedding day must also be prepared for the bad ones. If the betrothed had remembered the rhyme that stated, 'Marry in the month of May, and you will surely rue the day', they mightn't have been so surprised when things quickly started to fall apart at the seams.

***

Colin had been standing in the kitchen when he heard a scream from the bathroom upstairs. Having just returned from a short honeymoon to County Clare, he had immediately moved his new bride into the Saint James household and, seeing as the property was akin to a small hotel, nobody was getting under anyone else's feet. In fact, Mr and Mrs Saint James, their son and their new daughter-in-law were proving to be quite the formidable quartet. Day by day, Colin and Trish's appreciation of each other grew, and while they'd probably never have formed an alliance if it wasn't for the actions of a pair of unscrupulous men, they were aware that things could have turned out a lot worse. At long last, it appeared that the future might not be so bad after all.

Until that scream came.

When Colin reached the landing upstairs, he found Trish, who was now six months into her pregnancy, standing in the doorway of the newly decorated nursery, frozen. He followed her teary gaze towards her hands, which she held aloft. They were covered in blood.

As he carefully led her down the stairs and out into the car, she kept repeating the words, 'It's too late', over and over again.

While Trish's instincts might not always have been sound – as her encounter with that randy travelling salesman would have attested – in this instance, she was entirely correct.

***

Following the miscarriage, Trish received great support, not only from Colin, but from the many callers who arrived at the house armed with chocolates, flowers and words they were sure would be of comfort to her.

'It is nature's way, pet.'

'You'll get another chance, don't worry.'

'Time's a great healer.'

While she was sure that their intentions were noble, Trish just wanted to hurl the bouquets at them and scream, 'Yes, it is a great healer, but it's me who has to live through every single second of this nightmare until that magical time arrives! And if it is nature's way or God's way, why would I want *another* shot at it – how do I know that He won't do the same thing again?'

She didn't have the energy to say more than 'Thank you' and 'You're probably right', so her friends and family assumed that she would be back to her usual self in no time.

They couldn't have been more wrong.

Over the next two years, Trish and Colin tried again. And again. But a baby always eluded them. Trish experienced several more miscarriages and several more breakdowns. When, after the last one, Colin delicately enquired whether she wanted to take one final punt at parenting, she declined. Simply put, she was damned if she was going to risk going through all of that once more.

Instead, Trish found comfort in her husband's baking. Every time she felt a pang of emotion, she would ask him to rustle up a batch of chocolate éclairs, or a Swiss roll or two. Being the gentleman that he was, Colin never refused, even as her form ballooned; he had far too much experience in having things that were incredibly precious stolen from him. Trish mightn't have ever shown it or expressed it, but she truly appreciated the silent support she received from her kind and sweet husband, and hoped that one day she would be in a position to return the favour.

Which was why, one night, as the end credits of *Melrose Place* rolled, she didn't hesitate for a second when, for the first time in their eleven-year marriage, Colin asked her for a favour.

'Trish, is there any way in the world I can persuade you to enter this wife-carrying competition-thingy with me?'

'Yeah, no problem,' she replied.

(Admittedly, the promise of tickets to next year's Eurovision Song Contest if they won the event had also played a small part in her agreeing, particularly as it was going to be held in Ireland following Linda Martin's magnificent win in Sweden that May.)

'Let's show this town what we're made of!' she declared.

THIRTY-THREE

It's time I showed him what we Turks are made of!

Azra was tired of being told by her new boyfriend that Ireland was the 'best country in the world' and decided that she must embrace her inner Turkish patriot, put on her tour-guide hat and show him some of her favourite spots in Istanbul.

'Meet me here at two o'clock and bring your walking shoes,' she instructed as she kissed him on the lips, and by 'here' she was referring to her flat, the location where her meetings with Oliver now always took place.

Oliver had already seen much of what Istanbul had to offer since beginning his employment with the Irish Embassy two years earlier, but his mind was somewhat distracted when she made the suggestion, and so he found himself agreeing to an itinerary he had already completed multiple times.

A few hours later, the lovebirds set off. Azra's trail began with a visit to the sixth-century underground Basilica Cistern, originally carved out of the earth by over seven thousand slaves. The enormous space commanded a size close to two football pitches, and was peppered with 336 marble columns, which impressively held up the vaulted ceilings.

'Well, what do you think? Your eyes have to adjust to the darkness, yes, and it has musty smells – but it's also very dramatic, don't you agree?'

'Sure,' he replied, feigning enthusiasm.

The cistern's main talking point was a well-known mythical figure, secretly submerged under the water towards the back: Medusa's grisly, snake-covered heads, which were chillingly located at the bottom of a couple of pillars.

If they don't generate a reaction from Oliver, nothing will!

As they stood between the pillars, Azra was surprised to

discover that the mysterious treasures did not seem to impress her guest in the slightest – particularly seeing as he had previously mentioned his penchant for the peculiar. In fact, he had been out of sorts ever since they left her flat earlier that afternoon. Was it something she had said or done? Medusa was famed for turning people to stone and, looking at her lover now, it seemed that the Greek gorgon continued to possess that ability.

'One of Medusa's heads is upside down while the other is sideways – do you see?'

Oliver managed a nod.

'There are many theories,' she continued, hoping that her anecdotes about the space might awaken him from his slumber. 'One is that they were, in fact, nothing more than rubble from the Roman era – an early example of recycling!'

'I see.'

'Another theory is that it was the early Christians making a bold statement about their religion by giving paganism short shift.'

Shrift. A smile appeared on Oliver's face for the first time that day but quickly faded as they continued to stroll across the wooden platforms, passing some barely lit musicians playing eerie music.

Azra was unaware that Oliver's lack of conversation was not owing to cool indifference; it was due to the nerves that he and every other man battle when on the verge of proposing.

Another highlight of the cistern was the intricately carved Column of Tears, said to bring good fortune. Azra was on the verge of leading Oliver towards it in the hope that they would benefit from such positive omens. Noticing his sluggish gait, however, at the last minute she instead decided upon another course of action entirely – one that she felt would definitely improve his humour.

'Okay, I know somewhere that will leave you – how do you say – on cloud ten!' she promised before dragging him away from

Medusa's unsettling glare. 'There's nowhere in the city I cherish more.'

En route to the next location, Azra couldn't help but notice the many flower girls traipsing the streets, armed with tulips. She took some lira from her purse and handed it to one of the girls. Azra placed the flower in Oliver's lapel.

'You're now dressed for a wedding!' she joked, although her words were met with a startled look – one that Azra couldn't quite interpret.

Had Oliver gone off her?

It only took the pair about fifteen minutes to position themselves in front of the masterpiece that had been instrumental in taking the young flower girl away from the streets and into the world of being a high-class concubine: her prized Spoonmaker's Diamond in Topkapi Palace. She was positive that this setting would warrant a more upbeat response from her lover.

'Isn't it the most magical object you've ever seen?' she whispered, as they stood a metre away from the jewel, both paralysed by the sight. Unfortunately, Oliver's current speechless state was no longer on account of his nervousness about asking for Azra's hand in marriage; instead, it was because the ring that skulked in his jacket pocket felt wholly inadequate in comparison to the object before them.

'Yes, I suppose you could say that,' he mumbled, ruling out the possibility of presenting Azra with the modest rock that he had acquired the evening before. Worse again, Oliver began to question whether monetary matters, rather than emotional ones, solely motivated this stunning lady standing beside him. Was he an idiot for thinking that she saw him in a different light than all the other men who crawled on top of her?

What did you expect, you idiot? he berated himself when he finally managed to part her from the jewel. *She is a prostitute after all.*

No matter how she tried, Azra couldn't work out why a melancholic cloud had fallen upon her companion. She decided against disclosing to him the fact that her lifelong dream of owning a rock on a par with the Spoonmaker's Diamond had now been replaced by a desire to be given a ring by him, her one true love – even one fashioned from a piece of wire found on the street would do.

You're as sentimental today as you were when a child, Azra, she realised, before blaming herself for getting swept away by the pair's unique connection. *And, you know, what harm? There's a reason that this Irishman has come into your life – embrace it!*

She had great plans for that evening – in both the bedroom and kitchen – but was devastated to learn that even though it was a balmy May evening, Oliver had to 'rain check'.

'I've a long day tomorrow, so I best get to bed early,' he feebly lied. 'I'll call in before I head to the train station to say goodbye, how about that?'

'Oliver, what's wron–'

'Sleep well.'

Azra didn't get a wink.

***

The next morning, filled with uncertainty, Oliver wished his one true love goodbye. Unbeknownst to them both, it was to be the final time they would ever see one another. Not because Oliver decided to put an end to the affair – for a more tragic reason, in fact. It would emerge that St Peter would be demanding Oliver's presence at the pearly gates in a couple of months' time.

As his health waned, Oliver couldn't resist returning one last time to the role of Azra's would-be saviour. Despite his fragile and decreasing health, the Navan man made a private vow that, before he gave up the ghost, he would offer her a fresh start in life – one that didn't involve clients or financial exchanges.

So long as that was what she wanted, of course.

Yes, sometimes in life, everyone needed a little helping hand from others; from his deathbed, that's exactly what Oliver planned to give Azra.

THIRTY-FOUR

Colin gave Trish a helping hand into the bath, one that wasn't filled with bubbles and heat but, instead, with freezing water. The exhausting training that the formidable duo had subjected themselves to in preparation for the wife-carrying competition was taking its toll on their bodies. If they were to keep the dream alive, they concluded that they would have to embrace extreme remedies like this ice bath. They hoped that it might prove to be the perfect antidote to the horrid chafing that was running riot in places that they previously hadn't even known their bodies possessed. That was saying nothing of the muscles, knees and feet which were all at loggerheads with each other over what ached the most.

'Oooooh,' Trish exclaimed, getting some perverse enjoyment out of the shock to her system.

Colin was overwhelmed by how devoted his once exercise-shy wife had been to the full-on training programme. Instead of dozing off at four in the morning, having watched some silly night-time film, Trish was now getting up at that ungodly hour to begin the first of her thrice daily five-kilometre runs – and there wasn't a sigh or a 'do-we-really-have-to-do-this?' in sight. When it came to sit-ups and press-ups, without fail she disregarded the heart palpitations and dizziness, and persevered, meeting all the targets her husband set and more. If life allowed a person to start again, Colin would most certainly have encouraged her to enter the Olympic Games – that's how vigorous she was revealing herself to be.

Most admirable of all was the discipline and self-control she was showing when it came to her diet. She encouraged Colin to pack away his – and his late mother's – prized baking utensils and replace his mouth-watering delicacies with a regime that would leave even the pernicketiest of nutritionists in a swoon. Over the three-month period the weight fell off her and, for the first time in a long time, Colin saw the woman from before those terrible miscarriages. He had no idea what was motivating her to show such commitment and enthusiasm, but he wasn't going to question it.

Something else that took him by surprise upon signing up for the competition was the connection that they had forged anew so late in their relationship; if it wasn't going to continue beyond the event, Colin was hell-bent on enjoying it while it lasted. If someone had told him a few months ago that he and his wife would be taking a bath together, he would have laughed in their faces. Who knew – before the competition concluded, they might even engage in some of the biblical relations that had been absent from their marriage for many, many years.

Trish continued to find pleasure in the horrendous temperatures of the bath, giving Colin an opportunity to ruminate over the exact reasons why he had been putting this woman through the mill: just so he could emerge triumphant against his brother in an absurd competition. He would have been the first to concede that there were many moments over the past number of weeks where he had questioned his motivation – after all, how was a win in this community competition going to nullify so many years of heartache? As a child and a teenager, he had always known deep down that Freddie hated him, although he was still at a loss as to the reason why. Looking back, Colin realised that his genuine attempts at forging a connection between them had probably made matters worse, despite his noble intentions.

However, as disappointing as it was to have been a stranger in his brother's life, nothing came close to the irreparable hurt Freddie had caused him by stealing the woman that he once loved; the woman he'd been due to marry. Beauty aside, Colin knew only too well that the man never had any interest in Mamie May – in fact, all the things that he found endearing about her would have repulsed his older sibling. Freddie did what he did simply because he wanted to hurt Colin, and to get his hands on the family's pear-shaped diamond, which Colin later discovered had been lost in a poker game practically before the confetti had even fallen to the ground.

No, there would be no forgiveness – not that the scoundrel had ever looked for it. He was positive that Freddie relished the idea that not only was his brother unable to marry his one true love, but also that he had settled down with a woman who was probably ridiculed by some in the town for her proclivity for sweet things. These two facts, Colin thought, would have brought Freddie much consolation in those moments when he wanted to throttle his gullible and doe-eyed wife.

Now Colin had one shot to demonstrate that his older brother had not, in fact, beaten him in life and, more importantly, in matters of the heart. As Trish's recent loyalty and allegiance had shown, Colin genuinely felt that he currently had the best wife in Navan and he was adamant to prove this point to everyone.

'You may have won the battle, Councillor Alfred Saint James, but you most definitely will not win the war!'

Trish gave a little jump – she had been on the verge of dozing off, and she knew that that would not do; they had their third and final run of the day to complete, after all, as well as forty lengths of the swimming pool to tackle before there could be any talk of sleep.

'Will we march forth, Colin?' she asked, reaching for the towel.

'I couldn't have put it better myself, dear heart.'

THIRTY-FIVE

Several weeks after her sweetheart returned to Ankara, Azra was fully informed on Bosnia and Herzegovina's declaration of independence from Yugoslavia and was looking forward to debating the consequences of such a bold move with Oliver, whom she hoped would soon make an appearance.

'If you're too busy to come down to Istanbul, I can take the train up to Ankara some weekend,' she suggested in one of the many unanswered letters that she wrote to him. 'I promise, I will make it worth your while!'

Initially, she questioned whether his silence was down to a change of heart on his part and cursed him for conning her into believing that he was different from the other men. The more time that passed, however, the more she concluded that something else was at the root of his silence.

She had even called the embassy, but they provided her with scant information other than the fact that he had returned home to Ireland indefinitely. When they abruptly ended the phone call after she asked when they were expecting him to return, Azra's instinct informed her that there was another, more sinister reason at play.

Her companion was dying – she could feel it in the pit of her stomach.

After calling operators in Ireland, she managed to locate a telephone number for him, but every time she attempted to reach him, the call would just ring out.

When the day of his birthday arrived in late July – just two short months following the lovebirds' last encounter – Azra, heartbroken, bought a bottle of Jameson whiskey, Oliver's favourite drink, and in her lonely flat, she toasted his health and prayed for a miracle. For the first time since that sip of Martini in the Pera Palace Hotel, she allowed alcohol to pass her lips.

She had not realised the extent of her sadness until that evening, when tears cascaded down her cheeks. In fact, the loss of the love of her life had rendered her so off-course that she was unaware that she had consumed the majority of the bottle – a feat by which even the hardiest of drinkers would have undoubtedly been impressed.

She staggered towards her bed only a couple of feet away but didn't make it, promptly crashing to the floor with a bang. In moments she was snoring, sleep offering her a brief reprieve from the wretchedness that she felt.

***

When Azra awoke the following morning with a head so sore that she was convinced she was about to follow her one true love into an early grave, there was a letter waiting for her from Ireland. Her bloodshot eyes first noticed the stamp, and when she realised its origin and recognised the familiar penmanship, she began praying that Oliver was in fact still alive and well. As she scanned the letter, however, her worst fears were realised. But her sorrow was challenged by shock as she took in the offer put forth by Oliver.

Azra,

I write this to you as my beloved town of Navan gets swept away by a peculiar event called the wife-carrying competition – ironically, a contest that neither of us would have been entitled to enter even though my love for you is stronger than most of the husbands who are training for the big race.

Thanks to round-the-clock coverage on the local radio and news-papers, the mania is hard to miss and while we won't be at the starting line, it has given me food for thought (and not 'bread for thought' as you always adorably say!)

In May, as you gave me a tour around your magnificent city, I was planning to propose to you but, like so many times in the past, I allowed the voices in my head to get the better of me. When I finally managed to silence them, I boarded a train to Istanbul, but no sooner had it left the station than I began to feel ill. Very ill. It appeared that the cancer that I'd encountered a few years ago had made a return – and it was more aggressive than ever.

Marriage is something that I can no longer offer you. Azra, I am dying. I have begged and pleaded with the hospital to allow me to travel to Istanbul to see you one last time but I am just too sick. I even tried to sneak out one night, but I only got as far as the car park before falling in a heap. I have no other choice now but to listen to my body.

And, more importantly, to now listen to my heart.

After I'm gone, I want to offer you a choice, which is entirely yours to make. During our final date together, I observed how the Spoonmaker's Diamond had left you completely smitten, which is fitting seeing as I, like many others, view you like a queen and it's only right that you should be showered with jewels! To that effect, you might recall me telling you that Navan is the principal town in Meath, which is affectionately known as the Royal County, owing to its history as the seat of the High Kings of Ireland. So it gives me much joy to think that when this horrid journey with cancer concludes, I will finally be in a position to make you a monarch, even if your rule will only be over my house in Navan. If you'll allow me to bequeath you my property, that is …

And as for the jewel. Well, all you have to do is realise that you shine brighter than any diamond in the world.

Love, Oliver.

This beautiful offer from her one true love had the potential to change the direction of her life completely, Azra realised.

If the blasted hangover didn't kill her first, that was.

THIRTY-SIX

The Meath Chronicle, 15 August 1992:

The fine residents of Navan have never needed much of an excuse to throw a party. Be it the St Patrick's Day parade, the annual Rotary treasure hunt or the homecoming of the winning – or, in recent years, losing – Meath football team, the crowds have always been guaranteed to come out in force. The festival to celebrate the heritage of Tara Mines' Finnish shareholders was certainly no exception.

Officials overseeing proceedings revealed to The Meath Chronicle *that, at last count, more than a thousand people had descended upon Navan's Claremont Stadium to ensure that their Nordic friends received the recognition they deserved.*

While a knees-up was always guaranteed, kind weather was not. Fortunately, as the attendees gorged themselves on beautiful Finnish Karelian pasties or fresh-out-of-the-oven cinnamon rolls, there was not a drop in sight – so long as one discounted all the ample drops of mead – or Sima, to give it its Finnish name – shots of Koskenkorva Vodka and pints of Guinness being guzzled by all the mammies and daddies present.

And for those who wanted an additional dollop of heat, the small selection of saunas specially constructed for the day in tribute to our Finnish friends were available.

'Here's a good one for ye,' local undertaker Mr Ó Cofaigh was heard telling anybody who would listen. 'There are over one and a half million saunas in Finland – that is almost one for every third person!'

Speaking of good ones, many decided that the record books needed consulting in an attempt to discover whether that fine Saturday in August was the earliest date in which Santa Claus, Finland's most famous son, had visited Irish shores. Either way, the youngsters were falling over themselves in their quest to get their mitts on one of the many presents being shared out by Father Christmas.

'I got a big bag of liquorice,' eight-year-old Stephen Newman told Lucy Breathnach, a reporter from LMFM radio, although the only evidence of this was the black stains on his teeth and braces. 'I can't remember the exact name of the sweets because I never done Finnish at school.'

'Rather than taking a punt at another language, I am certain your teacher would be more than happy if you just focused on improving your English for now,' Ms Breathnach tartly quipped. 'Oh, for interested listeners, a source tells me they are called Salmiakki and while quite salty, they are a heaven-send for digestive complaints and maladies of the throat.'

If the magical harmonies that were coming out of the mouths of the St Mary's Boys' Choir were anything to go by, it was clear that they, too, must have had their fair share of Salmiakki earlier in the day. They sounded angelic, with many acknowledging that they had provided one of the highlights of the day's celebrations.

'I loved the "Ave Maria". But was it just me or were they a little off towards the end of "Scarlet Ribbons"?' critiqued hard-to-please local woman, Mrs Brady.

If there was one other part of the day that deserved a particularly favourable review, it was, of course, the nail-biting and often hilarious wife-carrying competition, which took place throughout the day. With over one hundred Irish and Finnish lovebirds taking part, the structure of the contest was as follows: two husbands, carrying their respective wives, had to race each other through a tricky and muddy obstacle course, which consisted of an assortment of climbing walls, rickety bridges, balancing beams, tyres and ropes. Judges from both countries kept a keen eye on proceedings, which, in truth, bore more of a resemblance to Beechmount Hotel at three o'clock on a Saturday night than a proper competition, such was the propensity for bandy-legged contestants to face-plant to the ground. Even our Finnish friends struggled to remain vertical throughout.

Rarely had Claremont Stadium witnessed such pandemonium – and if the athletics field had a roof, it would surely have been lifted thanks to the ear-deafening screams that sounded throughout (thank goodness those liquorice sweets were in ample supply to soothe overused tonsils).

For better or for worse, happy marriages found themselves being tested like never before, and the way in which many wives yelled at their nearest and dearest over the course of the 253.5-metre track left no doubt in anyone's mind who wore the trousers in those relationships.

'We would have achieved a better time if himself had not devoured that takeaway from the BC Diner last night,' one aggrieved wife, who insisted on remaining anonymous, informed The Meath Chronicle *after their unsuccessful attempt to make the Final Four.*

Speaking of dieting, there was much chatter about the dramatic weight loss of Trish Saint James, whose new, slimmer physique was the envy of the parish. 'What's her secret?' was the question on everyone's lips. Whatever it was, it certainly played a part in her husband's extraordinary light-footedness across the obstacle course, ensuring the heats' fastest time – a hugely impressive 1 minute 3.8 seconds. To put that achievement into context, it was a whopping 8.4 seconds ahead of nearest rivals, Mia and Ilja Ylönen, who were somewhat unsporting when they blamed pesky midges for their second-place finish.

But heats are just heats and, as many athletes will attest, anything can change in the final – which, last Saturday, they invariably did.

At precisely eight o'clock, as the sun started to disappear into the horizon, tired of being so accommodating all day, the four finalists – Mr and Mrs Colin Saint James, Mr and Mrs Ylönen, Mr and Mrs O'Brien, and Mr and Mrs Sorjonen – lined up at the starting line.

Rather surprisingly, they were joined by a fifth couple – Councillor Alfred Saint James and his wife, Mamie May, who, despite their poor showing in the heats, had been given an automatic pass to the final in appreciation of the councillor's 'tireless efforts to organise the day's events', as it was explained to those standing close by.

'I spent the guts of yesterday mowing the pitch,' Gerry, the grounds' maintenance man, was heard to complain. 'Why didn't Dolores and I get a free pass to the final?'

As many debated whether it was fair or not, the councillor's inclusion meant that the final became less about two nations, but instead, two rival siblings – a feud that has been well-documented within the community for years. And, having proven so impressive earlier in the day, all eyes were on the younger of the two brothers, who was not taking his success in the heats for granted if the steely-eyed determination he sported was anything to go by – a singular focus that was mirrored by his wife, perched proudly on his shoulders. If the prize was to be awarded based on preparation alone, it was clear to everyone which couple would win.

But nobody said sport was fair – and what soon transpired endorsed that claim.

Just as the Finnish judge was about to shoot the gun, Councillor Alfred Saint James held his hand aloft and requested a private word. Following a short tête-à-tête, the judge then announced that in an effort not to alarm the many birds and animals in the area, he would not use the gun. Instead, a light handclap would indicate the beginning of the race.

'I don't want to be mischievous, but I am convinced that I saw Councillor Saint James kick a cat out of the way earlier in the day,' a suspicious ninety-four-year-old Sister Agatha from the Order of Saint Aloysius later claimed. 'So his sudden concern for the welfare of animals was a little out of the blue.'

The clap arrived but, unfortunately, Mr Colin Saint James, on account of inadequate hearing, didn't quite catch it. As the four other couples began to navigate their way through the swamp-like obstacle course, the competition's favourites remained rooted to the spot. When Colin eventually realised that the reason Trish was kicking him was because she was instructing him to start, he became so flustered that instead of climbing over the initial obstacle, a wooden fence, he ran slap-bang into it.

'Don't give up! Keep going, lads!' Words of encouragement from the onlookers inspired the couple and thanks to an abundance of inner strength, they regrouped and quickly hopped over this first obstacle. Despite their unfortunate start, they ploughed forward with extra-ordinary speed. 'Go Colin! Go Trish!'

As the sweat cascaded, the pair began making excellent ground, effortlessly climbing nets, swinging from ropes and jumping over muddy waters. Soon, they were neck-and-neck with the other finalists. The crowd went wild.

'You can do it, lads! Just a few metres further!'

With extraordinary skill, Colin made light work of the tyres and tunnels along with the various other obstacles – apart from one.

His brother.

Now a two-way race between the siblings and their respective wives, it quickly emerged that the younger of the pair was enjoying a slight advantage that was almost certain to see him walk away with the win. However, within metres of the finishing line, misfortune struck again for the younger Saint James sibling. While it was difficult to tell what exactly occurred from the stands, it appeared that in her excitement, Mamie May's leg suddenly swung in front of her, walloping poor Colin across the side of his head. Many later speculated that it was intentional – an accusation Councillor Saint James strenuously denied after the race. (His wife was unavailable for comment.) Whatever had transpired, it led Colin to lose his footing, resulting in Trish being thrown from his shoulders. As Colin's ankle became ensnared in the muddy ground and audibly snapped, his gaze remained fixed on his sibling and former love who had just crossed the finishing line, snatching gold.

'The people around me were adamant that they had heard a window break somewhere close by,' said an observer who described himself to The Meath Chronicle *as a poet. 'I am entirely convinced that the sound they were referring to was that of the poor man's heart*

being shattered. Not even Cain and Abel could lay claim to such frosty relations.'

Probably not, but let's hope this pair won't suffer the same fate as those two doomed biblical figures.

The awards ceremony took place just before midnight, directly after the Finnish taught the Irish some of their local dances, such as the humppa, polkka and jenkka. Unsurprisingly, Colin and Trish were not present to cheer on the winning duo. On the suggestion of the Town Clerk, Councillor Alfred Saint James dragged a reluctant and surprisingly downbeat Mamie May to her feet to lead the group in a round of 'The Bonfire Dance' – rather appropriate given the sparks that had been flying earlier that day. Lord knows what will transpire between the duelling rivals next.

1993

THIRTY-SEVEN

Within hours of arriving in Navan, Azra was taken aback by how differently things worked there in comparison to her motherland.

One aspect in particular shocked her.

It wasn't the change in climate – thanks to Oliver's previous warnings, she had been prepared for the biblical weather and wrapped herself up to combat the wet March conditions. Besides, where was the harm in a good lashing of rain? Indeed, when she first caught a glimpse of the green and lush countryside on her way to her new home from the airport, she realised that a cloudburst every other hour was the pay-off the country had made with the gods for such a verdant landscape.

When it came to one of the other main societal differences between Turkey and Ireland – alcohol consumption – again, Azra hadn't been fazed in the slightest. During her week-long stint in Remzi Bey's seedy brothel, the lion's share of her clients had either been drunken sailors and soldiers, or tourists of the guzzling variety, so being surrounded by some boisterous intoxication was not a totally unfamiliar experience.

No, what struck Azra the most was having to forfeit her anonymity.

As she familiarised herself with the town of Navan, rambling up and down the shop-filled Trimgate Street or passing teenagers walking in laps around the shopping centre, the new arrival quickly noticed that not just one or two heads turned in her direction, but *every single one*. And they didn't just belong to those who shared a path with her; nearly every car that drove past her slowed down, the drivers peering out the windows to take a good look at her.

Should I say hello? she wondered during these uncomfortable moments. *Or just strike a pose and let them examine me from head to toe?*

Initially, Azra felt a little unsettled, being the focus of this curious town's gaze, seeing as she was so accustomed to being just one out of millions in overcrowded Istanbul. Worse again, she detected a little aggression in their stares and that made her ill at ease. Was she going to be the town's freak-show indefinitely, or would there be a reprieve from these people's curiosity?

Fortunately, after a couple of weeks, Azra noticed that the initial glares had been replaced by a smile, a wave or even a helping hand.

'Do you need a lift anywhere?' became a common invitation, as was the phrase, 'Are you looking for anywhere in particular, pet?'

Azra was pleased by this turn of events. After all, one of the principal reasons she had been so excited about uprooting to the Emerald Isle was due to the accounts Oliver had given her about the warmth and conviviality of its citizens, and it was becoming apparent that the people of Navan were proving to be the perfect ambassadors.

It wasn't lost on her that she was being welcomed into a community that was completely ignorant of her colourful past. Navan was offering her a fresh start. So long as she was prepared to accept it.

Except, she quickly discovered, she wasn't.

When she initially boarded the plane in Istanbul, she had been convinced that her days of sexually satisfying the men of the world in exchange for money were in her past. But as soon as she started to familiarise herself with the charming town, she realised that the transition was not going to be as smooth as she had envisioned.

Everywhere around her were couples – husbands and wives; boyfriends and girlfriends – and even though from a spiritual point of view, she'd never felt closer to the love of her life, Oliver, in reality the sight of these partnerships left her feeling more alone than ever.

Despite the many tricky situations she had found herself in over the years, now that she had left it behind her, Azra was surprised to learn that the life of a concubine had suited her for a multitude of reasons, and not just because it offered her the possibility of being able to do what Julia Roberts had done in that *Pretty Woman* film. If she were honest with herself, Azra would have admitted that being surrounded by men admiring her beauty day in, day out, went some way towards filling the void of loneliness in her life, a feeling that she sometimes suspected had something to do with the early loss of her parents. Now, without that adulation in her life, she was, quite literally, in no man's land. That didn't suit her in the slightest. She longed to be fawned over again, worshipped and admired. Nothing could beat the giddy thrill she felt when a new client mentioned that she had come 'highly recommended'.

What's more, a gal has got to eat, and even though Ireland had experienced a recession just a few short years earlier, she quickly learned that it was still quite an expensive place to live and the memories of those horrid days where stale bread was her daily diet rendered her panicked.

But, most of all, she continued to ache for her dear Oliver. How she missed him – his smile, his ability to make her laugh, his love. As a result, her heart was still far too broken to think about anything like a proper relationship with another man.

No, if Ireland was going to continue playing host to her, Azra decided that there would be no new man, no new career. Instead, she wanted to spend her days doing what she did best.

THIRTY-EIGHT

Colin did not become aware of his neighbour's death until many months after the event. Even though there had been a hearse along with an army of mourners in and around the estate at the time, thanks to the public humiliation he had suffered at the wife-carrying competition, Colin had elected to shut himself and his broken ankle off from the pitying gaze of the town and lick his many wounds in private. He had even finally welcomed Dr Cassells' recommendation of sleeping tablets.

This decision to become recluses was welcomed by Trish who, having fulfilled her marital obligations and partaken in the blasted contest, was now more than happy to revert to her old ways of lazing on the bed and feasting on whatever treats her husband removed from the oven that day. She had also come to terms with the fact that, instead of front row seats at Millstreet's Green Glens Arena in May, she would have to watch the Eurovision Song Contest from the comfort of her bed.

As most people who have enjoyed dramatic weight losses will attest, it does not take much to pile it back on. The most significant change since the contest was not the weight that Trish had reclaimed, however, but Colin's personality. The gentleness he once possessed as a child had utterly abandoned him. Now, as the occasional concerned visitor who called to the house would have attested, the guy's demeanour was slowly coming to resemble that of the Christmas Grinch. He had no problem shutting doors in their faces or slamming the phone down when they rang. The delivery guys from Quinnsworth had the sense to leave the groceries on the doorstep and hightail it. Even Raymond, his lifelong friend, had been at the receiving end of his rudeness and was often reduced to tears on the doorstep. Following the wife-carrying competition, Colin no longer cared; if he thought that the botched wedding in

1977 had been his nadir, he was gravely mistaken.

Torturously, every time he filled his mixing bowl with flour, eggs and whatever other ingredients the day's recipe required, he would replay the humiliating moment of his brother's victory over him in his head and, on each occasion, his body would seize up when he recalled how easily his brother had made a laughing stock out of him. He was certain that it was Freddie and not Mamie May who had orchestrated her hitting him with her leg – although maybe she'd been in on it, too; nothing would surprise him at this stage.

Everybody is laughing at you, you silly sod, he would say to himself, releasing some of his frustrations as he vigorously whipped the mixture in the bowl. *As well they might because you have been disgraced once more.*

He had only himself to blame, he decided. Unlike his sibling, Colin concluded that he was clearly ill-equipped to reach the top of the podium. The only place where he felt of use was his kitchen where he now spent all his time – much to the delight of his wife – and the talented baker soon went from creating one batch of buns a day to ten or twelve. The icing was the only dash of colour in the entire property.

Elsewhere, the curtains remained drawn. The doorbell went unanswered. The telephone rang out. The house grew messier and messier, neither bothered by the idea of cleaning.

It was only when a stairlift was being fitted into the house one morning in April that they discovered the news about Oliver's demise.

'We used to play football against each other, you know?' the worker, who'd mentioned he was a native of Blanchardstown, said, eager to make conversation as a way of distracting himself from the hideous cesspool in which he had found himself.

'Sorry, what?'

'Oliver and me. You probably don't miss him too much, seeing as he was away in Greece so much. Or was it Turkey? I said we used to play against each other – I mean, it was only a couple of times. He wasn't bad, I'll give him that!'

'Did he die?' a flour-covered Colin muttered, secretly envious of his former neighbour's fate. What comfort death must have afforded him. 'When did that happen?'

'Last year, man! Didn't you know?'

'We keep ourselves to ourselves these days,' Trish interjected from the bedroom above, eager for the idle chitchat to end. (The latest episode of *The Sally Jessy Raphael Show* was only minutes away from being broadcast and nothing got in the way of this gal and her favourite bespectacled talkshow host.)

'Right, so you haven't met the new resident yet then?' the Dubliner continued. 'I bumped into her earlier on and, Jaysus, she's quite the looker. No wonder Oliver fell in love with her over in Turkey. Or was it Greece?'

Colin didn't even acknowledge these claims; he just wanted to get back to the stove.

'So tell us, why are you getting the stairlift installed? Neither of you has hurt yourself, I hope?'

How could Colin confess that this new addition was due to his wife's continued outward growth, meaning she now needed extra support negotiating daily life around the house?

'Are you gonna tell me or do I have to keep guessing?' the handyman enquired, unsure of how best to interpret the trance-like state his client had found himself in for the past ten seconds. 'Mr Saint James?'

'One must be prepared for all eventualities,' Colin snapped – an answer that was received with a most disappointed sigh.

'Oh, right. Well, before I leave you both in peace, let's press this button here and see if she's in working order.'

She was. From the bedroom, Trish released a sigh of relief, delighted that the work was done and she could now watch her television shows in peace. She curled up under the duvet, as content as the cat that got the cream.

Colin paid the chatterbox what was due before sending him on his way.

'You should think of joining the five-a-side team here in Navan, man – you know, get out of the house,' the concerned worker mentioned as he got into his van. 'They're actually not bad.'

Even if Colin had his full hearing faculties, he would not have heard him, as he was too distracted by the strange woman running up the driveway towards them. There was something wily about her demeanour, he noticed, aware also that he was taking an immediate dislike to her. She looked to be about thirty, maybe younger, maybe older, and as she made her way up the driveway, Colin couldn't take his eyes off her. This was the new neighbour, he presumed.

'Hello!' she called out, waving.

However, her friendly wave received no reply but a blunt slamming of the door.

After a moment's surprise, Azra realised that his impolite act suited her down to the ground. She was worldly enough to realise that if her recent plans to open a brothel were to prevail in a town as small as Navan, she didn't need meddlesome neighbours prying into her affairs. If they were happy to keep out of her way, then everything would work out perfectly.

Little did she know that things would not quite work out that way ...

THIRTY-NINE

Azra's first client in Navan was a local, fifty-three-year-old school caretaker called Dominic, whom she had lured to her new lodgings with the promise that her expertise in massage therapy would transform his troubled back.

'The town hosted a silly competition last August where we had to carry our wives on our shoulders,' Dominic informed her as they both leaned against the railings overlooking the River Boyne earlier that day, the ruins of Athlumney Castle looming in the background. 'I've not been right since.'

'Well, lucky for you we crashed into each other,' she replied, before quickly correcting herself. 'Bumped! Isn't that the expression you use? I need to sweep up my English.'

'Brush, you mean.'

While Azra might have remained unsure of her English idioms, she knew that Ireland wouldn't be too welcoming of ladies in her profession, even if it was the country of a hundred thousand welcomes as Oliver had often mentioned. She deduced that the best way to get word out amongst its more lustful inhabitants was to take advantage of their willingness to converse with strangers. She would then happily inform them of her proficiency as a 'masseuse'.

'We Turks are famed for it,' she explained.

'Is that so?' he replied, resisting every urge to cast off his clothes and dive into her beautiful hazel eyes there and then. Like some of his Irish counterparts, he wasn't one hundred per cent certain what a massage actually entailed, but he was game to give it a try. In fact, there was very little Dominic wouldn't have done in the company of this alluring and exotic lady.

'Call up to me sometime, and I'll soon have you as fit as a guitar!'

'Fiddle.'

'Let's not talk about fiddling in public,' she whispered while giving him a knowing wink.

'How about tonight?' Dominic suggested. 'My wife has taken the children to her mother's in Virginia for a couple of days. The old doll hasn't been feeling too well of late, poor thing.'

'What a shame,' Azra said, 'but lucky for your shoulders and upper back!'

'See you at, say, ten?'

'Until then.'

***

Dominic was extremely familiar with the property that Azra now called home – not only in its current incarnation, but also from the time before it had been divided, when it belonged solely to the Saint James family. Even though he lived in a modest, terraced house in the centre of the town, and his penchant for gambling meant that he was always on the hunt for a few bob, not in a million years would he have changed his lot with Colin Saint James.

That poor fecker, he thought, as he emerged from his car and walked towards Azra's front door. *I wouldn't fancy the odds he'd be offered for getting even with that brother of his.*

When the door opened, what stood in front of him appeared nothing short of angelic.

'You look ...' the gambler uttered, convinced that, at long last, luck was on his side.

'You better enter,' she encouraged. 'You might get a chill standing outside, and your back will never heal if that's the case.'

She ushered him in.

'So, you like my uniform?' she playfully asked about her negligee as she led him up to the master bedroom. 'It's quite hot this evening – I hope I won't have to strip.'

Dominic thought he had died and gone to heaven – a place he

would literally end up should his missus discover that he wasn't, in fact, at home tending to his stamp collection.

When they arrived into the candle-scented bedroom, Azra told him that she would give him a moment to disrobe before instructing him to lie on top of the massage table she had fashioned from a table and a couple of sheets.

'Call out "Istanbul" when you're ready and I'll re-come.'

As Azra waited outside the bedroom, she could hear Dominic tumble and stumble about the place.

'Istanbul! Istanbul! Istanbul!'

'Ready or not!' she teased as she returned. 'Now let's see if we can make right some of that back pain.'

As if all his Christmases had come at once, Dominic found himself being the fortunate recipient of Azra's womanly touch, as he lay face-down on the makeshift massage table.

'Time to turn over,' she ordered, and when he complied, it was evident that this newly appointed seafarer was sailing full mast. She wasted no time and jumped on board. 'Aye, aye, Captain!'

'Istanbul! Istanbul! Istanbul!' he yelled out with enthusiasm, not long afterwards.

'How does your back now feel, Dominic?' she enquired, adopting a professional tone.

No answer was needed – the rapture etched across his face indicated that the fellow was in fine fettle.

Azra would soon be thrilled to learn that details of the arrangement reached between Dominic and herself travelled around the town with greater velocity than even the speediest of ships.

Little did she realise, however, that the harmless-looking man · from next door would do his best to capsize the entire enterprise.

FORTY

After the sighting of Azra, Colin's mind went into overdrive – not even the sleeping aids that he'd recently agreed to take could calm his active mind. If Dr Cassells had had an opportunity to give his professional opinion on this recent turn of events, he might have warned the fellow that he was developing an intense and unhealthy obsession with his new neighbour, but Colin would have argued that it was nothing of the sort – he simply did not trust her, particularly when he noticed the lights of a car pulling up the driveway late that same night.

'Who has visitors at this hour?'

With that, the squalid bedroom that had been Colin and Trish's living quarters since the disastrous wife-carrying competition soon lost one of its residents. Without even consciously realising what he was doing, Colin upped sticks and relocated to the front sitting room – an area of the house that was now submerged in dust, given its complete abandonment in recent months. What a stark contrast from his happy childhood days when he used to curl up in his mother's arms and watch and rewatch footage of her many television appearances, such as her Housewife of the Year victory or her subsequent interviews on the *Six One News* or talk shows like *The Late Late Show*.

That night, amidst the cobwebs and the mildew, and without a word passing his lips, Colin pushed the armchair close to the window and kept watch – convinced that, despite it being pitch-black outside, he would enjoy a good view of the comings and goings of his next-door neighbour and her mysterious guest with the help of the net curtains, which stopped nosy visitors peering inside.

There is something I don't like about her, he muttered for the umpteenth time that night, oblivious to the fact that there was very little he liked about anyone or anything these days – including the milkman, who'd sworn never to deliver so much as a sliver of cheese again to the Saint James household following the aggressive dismissal he had received earlier that day.

If pushed, Colin would have admitted that the exotic lady simply didn't fit in here – her vitality only served as a constant reminder to Colin about how horrid his own life had turned out. In addition, he felt that she possessed an air of mischievousness, although he couldn't articulate why he thought that way. Furthermore, what was this woman's relationship with Oliver – how did she manage to convince him to hand over the keys to the property?

Or could it also be that, like so many men that Azra had encountered over the years, *Colin was just a teeny tiny bit captivated by her?*

Whatever the cause of this sudden interest in the woman, it was only when Colin heard the engine of the stranger's car turn on some twenty minutes later that he realised that he hadn't been watching anything at all. Thanks to his and Trish's slovenly ways, the dirt on the windows was so thick that it had formed a complete barricade between the inside and outside worlds.

After discovering the error of his ways, he shouted a stream of expletives – words he didn't even realise he had in his vocabulary – and dashed to the front door, but it was too late. The car had disappeared out of sight and the lights in Azra's side of the property were now turned off, the curtains drawn.

A sweat-drenched Colin returned to his chair, disappointed, wondering whether his compromised vantage point had prevented him from finding out something sensational – which, as it turned out, was the exact word that Azra's first customer, who'd just escaped the property unseen, had used to describe his own experience.

FORTY-ONE

The following morning, just moments after the grandfather clock had struck six o'clock, Colin was battling a pounding heart having just caught a glimpse of Azra again through the now-clean sitting-room window. It was clear to him that she was venturing out of the house to go for a jog, seeing as she was kitted out in full sporting regalia, from pink wristbands to pink headbands to pink leg warmers.

As Azra scampered down the driveway, Colin couldn't help but mock. *Wouldn't she look only perfect on top of a cake!*

'A cake!' he shouted, almost waking his sleeping wife in the room above. *I will take my lead from the Trojans and gain access to her house by pretending to welcome her to the community with a homemade cake.*

Maybe he was more like his devious brother than he'd previously imagined.

And with that, Colin finally had an objective in his wretched life once again: to channel his wife's favourite detective, Jessica Fletcher, and see if his strong suspicions about his new neighbour had any merit.

Before that, however, he had work to do in the kitchen.

***

Colin knocked on Azra's door, which stood a couple of metres to the left of the house's original door. He ignored the cheap bell that had been installed following the house's division, as it had never properly worked and, judging by the manner in which the push button continued to jut out unevenly from its post, he deduced that the new resident hadn't gotten around to rectifying the situation.

Colin decided to count to twenty before undertaking another attempt at making contact. He knew that Azra was inside; he had seen her pull the curtains in her bedroom only a few minutes earlier and even though she was probably on the verge of having a mid-afternoon nap following her early start, Colin decided to ignore the strong likelihood that she didn't want to be disturbed, for he was a man possessed, which superseded all social etiquette.

He had spent hours baking the most immaculate cake that he was sure had ever existed – the white, log-shaped baked Alaska that he currently held. She could hardly fail to be impressed by his kind, neighbourly ways, although whether it was enough to cause her to confess whatever dark secrets he was sure she harboured remained to be seen.

Even though the kitchen was the only place where Colin found any peace and reprieve, his excitement had proven to be quite a hindrance that morning, resulting in the first effort having to be relegated to the dustbin. To make matters worse, when the second attempt proved to be more successful, Trish, lured to the kitchen by the overpowering smell of home baking, wrongly assumed that the baked Alaska was for her and swiped it from his hands.

'I'd love to say, "You shouldn't have",' she remarked as she ascended the stairs with the help of the stairlift, 'but that would be a big lie!'

Having learned the error of his ways, Colin closed the kitchen door and opened all the windows as he retrieved his third effort from the oven, so that the enticing smells would be directed towards the intended recipient of his morning's toils rather than herself above.

Fifteen, sixteen, seventeen, eighteen, nineteen, twenty.

He knocked on Azra's door for the second time and following this latest attempt – despite his limited hearing – he heard surprisingly heavy footsteps running down the stairs, suggesting that she wasn't as light on her feet as Colin had originally thought. Actually, whether she was or wasn't remained to be determined because, through the panel window, he noticed that the footsteps' rightful owner was not Azra but some broad-shouldered male who was now dashing through her living room in the direction of the back of the house.

'What in the …?'

Armed with nothing other than his cherished baked Alaska, Colin hobbled around the side of the house – the ankle that he broke during the wife-carrying competition still gave him a little grief every time he put too much pressure on it. A profusion of ghastly images raced through his mind – something that was quite common recently, seeing as he was being completely deprived of sleep, nourishment and good old-fashioned fresh air, and exposed to too many second-rate detective series, courtesy of his wife. Was there a drug den within a section of his old home, perhaps? Or worse again, had his neighbour been the victim of a grisly murder?

When he reached the back garden, it appeared that his suspicions seemed to be well founded as, in front of him, a large, curly-haired head was trying to escape from the window of the downstairs toilet.

'Stop this instant!' Colin demanded, his delight that his instincts about his neighbour were sound trumping any fear he might have felt being in such close proximity to a possible murderer.

When the supposed miscreant continued to worm his way out the window, Colin flung his culinary masterpiece at him with as much force as he could rally, hitting him square in the face.

'Don't move another muscle,' Colin yelled, 'or I shall call the Guards!'

Before the so-called transgressor could give any response, Azra emerged from the house, taking the more traditional route of the back door.

'It is okay, neighbour – this is just my friend who gives price to me for two-glazing windows. No need to be alarmed.'

Colin, surprised that his new neighbour was uninjured, re-turned his focus to the cake-covered man.

'Then why is he climbing out the window like a hardened criminal?'

'He is not! He is giving the windows the twice over, that's all.'

'I see,' Colin mumbled under his breath, giving them his own once over. 'Yes, they look like they could do with being updated, it's true.'

Before he could make the situation any worse, Colin returned to the front of the property and back into his house, his tail between his legs. He thought it best to keep a low profile for a few days until the blushing on his cheeks subsided.

Oh, what a waste of cake!

At the other side of the house the curly-haired man, who was still struggling to free himself from the narrow window, had the exact opposite opinion of the cake.

If it was not for all this ice cream covering my face, thought Father Cutbirth, who'd heard about Azra's enterprise as he forgave Dominic in the confessional that morning, *Colin would have known exactly who I was!*

FORTY-TWO

A week later, Colin, determined not to assault any honest, hard-working people on this occasion, positioned himself outside Azra's front door once again. While he was left red-faced following the incident with the baked Alaska, he still wasn't prepared to admit defeat. He simply didn't trust this exotic woman – especially seeing as their driveway was nothing short of a car park these days.

Why all the visitors?

He raised his arm and this time Colin's determination was so impassioned that he ended up hammering on the door, resulting in it flying open.

With the audacity of a school bully sauntering into the playground, Colin entered an area that had once belonged to his family – a place he hadn't darkened the door of for quite some time. He tried not to allow memories of all that the Saint Jameses had been through together here to flood back into his mind.

Easier said than done.

It was here in this sitting room that his beloved mother had been laid out to rest just a few short years earlier. How peaceful she had looked after going to war so valiantly with cancer for six months, although she would have been the first to admit that her actual battle had been with her eldest son. As for that 'Jezebel', Mamie May Mooney – what his mother had threatened to do to her! The only comfort Colin received during that period was that Freddie had complied with their wishes, for once in his life, and kept his distance from the funeral. Their grandmother was not a violent person, but she had sworn blind that she would make light work of her eldest grandchild should he come within 'an ass's roar of the church'. As the lid was placed on the coffin, it was left to Mrs Brady – who still harboured a grudge over being pipped at the post by the deceased in 1967 – to lighten the mood and take the conversation away from Freddie.

'I was hoping that Mrs Saint James would die earlier in the week,' she announced. 'I was supposed to have a hair appointment tomorrow, but I had to cancel it because of the funeral. It seems the woman is determined to be as difficult in death as she was in life.'

Not having set foot in the place since Oliver had purchased Freddie's portion of the house, Colin became quite distracted by the changed surroundings and unique decorations. Gone were the opulent satin curtains and antique paintings and, in their place, were colourful fabrics hanging from the ceilings with a series of blue and navy glass ornaments that had the appearance of some kind of evil eye. Wherever this shady lady was from, it was not Clonmel or Cahersiveen, that was for sure.

'Hello?' he called out, now unable to conceal his irritation that his hostess hadn't received him yet.

'Upstairs, if you want a good duck,' was the reply Colin heard, confusing him. Was she some unauthorised butcher, perhaps specialising in waterfowl? Maybe that was how she got one over on Oliver in the first place – taking advantage of his love of animals?

'Come on!' she called again, a note of irritation in her voice.

Now a man on a mission, Colin climbed the stairs. As he did, he noticed a selection of objects strewn across the floor that only furthered his suspicions that she was involved in the meat market: ropes and leather gloves and chains – probably for the gates of a hen coop, say. But, in his excitement to reach the landing above, he tripped over a handful of clamps.

'Hello, neighbour. Twice in one week – I am lucky!'

When he looked up towards the suspected covert meat dealer, the sight in front of him was so scandalous and shocking that, were it not for all the rest that he had gotten during his many months in hibernation, he would surely have had a massive coronary there and then.

'Where are your, em, clothes?'

FORTY-THREE

When Azra first heard the story of how the Tara Brooch had been discovered on Meath's eastern Bettystown beach, it had immediately reminded her of her beloved Spoonmaker's Diamond.

Created in AD 700, the ornate, early-Christian masterpiece had been unearthed – or unsanded, rather – a whopping eleven hundred and fifty years later by an observant peasant woman. She claimed to have found it in a box buried in the sand, though many suspected that it had been uncovered somewhere inland and her fanciful, seaside account was an attempt to avoid any legal claims by pesky landowners.

At least the gal had more sense than that poor, unfortunate fisherman whose miraculous eyesight was rewarded with a handful of spoons, Azra reflected as she walked towards Navan's lively Market Square, where she planned to take a bus to the beach in question. Even though it was the start of May, this was the first time since her arrival that the sun had had the decency to properly reveal itself.

While she certainly did not expect that lightning might strike twice and, at long last, help realise one of her lifelong dreams of owning a priceless jewel, she believed that a little sea air would be the perfect tonic to so many hours cooped up in the house.

As Azra waited for her bus to arrive, she felt familiar pangs of remorse. She knew that she was probably not living the life that Oliver had imagined for her when he bequeathed her his house. She also knew that the intentions behind his act were to afford her a change of scenery and, hopefully, a fresh start. While they were together, he'd always been forced to bite his tongue regarding her work arrangements. How could he complain? Had he not benefited the most from her chosen career path? Yes, and yet she knew he had been privately distressed every time he would return to Ankara, knowing that he was leaving her in the arms of another.

And another.

And another.

With sixteen years' experience under her much-loosened belt, she had the self-awareness to conclude that her career had become an addiction – a quick fix for a lack of true love and affection. Walking away, however, did not appear to be an option.

Besides, Oliver can hardly pass judgement, she thought. *Since he died, he's been lying on his back as much as me!*

The bus was due in ten minutes. Having no car, Azra depended on her two little trotters to get her from A to B, and even on those miserable days when she got caught in the pouring rain, laden down with shopping bags, she never wished for a car. Unlike so many of her contemporaries in Istanbul who were fast on their way to middle-aged status, the thirty-eight-year-old's beauty had not gone the way of those on board the *Marie Celeste* and disappeared into the ether – a feat she credited to a disciplined and healthy lifestyle, of which walking was an integral part. Her body was her temple – and her bread and butter – so she had to be dogged in her exercise regime. She always enjoyed it when her clients attempted to guess her age – the only person ever to come close was a bachelor farmer from Ballivor, a man who had close to fifty years' experience pulling teats, so he firmly believed that he knew a thing or two about body parts.

'The Year of our Lord? Ye thirty-three? No, thirty-five.'

The chap did not receive an answer, just a slap across the face.

With a few minutes to spare until the bus arrived, Azra popped into Tierney's Newsagent's to get a magazine for the journey. It was while she was scouring the shelves for a suitable pick – *Woman's Way*, perhaps? – that she became convinced that someone was watching her. She looked around the shop but, apart from a preoccupied staff member, Azra was the only person there.

It must be my imagination, she conceded.

As soon as the bus arrived, Azra swiftly embarked and relaxed into her seat, although given the sunny conditions, it came as no surprise to her that she was not the only person who had had the idea of heading to the beach. She didn't even mind that they were all sitting cheek to jowl – it almost gave the trip a sense of fun and camaraderie. How she looked forward to an afternoon away from the house and her eerie and reclusive neighbours. Azra remembered that Oliver had described them as quite an unusual couple who kept themselves to themselves, but she was alarmed to see how much their portion of the lovely property was crumbling around them – although that opinion was based largely on their wild and unkempt garden; heaven knows what the inside of their house was like. And this from a person who primarily grew up on the streets!

Azra had come face to face with Colin on only three occasions, but the last two times they'd encountered each other it had been, well, somewhat messy – especially their most recent exchange. Having been so intimate with men over the years, she had a good sense of those who were damaged and wounded – whose light had lost its flicker. From the fleeting moments they had shared, Azra knew that Colin definitely fell into that category. He was in need of companionship – it was such a shame that he had bottled it at the last minute.

Anyway, she reminded herself that the goal of today's outing was to forget about her life for a few hours, so she parked her analysis of her curious neighbour and, instead, read about other people's concerns in her magazine. With interest, she studied an article praising the upcoming and ground-breaking Criminal Law (Sexual Offences) 1993 Bill, which was set to decriminalise homosexuality in the country, and laughed at the absurdity of the sole contributor to argue that it would undermine traditional marriage. ('The stories I could have told that woman about so-called "loyal" husbands.')

As she was about to turn the page, she felt, once again, that somebody's eyes were on her. She looked around and scanned the crowded bus, but everyone seemed to be minding their own affairs apart from one – a man kitted out in an ill-fitting trench coat and an oversized peak cap, sitting a few rows behind her. She noticed that his head had moved the very second she'd turned hers. Was he a potential customer, too afraid to call to the house?

She had often seen men nervously creep up the driveway, but before they reached the door, they performed sharp U-turns and scampered off. From her bedroom window, she recalled seeing one such yellow-bellied rascal standing at the gates of the house, blessing himself repeatedly. The scaredy cat appeared so mortified that one would think he was about to enter the ring with Attila the Hun. At the last minute, he'd fled, morality intact. Was this pursuer the same person, perhaps?

Either way, she decided that it was unfair of him to interrupt her on her day off, so, deciding to ignore him, she resumed her reading. She'd only gotten a brief opportunity to scan a few further pages of the magazine, including an advertisement for some annual contest for the country's best housewife, when the driver informed the passengers that the next stop was Bettystown beach.

Azra thought it novel that no matter where you were on the island of Ireland, you were always only a stone's throw from the sea, and as she stepped off the bus and strolled towards the water, she decided that she should make more day trips like this.

Facing the calming waters, she closed her eyes and took a deep breath. How good this felt! She envisioned that this was what Oliver had in mind for her by inviting her over to the Emerald Isle. Istanbul, the brothel, her father, Mustafa Bey – they all seemed like a different lifetime.

But her moment of tranquillity was rudely cut short when a loud cry sounded somewhere behind her. With the sun in her eyes, she struggled to make out the exact details of the incident. Based on the graphic insults that an elderly woman was shouting, Azra deduced that someone was hiding behind a car, and when the driver – the aforementioned old lady – had reversed, she rolled over the person's foot.

'What in heaven's name are you doing skulking behind my car? Are you a Peeping Tom?'

Even though she had never heard that expression before, Azra suspected that the charges being made against the culprit were possibly true. Thanks to a helpful cloud, she could now clearly see that he was the same, trench-coated brute who had been staring at her on the bus and it was clear to her that he had been watching her from his surreptitious vantage point before he was so painfully revealed.

Feeling a little exposed and vulnerable, Azra thought it best to cut her day trip short and return home. She had always known that she was not going to share the same luck that the woman in 1850 had experienced by finding a second Tara Brooch, but she certainly hadn't expected that her seaside jaunt might result in her being attacked in broad daylight!

It is not easy being so desirable, she complained, running as far away from her stalker as she could, as quickly as possible. Before she left the beach, she turned and looked back towards him one more time, relieved to discover that he wasn't pursuing her as he continued to receive a scolding from the woman, who now enjoyed the support of an army of bare-chested men.

As she walked towards the bus stop, Azra passed an ice-cream van. Inspired, she decided to treat herself to a 99 cone when she returned to Navan.

Forget the diet, I will have plenty of time to watch my figure when I am in a box in the ground – which might be much sooner than I think if these antics continue!

FORTY-FOUR

The following week, Azra thought that she could have gotten a job as a telephonist such was the volume of calls she received. If the nature of the conversations were anything to go by, however, she would soon be in need of new opportunities. Everyone was cancelling. And it was Friday, usually her second busiest day of the week.

Being a lady of the night – and, in this industrious gal's case, day as well – she had accepted that her clients were sometimes forced to cancel last minute for a variety of reasons.

'The boss insisted that I do a double shift.'

'The wife returned home from her sister's house unexpectedly.'

'The blasted baby has the mumps.'

But she had never experienced anything like the flood of cancellations she received this night. Her diary had over a dozen appointments for the weekend, but half of them had cancelled. They had come up with a rainbow of excuses that Azra knew were plucked out of the air. ('I have to defrost the fridge' was an especially lame example). The other half were no-shows.

To add insult to injury, the handful of walk-ins that she was usually guaranteed had also abandoned her. There wasn't a sign of anyone wanting to purchase her wares – not a single sinner!

What on earth is going on?

She knew that this downturn in business had nothing to do with her skills. Following a rendezvous, her many clients would spend an eternity praising her performance. What's more, the manner in which word of mouth had spread across the town since she had flung open the doors over a month earlier indicated that her talents were receiving five-star notices.

She knew this sudden ship-jumping had nothing to do with nerves either – it was the weekend, after all, a time when pints of

Guinness chased by shots of Jameson were the perfect antidote to any anxiety by which new or returning customers might have been crippled. When it came to inhibition, she had discovered over the years that few things held a drunken person back.

There was no large-scale community event to pilfer her patrons either, not that she knew about anyway, so her only conclusion was that some brute was warning them off. She had recently established a special arrangement with one of the local Gardaí, so she was not convinced that the Boys in Blue were at the root of this unusual turn of events.

Could it have anything to do with that Peeping Tom from last week? she wondered as she inched tentatively towards the window so that she could scan the large garden outside.

She felt queasy in her stomach.

The brothel in Istanbul had been equipped with burly men to protect the ladies from any disturbances. When, in recent years, technology became more readily available, the entire establishment had been kitted out with cameras, which provided more protection than she could ever have imagined.

'You don't want to pay?' Solak Bey would shout. 'Well, how about I show your wife or your boss this footage of you doing incredibly perverted things to one of my girls.'

However, since Azra had launched her enterprise in Ireland, she'd become so seduced by the warm and friendly nature of its residents that she felt there was only a need to call upon her old trick of taking a snap of each of her clients with her handy Polaroid camera. (Unbeknownst to them, she'd secretly placed the apparatus in an open wardrobe, which she easily operated with the assistance of a wire. She then stashed the incriminating images in an envelope somewhere safe.)

Now, as she studied the property for trespassers, she concluded that she had been just like her newly adopted country – green!

She was about to leaf through the *Golden Pages* to rectify her security concerns when she noticed a car's headlights illuminate the front gate.

Business at last, finally!

She berated herself for being so melodramatic, before reaching for her lipstick and powder puff so that she could look her finest for what she hoped would be the night's first of many customers.

That incident at the beach has made you nervous and jumpy!

When she returned to the window to ensure that the chap had managed to negotiate the jungle of weeds currently plaguing the driveway, she noticed a second man approach him from behind the garden's many trees. Azra squinted, but the darkness made things tricky to distinguish. She tried to open the window, hoping that she might be able to hear some of the action but, just like the gate, the handle had seen better days, so it took her an age to loosen. When she finally succeeded, her would-be client was hopping back into his car and speeding off. The way in which the remaining, strange figure folded his arms after he closed the gates suggested to Azra that he was delighted with this result.

The rotten sahte*!*

Was he the same man from Bettystown beach and, if so, who was he?

Was he some besotted former client who wanted her all to himself? She was reminded of the possessive but can't-leave-my-wife septuagenarian from Maslak who had shot dead one of her other regular customers in a fit of jealousy.

There was only one way to find out if history was repeating itself, and that was to venture into the dark of the night. She threw on her coat, grabbed the knife that she kept in between the mattress and bed frame, and charged down the stairs and into the garden, making a beeline for the interfering individual who was positioned behind a tree.

'Reveal yourself, you coward!' she shouted, allowing her temper to get the better of her. 'I am not afraid of you!'

But the offender would not budge, leaving her with no other option but to grab his sleeve and drag him out from his hiding place. In doing so, the man tripped on a large rock that sat idly on the grass, landing face down at her feet.

'You are not such a big man now, are you?' she roared as she turned him over so that she could get a good look at his face. She gasped when she realised who it was: her eccentric, hermit-like neighbour.

'It's you!'

Colin took full advantage of her confusion and flung her hands from him.

'Your list of misdemeanours is getting longer by the minute, my girl. Firstly, operating an illegal brothel and now attacking a citizen on his own property. I needed to get my ducks in a row, as it were, and now I have all the evidence I require.'

Azra, still shocked, thought it best to rein in the aggression, regardless of her connections with the local Garda station.

'I am sorry, fright came upon me – I didn't know who you were.'

'Could you speak up?' Colin barked. 'My hearing leaves a lot to be desired.'

'Is it normal behaviour to hide behind trees at ten at night?' she happily roared. 'And to follow me, a helpless woman, on buses and beaches? Where is your scarf and hat tonight, huh? All I wanted was a quiet afternoon by the sea and you ruined it.'

'I apologise for that,' he said, temporarily falling out of character. 'I thought you might have been soliciting customers.'

'What are you going to do?' she questioned, introducing a splash of child-like innocence to her voice. 'Maybe we could come up with an arrangement?'

But her advances were futile.

'This is Ireland, my girl – we do things differently here, and prostitution is something we abhor!'

Azra thought it best not to argue that she could find at least thirty men from the town who would beg to differ.

'Tomorrow, I shall go to the police station where I will be making a formal complaint. You have until then to gather your belongings and vanish back to Turkey or Greece or wherever it is you call home.'

And as if to illustrate what he had meant – in case anything was lost in translation – Colin turned on his heels and disappeared into the house.

FORTY-FIVE

Colin walked towards the Garda station on Abbey Road the following day, the streets of Navan livelier than usual because of a football match in Páirc Tailteann. There was a time when Colin would have been one of the many enthusiastic supporters, cheering on the boys in green and yellow. In the company of Mamie May and his parents, they would have positioned themselves slap bang in the middle of the stand, their pockets bulging with reduced-price chocolate that they'd acquired from one of the confectionery sellers dotted throughout the grounds. Win, lose or draw, it would have been next to impossible for the quartet to find a better way of spending an afternoon. Needless to say, like everything following that treacherous afternoon in 1977, those sorts of outings had become a thing of the past, and it had fallen upon the local media to educate Colin on who the movers and shakers were in the world of Gaelic football.

Besides, he currently had no time for any distractions – he was far too busy safeguarding the town from his neighbour's wickedness.

As he approached the station, however, his lively stomach suggested that he continued to have some doubts about exposing his neighbour's behind-closed-doors activities. He had set off from the house three times earlier that day, but only made it as far as the gates. All night and all morning, he had thought very carefully about the ramifications of his actions and why, in fact, he felt so compelled to unmask her shameful secret. He lived in Catholic Ireland, for goodness' sake – of course, he was expected to frown upon such indecent and immoral darkness and bring it to light he told himself.

But that was not it.

What about the dangers he and his wife faced living, literally, slap bang in the middle of such an unsafe environment? At any given moment, there might be an outburst of violence – or worse, murder – and that just would not do. The pair was vulnerable enough as it was, what with Trish's limited mobility and his compromised hearing; they didn't need to spend their days being endangered by such anti-social behaviour. What if one of Azra's clients was so drunk that he staggered into their home by accident and demanded that Trish engage in unmentionable relations during one of her favourite soaps? Oh, that just wouldn't do!

But, no, he admitted to himself, that was not the reason either.

The real truth, he knew, was that thanks to being repeatedly humiliated by his brother over the years, he had now become a cantankerous and resentful so-and-so, irritated by everybody and everything that he came across, whether it was on the television, in the papers, or, like now, in everyday life. The concept of happiness had become alien to him, and his former self – the one who boasted a warm heart and a smile at all times – belonged to a different person altogether. Not even Charles Dickens could create a character so full of anger and melancholy, he felt, and seeing as there was no feasible way of remedying the situation – his brother would always find a way of sabotaging his attempts of happiness, after all – Colin had decided to play the part of the grumpy sod with conviction.

I have finally found something that I am good at, he told himself as he ignored the vibrations of his conscience.

The station was quiet. In another hour or so, Colin thought, when the Saturday evening festivities properly kicked off, the on-duty officers would be swamped. After Colin had congratulated himself for his excellent timing – he didn't want to compete with others for the Gardaí's attention – he rang the bell that sat on the counter and waited. The apathetic 'How can I help you?' arrived before the Garda had even opened the hatch, indicating to Colin that he might have his work cut out for him.

Once the hatch opened, he recognised the tall, bearded man opposite him. 'Ah, Garda Maguire, you are on duty tonight. I would like to seek your assistance in something that can be best described as a delicate matter,' he revealed.

'I see. What is it, Colin?' came the response, unconcerned.

'What is the legal protocol for declaring the discovery of a brothel?'

On hearing these words, Garda Maguire's manner changed completely, but not quite in the way that Colin had anticipated. The man standing opposite him looked crestfallen, as if his mother had just told him that she would be withholding his pocket money.

'What is it you know?' he asked in a whisper, forgetting about Colin's hearing difficulties.

'You will have to speak up, Garda!'

Raising his voice was something that Garda Maguire was ill-prepared to do for reasons that were slowly becoming apparent to Colin.

'Wait,' he continued, placing a notebook on the counter before scribbling the question on one of its pages: *What is it you know?*

With Garda Maguire's superior lurking in the background, Colin had a strong suspicion that this family man who was charged by the country with being a moral beacon was, in fact, anything but. Colin had little interest in playing games and brazenly cast aside the pen that was being offered to him and, instead, replied in the loudest voice he could muster.

'Yes, Garda, I do know something, and if my instinct serves me correctly, so do you!'

Garda Maguire swiftly slammed the hatch shut and dashed out into the reception area.

'Colin, would you mind following me this way?' he pleaded, pointing towards one of the interview rooms.

Relishing the power, the delighted troublemaker did as instructed and sauntered down the corridor, full of pretension and smugness, before entering the room as directed.

'Allow me,' the Garda said, pulling the chair out from under the table – it was a wonder that his sudden impulse for chivalry wasn't leading him to serve his guest a flute of Dom Perignon and a plate of caviar. 'Now, what's all this nonsense about brothels, Colin?'

'Oh, it is far from nonsense, my good man, and I have proof. Plenty of it.'

'Proof?' Garda Maguire replied, his voice quite fragile. 'What kind of proof?'

'You know, photographs – that sort of thing.'

Garda Maguire looked quite sickly. For Colin, this exchange was proving to be far more satisfying than anticipated.

'How have you been over the past few months, my friend?' Maguire asked. 'I believe you and Trish have not left your house for quite a long time? Maybe the lack of fresh air is leading you to imagine such wicked things? Could it not be possible that Azra is just a friendly woman who likes inviting people over to her house on a regular basis? Who doesn't enjoy a bit of company in the evening?'

'Azra? Who mentioned anything about Azra?' Colin enquired, and even though he had known the man sitting in front of him for many years – as teenagers, they had often collected money together for various charities outside the church on Sunday mornings – he could not help but relish every single moment of their exchange.

'Didn't you mention her outside in reception?' Garda Maguire attempted to bluff. Realising that he had put his flipping foot in it, he looked ready to hack the appendage off.

Colin leaned forward.

'I think it is time I had a word with your superior, don't you?'

'Colin, this is not like you. You've always kept yourself to yourself over the years – why start sticking your nose into matters that don't concern you now? You're better than this.'

'You don't think that a person living next door to a house of ill-repute has the right to be concerned? Is that what you're telling me?'

'Colin, sometimes people get lonely and they crave companionship. Where's the harm in a little innocent fun?'

'Absolutely none, Garda Maguire, as long as you don't have to pay for the pleasure of it.'

Becoming quite hot under the collar, Garda Maguire rubbed his clammy hands on his trousers and tried to determine how best to resolve this matter. His shift was due to finish in half an hour, and he had promised his wife that he would bring home a takeaway from the China Garden, but if she caught wind of Colin's allegations he felt certain that the Dish of the Day would be dumped rather than dumplings.

'Look, Colin – you know what wives are like. Sometimes they can be a little ...'

'A little?'

'You know, frigid. Husbands have no other choice but to look elsewhere. So I have been told, that is.'

Colin had heard enough.

'I don't mean to pontificate, but I think it's best if I discuss my concerns with someone more in tune with social etiquette. Thank you for your time, Garda Maguire. Give my best to Mrs Maguire, won't you?'

He stood up and strolled out the door, delighted to have left his one-time philanthropic companion drowning in a sea of his own sweat.

'Stop!' Maguire shouted after him, an order that Colin adhered to, but not on account of being told to do so by that philanderer;

the complainant had noticed something striking on the notice board on the wall in front of him.

'I don't believe ...'

He bolted towards one of the many posters that littered the display and read it aloud with the same zeal with which Patrick Pearse had read the 1916 Easter Proclamation. He scanned it twice and then a third time to ensure that what he saw was correct. And at that very moment, the lightness of yesteryear came flooding back, trumping the sour and sanctimonious version of himself that had reigned supreme since his defeat at the wife-carrying competition nine months earlier.

'Colin? Colin? Are you all right?' Garda Maguire asked, eyeing Colin's rigid appearance, secretly feeling that a stroke would not be the worst thing in the world to happen to him.

'Garda, you can forget what I have just divulged. I'm not sure what got into me. Apologies for wasting your time.'

Not since the time that his teenage sweetheart, Jane, revealed that she wasn't pregnant had Garda Maguire felt so much relief. He couldn't help but smile, even as he admonished Colin. 'Don't do it again, all right?'

But these words were in vain. Colin had disappeared out the doors with the same alacrity as the football teams were currently displaying on the Páirc Tailteann pitch.

As Garda Maguire closed the door of the interview room, he breathed a deep sigh of relief. He could feel his heart rate returning to normal. His standing in society would not vanish now, thankfully. When he positioned himself outside St Mary's church the following morning, the parishioners would once again commend his knows-no-bounds altruism.

And there was an added bonus. *No need to cancel my midnight appointment with Azra after all!* he said to himself. *Here was me thinking that the new aftershave I bought in Valueland would go to waste.*

FORTY-SIX

Trish had not believed her ears when Colin told her that he'd to pop out to run an errand. Not even if NASA had invited her to become the first woman on Mars would she have left her television set on the night of the Eurovision Song Contest final – particularly seeing as it was taking place in Ireland thanks to Linda Martin's phenomenal victory the previous year in Sweden with 'Why Me?' – a beautiful ballad penned by Eurovision legend Johnny Logan.

Two months earlier, in Dublin's prestigious Point Theatre, the enigmatic and full-voiced Niamh Kavanagh and her song 'In Your Eyes' had effortlessly emerged victorious in the national heats. It wasn't often that a country won the contest twice in a row – only Spain, Luxembourg and Israel had accomplished this feat so far – but, tonight, hopes were high that the soulful Dubliner would be adding Ireland to this illustrious list.

Niamh was scheduled to sing fourteenth on the night – a great position, Trish felt, as it would mean that her performance was neither too early nor too late in the overall running order.

Yes, it will be fresh in the mind of the jury as they make their deliberations, she decided, spread across the bed, full of positivity.

Would it be enough to convince them to award Ireland the prestigious prize for the fifth time in the contest's thirty-eight-year history? If anyone could do it, it was Niamh – after all, she had a wealth of experience having sung on the soundtrack for box-office smash *The Commitments* two years earlier.

Yes, Trish thought, *we can do this!*

Because of the day that was in it, Trish decided that she deserved a few additional treats to mark the auspicious occasion. Instead of the usual one log of Viennetta ice cream, she made light work of two. Why have a couple of KitKats when she could enjoy four? And why limit her intake of garlic bread to a single baguette when she was surely entitled to three? As a result, her belly was set to burst, but that didn't stop her from devouring the entire cheesecake that Colin had rustled up earlier in the afternoon. The Eurovision only happened once every year, after all, so where was the harm?

Trish was not in the slightest bit surprised by the speed with which she had piled back on the weight following her dramatic loss a year earlier. In truth, she was much more comfortable being a larger lady than the Skinny Minnie everyone had kept fawning over. During the time of the wife-carrying competition, she had been the recipient of endless compliments and praise, which, granted, had been pleasant to hear, but they also filled her with an unshakeable dread. People kept telling her that she was a 'changed woman' and that the 'world was now your oyster', but she would have been far happier devouring delicacies rather than transforming herself into something new and spangled.

Throughout that period, she had become panicked – though she hid this from Colin – and, in reality, she had wanted to free herself from the pressures of their great expectations. It was too much for her. When she was the size of the Sugar Loaf Mountain, nobody had imagined that she was fit for anything other than remaining alive, and that had suited her perfectly. That modest forecast for her future was one she could handle, so when she returned to wolfing down everything in sight, there had been no sense of guilt or regret. The consequences of her over-eating suited her nicely.

When the interval act – which included a special performance from Mr Logan and the Cork Music School Choir – came to an end, she let out a little, excited squeal.

The nerve-racking voting was about to begin.

Come on, Niamh! Do it for me!

On second thoughts, she was delighted that her husband had made himself scarce; he had an awful tendency to fall asleep while she watched TV, his loud snoring interrupting her enjoyment. Furthermore, when he was awake, he would always question what had just been said; so many episodes of *The Late Late Show* had been sabotaged by his irritating need for clarification thanks to his limited hearing.

'Gay said, "Roll it there, *Róisín*" like he always does! Why would he call her Rosemary, for God's sake?'

She should be kinder to him, she often felt. While she was certainly far from a social butterfly, she still answered the odd telephone call from her mother or sister. It was from these calls that she learned about the speedy demise of her husband's reputation following the embarrassing wife-carrying competition. It saddened her more than she would care to admit, hearing that everyone pitied him in the town. She also suspected that there were probably some who even laughed at him behind his back. It was so unfair, she thought. He used to be such a splendid man with character, compassion and integrity.

And now?

His only misfortune was to share parents with that brute of a man, Councillor Alfred Saint James. How she wished for the day to come when Colin would receive an opportunity to vindicate himself, but as the months went on, and he became ever more introverted and bitter, she wondered if that opportunity would ever arise.

I would almost be happy for Ireland to lose tonight if it meant that Colin could finally get his moment in the sun. Almost.

As the votes started to come in from the various juries around Europe, Trish temporarily forgot about Colin's difficulties, for it was becoming clear that the contest playing out in front of her was set to be a three-way race between Ireland, the United Kingdom and Switzerland, with the magnificent Niamh seemingly having the edge.

Don't get ahead of yourself, Trish – anything could happen yet!

And indeed, in the final stretch, it appeared that the anything-could-happen prognosis was going to materialise when Malta was given the final and deciding vote: the winner was going to be either Niamh Kavanagh or a fellow redhead, the Liverpudlian popstar Sonia. Going into the final vote, Ireland was ahead by eleven points but with a maximum of twelve up for grabs, Trish calculated that if Malta gave top score to the United Kingdom, and nothing to the host country, then Ireland would be pipped at the post by a single ruddy point!

Come on! Ireland was the best by a country mile! Trish argued as she turned her eyes skywards, begging Himself to award the prize to the most deserving contestant – for once!

She closed her eyes and crossed her fingers.

Please, please, please!

Trish, along with the entire country, held her breath and waited. Slovenia, Finland, The Netherlands, Bosnia and Herzegovina and Switzerland were all racking up scores but nothing yet for either Ireland or the United Kingdom.

'Greece, six points!'

Trish could feel beads of sweat beginning to form on her brow.

'Italy, seven points!'

After Spain and Luxembourg were awarded eight and ten points, the entire continent realised that the winner of the thirty-eighth Eurovision contest would be determined by whoever received Malta's final score. The memories of the wife-carrying competition came flooding back. Surely such a fall-at-the-final-hurdle outcome wouldn't happen to her twice?

'Come on, come on, come on!' Trish roared as she pulled the duvet over her and waited for the last vote to be announced – *with agonisingly slow speed*, she critiqued.

'And finally ...'

Trish peeped her head up, her heart pounding, her stomach churning.

'Ireland, twelve points!'

'Wahoo!'

Trish could not believe what had just occurred on her television screen. God had *finally* listened to her pleas and, deservedly, 'In Your Eyes' had won gold! Trish screamed and shouted and jumped out of bed, throwing the remnants of her snacks around the room – a reckless act that would normally have disgusted her.

'We won! We won!' she repeated until she had to sit back on the bed to catch her breath and wipe away the sweat.

The excitement was so great that she was initially oblivious to the shooting pain that ransacked her chest before travelling to her arm and neck. When she did become aware of these unusual changes to her body, she deduced that they were nothing more than a manifestation of the delirium that she had been experiencing following Niamh's stunning victory.

They will pass, she convinced herself, before lying horizontally on the bed. *Niamh's legendary status will not, though. She will be in our history books forever and a day!*

The final words she heard appeared to belong to her husband.

'It is a miracle, Trish – I know how I will finally get revenge on that brother of mine. But I need your help – again!'

Trish could feel a lightness descend upon her – and she had no intention of resisting it.

Colin paced the room, almost tripping over his words – and feet – in his excitement. 'You don't need me to tell you that Freddie has always delighted in the fact that he stole Mamie May away from me. His deceitful victory at the wife-carrying competition further suggested to everyone that it was he and not me who had the best marriage in the town – but I now know how we will prove to him and everyone that, despite his best efforts, it is me who has the best wife in the country! I can't believe I didn't think of it sooner! We will put an end to the feud at long last! So long as Mamie May enters, which, I've absolutely no doubt she will – as soon as Freddie gets wind of our intentions, he will force her to sign up, mark my words!' It was only then that Colin stopped pacing. 'Trish, my dear, we are going to follow in Mummy's footsteps and *enter you in the Calor Kosangas Housewife of the Year competition!'*

But the only thing that poor Trish would be entering was heaven. As she took her last breath, a surprising contentedness enveloped her. Not because of the Eurovision Song Contest or because she could see that Colin's fighting spirit had not entirely abandoned him. It was because, belatedly, she was going to meet her babies who had not been able to make it to the finish line.

I hope they all know how much I have missed them. Every day. Every hour.

If not, Trish looked forward to telling them face to face.

Yes, it was a great night for everyone.

FORTY-SEVEN

It was not uncommon for Trish to lie stretched across the bed, eyes closed yet still actively listening to what was going on around her. Sometimes, she even watched films in that manner – in particular, the ones with which she had casting issues. For instance, if she thought that Tom Hanks was wrong for the role, she would shut her peepers and imagine someone like Mel Gibson, say, or Harrison Ford playing the part instead. 'There is nothing stronger than our minds,' she would often say, completely unaware that that wasn't necessarily a good thing. Of course, there were other occasions when sleep just got the better of her and she dozed off.

Tonight, unfortunately, Colin was so engrossed describing his new plan that he missed the especially pale tinge to her face. Not that it would have made any difference; his wife was already utterly bereft of life, and not even a private concert from Niamh Kavanagh would have brought her back to rude health.

'It is the perfect opportunity for us to show Freddie once and for all that he didn't get the better of us, Trish – that we are not a pair of desperate losers after all, cooped up in a dirty house!' he explained, his arms flailing about with abandon. 'You've seen the show on the television – Mummy was the first winner, for heaven's sake – you know what's involved! According to the poster, the producers are claiming that it will be the very best yet!'

Colin glanced at the TV and, irritated by the orange Tango man running around the screen in front of him, he switched it off completely. 'Even though I wasn't even nine at the time, I'll never forget it. The instant fame. How proud my father was of her,' he added, praying that he, too, would get an opportunity to stand on that same stage, as the husband of the country's best wife. 'As an added bonus, Trish, Mummy and all the housewives since have walked away with cheques and split-level cookers. I've been saying that we need a new cooker for ages, haven't I? Haven't I? Think of all the cakes I could bake in it!'

He considered sitting down on the bed, but the flood of adrenaline in his system kept him pacing the floors.

'Which reminds me, maybe I should hang up my apron for the time being – not that this competition is a beauty pageant, but it would be no harm if we embraced healthier ways before the big night. It will sharpen the mind if nothing else!'

'Firstly,' he continued, 'we will have to compete in the local heats in November, with the winner then progressing to the national finals next April. If we qualify, you will get to meet Gay Byrne at long last! That alone would silence that beloved brother of mine beyond a shadow of a doubt!'

He looked around the room. Dissatisfied by its untidy condition, he removed his jacket and began picking up the rubbish and empty plates that lay strewn across the floor. He was adamant that their gluttonous, slovenly ways would now become a thing of the past.

'They are going to test your ability to produce a meal – don't worry, I know it's not your forte, so I will teach you a few simple recipes that will leave the judges in a swoon!' he promised. 'You will have to impress them with your conversational skills too, which, if tonight is anything to go by, will need a little work. Then you will need to finish with a party piece, like a poem or a song. Maybe you can do that thing with your lips and teeth where you look like a walrus? That always makes me laugh, and I know having a good sense of humour is important to judges,' he said, the thought of his wife's silly ways coupled with the prospect of winning gold producing a smile.

'You will need to get involved with some charity or other,' he continued. 'Civic spiritedness is of the utmost importance, I believe. I know we haven't been overly active in the community this past year, but we have a little time before the heats to rectify that. They are going to take place in the Beechmount Hotel, by the way.'

He took a break from the cleaning and made a dash for the wardrobe, pulling out various frocks – and if the mothballs were anything to go by, only God knew when they'd last been worn!

'Do you know what, Trish? I think, given the occasion, we should pop down to Geoghegan's and get you something top drawer – something sparkly and eye-catching. Although, maybe we should wait till a time closer to the event because, if I stop baking so many cakes and buns, and we recommence the training we did for the wife-carrying competition, we could transform ourselves again! What do you say? Not that you don't look great, dear heart – although, I must say, you do look a bit out of sorts tonight. I hope you aren't feeling too overwhelmed by the competition. Don't forget; I will be with you every step of the way! Now, I better jot down some of these ideas in my notebook.'

As he started rooting around his desk drawers for a pen that would work, his hands stumbled across a small box that was hiding towards the back of the top drawer – one that he had forgotten existed. However, as soon as he saw it, he knew exactly what was in it: the beautiful red train that Mamie May had given him for his ninth birthday, which his brother had subsequently smashed into pieces. Cautiously, Colin took it out of the box and held it in his hands. After keeping the sabotage a secret for many months, he had eventually confided in his father, who then helped him to glue it back together, although, as Colin well knew by now, the cracks tended to remain visible forever once something was broken.

Almost for the first time since reading the notice in the Garda station, Colin took a breath. His initial excitement for revenge now made way for a measure of reality: by entering Trish into the Housewife of the Year, were all those cracks that he had accumulated over the decades really going to be erased once and for all?

Unlikely.

He returned the train along with the notebook to the drawer and, rather than compiling a To-Do list for the heats, walked over to the bed and gave his wife and only ally an affectionate kiss on the cheek before lying down beside her.

'Ignore everything I just said, Trish – I got a little carried away, that's all.'

As he closed his eyes, a niggling worry demanded Colin's attention: why had his wife remained silent for the past number of minutes – even when he turned off the television set, an act she normally would have viewed as being on a par with high treason.

He jumped up and shook her body gently. When that had little effect, he tried a little harder. He then checked if Trish had a pulse or if there was still breath escaping from her mouth or nose. The answer to both was negative. There was only one conclusion: at the tender age of thirty-six, his wife had departed.

'Oh no.'

If he were honest, her death wasn't too surprising, given her terrible life choices. Not that he had provided much encouragement for her to get healthy; he had been too consumed with his own troubles. If anything, he'd exacerbated things, cooking her whatever she wanted. He lay down next to her again and clutched her hand. Neither of them would ever have claimed that they were love's young dream but, somehow, in the face of the difficulties they both battled in their respective lives, a loyal allegiance had emerged between them.

'I've let you down, haven't I, Trish?'

He was on the verge of apologising for his failings when he noticed the expression on her face. He had often heard that the serenity that escaped many in life found them in death – and by the looks of things, that seemed to be the case with Trish. This gave him some comfort.

'Goodbye, dear heart. You will be missed.'

He sat up and gently crossed her hands atop her chest, hoping that the next world would be kinder to her than this one had been. As tears rolled down his cheeks, he now knew for certain that, like with Mamie May's train, the cruel world would ensure that the cracks of his heart would always remain.

1994

FORTY-EIGHT

'It's really only for couples, Azra – you wouldn't enjoy it. See you for more aqua aerobics on Tuesday though!'

Thanks to the likes of she'd-as-soon-shoot-you-as-look-at-you Mrs Brady and some of the other ladies from aqua aerobics, Azra was beginning to develop a complex about being single, particularly because it resulted in her being marginalised from the local social scene time and time again. Those horrible emotions from her early life had come rushing back in recent months – feelings of isolation, loneliness and worthlessness that had, in large part, led her down this path in life in the first place.

Up until this point, Azra had learned to overcome the threat of tears in these situations by laughing at the absurdity of husbands and wives using their marital status to empower themselves over others – as if they were some kind of better person in the eyes of society simply for having said, 'I do.' Look at her father! He had hardly been a beacon of morality simply because he wore a wedding ring on his grubby finger – something he had pawned before his wife was cold in the grave. Additionally, Azra had the comfort of knowing that she was a part of a profession that, amongst other things, served to emphasise the hypocrisy of the institution every time married men, bored of domesticity, passed the threshold – something they repeatedly did.

Now, however, to alleviate her isolation, she was beginning to wonder whether she should take an if-you-can't-beat-them-join-them approach.

In Istanbul, to have a social life, she had never needed a husband or a boyfriend – being a city teeming with millions of inhabitants, there had always been somebody to accompany her to a concert or the theatre. Navan, with a population of fewer than twenty thousand, was a different beast altogether. Apart from visiting a brothel, of course, everybody seemed to do everything with their husbands or wives. And despite being in the town for over a year, Azra had yet to find a gal pal with whom she could do things like go for a nice meal or a drink. Despite being surrounded by men most days of the week, she was forced to admit that her old foe called loneliness was making a return appearance. It appeared to her that Ireland was no country for single women.

'That's fine, Mrs Brady – enjoy *Four Weddings and a Funeral*. I'll probably just see it when it comes out on video,' she fibbed, having every intention of seeing it in the Lyric Cinema on her own over the coming days – but wouldn't it be nice to have someone with whom she could share some popcorn or a bag of Maltesers every now and then?

It wasn't just at the cinema or evening meals where it seemed a woman must be in a couple; every time she did something other than her weekly shopping, she could feel the weight of the other women's pitying gazes. How she longed to shout at them: 'Don't feel too sorry for me, Betty or Yvonne or Sally – I had sex with your husbands only the other day!'

Maybe that was part of the problem, she conceded – she was a threat. These wives never invited her anywhere because they didn't trust her with their husbands. Had they heard something about her endeavours, perhaps? These human CCTV cameras knew everything about everything, so it wouldn't have surprised her, but, in truth, she doubted it – otherwise she'd have been frogmarched out of the town long ago. She just wanted a few gal pals – was that too much to ask? She kept returning to the same proposal – maybe the only solution to her isolation was to become a husband-hunter once again? It was a flawed logic, granted, but it appeared to Azra that there were many things flawed with the world in which she lived.

In darker moments, Azra often wondered whether she should simply pack her bags, sell the house and return to the hustle and bustle of Istanbul – at least there she would be able to enjoy something resembling a social life and not be judged for being a 'Miss' rather than a 'Mrs'. But each time she had reached for her suitcases, the memories of her sweet Oliver returned. She convinced herself that to leave his house would be a betrayal of his generosity. Besides, living in his home allowed her to feel connected to him, even beyond the grave.

Speaking of graves, as she had been leaving her home for aqua aerobics earlier that morning, she'd spotted her neighbour, Colin, making his way to the cemetery, flowers in hand. It was a year to the day since his poor wife had passed away. Azra remembered the night vividly – before the ambulance arrived, she had been knee-deep in boxes, packing and ready to make a run for it following Colin's threats. The only silver lining of that whole tragic incident had been that the man had lost any interest in playing the role of model citizen.

That's not to say that they didn't see each other. That morning, for instance, as the neighbours passed each other at the gates, they shared a simple hello, but, like each and every time she'd seen him in the past, the man appeared to be in another world. This time, however, she noticed that he sported a walking stick.

Maybe I'll call into him one of these days, she pledged. *See if he needs help with anything. Not today, though. I am still too upset about Mrs Brady leaving me out! If her husband thinks I'm going to let him anywhere near me tonight, he can think again!*

'Oh, by the way, Azra – did you hear the shocking news?' Mrs Brady asked as she got into her rusty Ford Fiesta, parked outside the swimming pool. 'It has just been announced that the next Housewife of the Year competition is going to be the last one. Can you credit it, after twenty-seven years, it's finishing up! An end of an era, you could say.'

Azra looked at Mrs Brady with a blank expression. What on earth was the woman talking about?

'What am I saying, you probably haven't even heard of the competition,' Mrs Brady continued, noticing Azra's puzzled reaction. 'It's an institution here in Ireland.'

'I see. Maybe we can have a coffee some time and you can fill me out.'

'Fill me in. Really, Azra, you've been in Ireland long enough. By the way, your house has a very big connection with the competition. Once, a winner lived there! Although, between you and me, I always felt she was a little overrated. I once found a cat's hair in one of her scones.'

'I think I might have read something about the competition. It sounds –'

'Anyway, some of the girls are thinking of entering – they've been too nervous up until now, but seeing as it's the last hurrah, they've decided to give it a go. We're going to meet next Wednesday so that I can share a few tips with them.'

'You entered? Did you wi–?'

'Mrs Wall is going to bake her famed carrot cake! You should try it!'

'I'd love to someti–'

'Listen to me, going on and on! Sure, you've no interest in the competition, Azra, seeing as you're not …'

'A housewife?'

'No. Anyway, must dash! I have to pop over to Mammy's grave before putting the dinner down – that shepherd's pie isn't going to cook itself, after all. You've no idea how useless my husband is around the house.'

He's even more useless in the bedroom, Azra thought.

'Sometimes I envy you, Azra – all alone!'

'Goodbye, Mrs Brady.'

'The end of an era,' Mrs Brady repeated before speeding off.

FORTY-NINE

'Three in a row, can you credit it, Trish! If it wasn't for the fact that you already died, you would most certainly have done just that!'

Colin had been looking forward to telling his late wife all about the night two weeks ago when Ireland entered the Eurovision history books after the country won the crown for a record-breaking third time in a row. His only regret was that it had taken him so long to inform her. He had missed his daily visits for the past couple of weeks as the ankle injury he had suffered during the wife-carrying competition had had the bad manners to play up on him again, rendering him housebound.

'The song was performed by Paul Harrington and Charlie McGettigan,' he added but suddenly stopped short and, rather than telling her about the sweet ballad, he decided to tend to some of the weeds around the sides of the headstone. Trish shared the grave with Colin's parents and he took comfort in the idea that they were looking after each other now. He imagined that his mother had proven to be just as wonderful a housewife and mother in heaven as she had been on earth and that she was keeping a close eye on her daughter-in-law. As he plucked a few dandelions that were creeping up through the gravel, Colin could hear his wife shout at him: 'Tell me about the song! What was it called?'

It was called 'Rock and Roll Kids' but since it had claimed victory, every time the melody and nostalgic lyrics whirled around his mind, Colin was sadly reminded not only of the untimely passing of his late wife and her devotion to the competition, but also of his own youth – his lost youth. Like the character in the song, Colin recalled how he and Mamie May would spend their days 'listening to the songs on the radio'. His chest would always tighten when he heard the lyrics, 'I was yours and you were mine, that was once upon a time. Now we never seem to rock and roll anymore.' As much as he tried to get on with his life, at every turn there appeared to be constant memories of the hurt of yesteryear.

'I'll tell you, Trish. The win wasn't the only highlight of the night – you should have seen the interval act!' he continued. However, before he could wax lyrical about the stomping Irish-dancing sensation *Riverdance*, he spotted Mrs Brady approach, a scissors and some weedkiller in her hand. The speed at which she hobbled along the narrow paths suggested that she had something important to say.

'Colin! I suppose you're here to tell your poor mammy the news just like I'm about to tell mine. You look awful by the way – she would be so disappointed in you. And to think of how much pride she once took in your appearance – always brushing your shiny dark hair.'

Colin had little interest in speaking to her today or any day – a sentiment shared by the majority of the town of Navan. She had an extraordinary ability to prise information out of a person without them even knowing it – before then sharing it with the rest of the community.

Mrs Brady persisted regardless of Colin's silence. 'It's the end of an era. That's what everyone is saying. If you notice something moving,' she said, pointing at the soil beneath them, 'it's because your mother is probably turning in her grave.'

'I must be making tracks,' Colin replied, picking up the various gardening implements. 'Please thank Raymond for all the newspapers.'

'Why don't you thank him yourself? He really enjoyed chatting to you on the phone last month.'

'Yes, it was good to have a little chat with him.'

'It's a shame that you are a widower, otherwise you and Trish could have entered. Everyone is going to, seeing as it's the last competition ever. The end of an era, all right. You could have gotten one up on your brother once and for all – I wouldn't say Mamie May could turn on the oven, let alone cook a dinner. I'd say there have been times when he wanted to shove her into the blasted thing! Why anyone would want to steal her is beyond me.'

'Take care, Mrs Brady,' Colin said, still only half-listening.

'The last ever Housewife of the Year competition.'

Colin stopped in his tracks and spun towards her. 'Sorry?'

'The end of an era,' Mrs Brady repeated. 'What would your poor mother think?'

Colin's complexion turned ghostly. With that, the busybody plodded off, delighted that her ability to stir the proverbial had not yet abandoned her.

FIFTY

Freddie hadn't spent too much time in Navan since winning the wife-carrying competition. Within mere hours of his sweeping victory, he found himself guzzling vodka with Mia Ylönen, one of the Finnish contestants who was drowning her sorrows after coming a disappointing fourth in the final.

'Do you think I'm pretty?' she'd asked Freddie as he led her to a taxi, a rare occasion where he played the gentleman. 'Ilja hasn't looked at me since I gave birth over eighteen years ago. He thinks I'm fat, I know it.'

Freddie had known it was the drink talking, as there wasn't a single pound on her skeletal frame.

'If he does,' he replied, holding a plastic bag aloft in case the vodka planned on making a reappearance, 'then he should head down to the optician first thing in the morning. I think you are beautiful.'

'Do you?' Her Nordic accent sent shivers up his spine.

'I do.'

Those three letters signalled the beginning of a passionate affair that saw them spend a lot of their time over the subsequent year in the Wexford summer house that she had insisted her short-sighted husband purchase soon after they'd moved from Finland. She never complained about playing second fiddle to Ilja's career so long as he didn't complain about playing second fiddle to her lovers. This structure to their marriage suited them perfectly.

While the 'Sunny South-East' wasn't exactly where Freddie envisioned spending his weekends, it was a break from his never-happy constituents and his familial obligations – and the Finnish woman was wealthy and very appreciative in bed.

'Do you want to go *away* away for the weekend?' she asked one rainy morning in early May.

'I do.'

It was when Mia was withdrawing funds for this last-minute trip to the south of France that Freddie heard about the demise of the Housewife of the Year competition. Initially, the news that the national event that had been so integral to his family's story was coming to an end didn't even register with him – several shrugs followed by 'Who cares?' were his replies to the many people who approached him to get his views as he waited across the road from the bank.

But when that busybody, Mrs Brady, approached him, the cogs started to whir in Freddie's mind.

'I bumped into your brother yesterday morning,' she announced, her hands laden down with shopping bags. 'He was at the grave, crying – wishing that his dear Trish was alive so that he could enter the Housewife of the Year competition in honour of your mother. He really was dear Mrs Saint James' favourite, wasn't he?'

'Is there something you wanted, Mrs Brady – or are you just going to spend your day interfering in other people's lives, like always?'

'Is Mamie May thinking of entering the heats?'

'I doubt it.'

'I'm sure your brother will be delighted to hear that, considering that he has no hand to play, if you catch my meaning. I'm sure he'd be devastated to see Mamie May enter, given all that's gone on.

'The end of an era,' Mrs Brady chirped as she crossed Watergate Street – the lost-in-thought expression on Freddie's face letting her know that she'd once again found her mark. As she passed the bank, she bumped into Mia who was emerging from it, her purse bulging with money and traveller cheques. 'Mrs Ylönen, be sure to give my best to your *husband*.'

'Of course.'

Mia joined Freddie, who seemed suddenly lost in thought.

'What's all this talk of a Housewife of the Year competition? I heard about six people mention it in the bank while I was in the queue.'

Freddie ignored her pleas for an explanation about this 'quirky' contest – a descriptor that was somewhat ironic given the fact that her own country had founded a competition that involved throwing their nearest and dearest over their shoulders and carrying them across a muddy obstacle course.

'Wouldn't it be funny if …' was all Freddie was able to offer the conversation, leaving his Finnish lover utterly confused.

FIFTY-ONE

A stall was assembled inside Navan Shopping Centre, in front of Quinnsworth, where two volunteers handed out and accepted entry forms for the heats of the Housewife of the Year Competition. The duo spent much of the day valiantly battling angry managers who were furious that the never-ending queues for the stall were blocking the entrances to the shopping centre – and it was Saturday, after all, the busiest day of the week.

'We didn't anticipate such a big response,' they argued. 'Hopefully, it will calm down soon.'

But, if anything, the exact opposite occurred. With only one chance remaining to be a part of a national institution, the housewives of Navan marched down to the shopping centre, application forms in hand, determined to get a place on the shortlist. The school summer holidays were fast approaching, and mothers wanted everything in place before swanning off for a few weeks to Kerry or Cork – or even Spain, where the wealthier housewives would take the opportunity to get a head start on their tans for the heats. (While looks were not being judged, many felt that a healthy glow wouldn't hurt their chances.)

Membership for aqua aerobics also rose around this time, which Azra discovered that same Saturday morning as she battled for a spot in the swimming pool. When someone suggested that she might like to forgo her place to make room for the housewives, Azra had to use all the breathing techniques she had previously learned in the classes to prevent her from channelling her inner Jack the Ripper.

It seemed there was absolutely no escaping the mania that was currently sweeping the town and when she popped into the shopping centre to pick up a few messages, Azra found herself slap-bang in the middle of the hysteria once again. In need of a breather, she decided to forgo her shopping and turned on her heels – but in her haste to escape the army of self-satisfied housewives, she ran straight into her neighbour, Colin, causing them both to crash to the floor.

'My ankle!'

'I'm so sorry, Mr Saint James,' Azra said, standing. 'I wasn't looking where I was going. Are you okay?'

'It's not your fault,' he assured her, trying to suppress his pain. 'This ankle seems to be going from bad to worse no matter how much I rest it.'

'Where are you going? Let me help you,' she offered, taking him by the arm and helping him to his feet.

'I need to get some weedkiller for Trish's grave. They are growing at a ferocious speed, blasted things.'

She led her neighbour by the arm and after pushing some of the women out of their way with unnecessary force, they reached the entrance to Quinnsworth. Just as she was about to pick up a basket for him, Colin stopped dead in his tracks.

'Is everything all right?' she enquired, noticing that his usual trance-like state was even more pronounced than ever.

'Why are they doing this to me?' he whispered.

Azra looked in the direction of his stare. Standing in front of the Housewife of the Year desk was a man who bore a striking resemblance to Colin. This man was staring back at Colin, grinning from ear to ear, as a redheaded woman, pretty and ethereal, waited behind him.

'Who are they?' she probed, hoping the ashen face that Colin now bore wasn't symptomatic of something serious.

'Just some people I used to know.'

FIFTY-TWO

That Sunday, the people of Navan were delighted to discover that a mini-heatwave had arrived and, covered from head to toe in factor 20, they wasted no time in getting the barbecues going and making the most of the sunshine. Colin also decided to embrace the warm temperatures and took himself outside into the front garden for no other reason than he needed to get out of the house – even for a few minutes. After discovering the previous day that Mamie May was entering the Housewife of the Year competition, he had been climbing the four walls – his dodgy ankle the least of his troubles now.

As he'd tossed and turned throughout the night, he'd questioned whether he should just pack his bags and leave Navan once and for all. A fresh start. The thought of having to listen to and read updates about the heats for the next few months would be torturous for him – given his late mother's success in the inaugural event, he was certain that journalists and reporters would make himself and his brother the go-to people for quotes in the lead-up to the final-ever competition. The phone had already rung several times that day – and it was a Sunday!

As he perched himself on the side of the fountain, the statue casting a cooling shadow on him, Colin feared that he was already starting to revert to his reclusive and bah-humbug days, which just wouldn't do seeing as he had made a promise to Trish as he buried her that he would endeavour to live a better life than the previous years.

Why are Freddie and Mamie May doing this to me? Haven't they done enough already?

His thoughts were interrupted by the emergence of his neighbour into the garden, dressed in a polka-dotted bikini which emphasised her beautiful form. He could now fully understand why she had proven to be such a success with the men of the town. After spreading a towel on the grass, she turned on a small portable radio, which blasted out some song that Colin had never heard before. He was surprised that neither her presence nor the ditty sung by some man claiming that love was all around him irritated him. When Azra hummed along, a smile even appeared on his face.

I really was horrid to that poor woman last year, wasn't I?

He rose to his feet and walked towards her. Colin wasn't sure exactly what he was going to say but he thought he would suggest to her that they start over. If he did decide to remain in the town, he'd need an ally in the run-up to the heats – and who better than a person who knew little about his turbulent past. (Unless the men whose company she kept had been talking, which they probably had, he acknowledged.) But before he could announce himself to her, the song on the radio ended and the DJ piped up about the one topic from which he wanted to be distracted.

'Wet Wet Wet say that "Love is All Around" – well, that remains to be seen, but what is a certainty is that the housewives of Meath are all around us as anyone who attempted to enter the shopping centre in Navan yesterday would have witnessed! I'm told that on account of the high demand, organisers have extended the deadline for applications so if there are –'

'Argh!' Azra roared before slamming the radio off.

'I couldn't have put it better myself,' Colin said, startling her.

'Was I disturbing you with the music? I've turned it off now – if I hear one more thing about that housewife competition …'

Colin was happy to learn that he wasn't alone in his scorn for the event.

'You're probably the only person in the entire country who isn't entering.'

'Well, maybe I would if I was married! Even better – my social diary wouldn't be so empty if I were a man's wife!'

Colin smiled, an idea forming in his head. 'What are your views on cooking – is it something you have any skills in?'

She perched herself up on her elbows. 'Why do you ask?'

'I hope you don't think me too forward ...'

FIFTY-THREE

The Meath Chronicle, 21 June 1994:

Mr Colin Saint James is delighted to announce his marriage to Azra Demir, formerly from Turkey's enchanting city of Istanbul but who has been based in Navan for the past year.

Hugely popular within the community, this social butterfly has had many admiring men fluttering around her since her arrival, although it was her next-door neighbour, Mr Saint James, who ultimately proved to be her preferred partner.

The nuptials were said to have been a private affair. Father Cutbirth, a personal friend of Azra's, officiated over the ceremony in St Mary's Church, with a quiet reception held immediately after at their residence. Apparently, the new Mrs Saint James was so keen to practise her culinary skills that, with the help of the new man in her life, she prepared their own wedding meal. They then spent the night in the Beechmount Hotel, but the groom was quick to note that this was for practical, preparatory reasons rather anything romantic. When pressed for further information, Mr Saint James explained that he was referring to the upcoming county heats of the last ever Calor Kosangas Housewife of the Year competition, an event where the newlyweds are determined to snatch victory.

This union follows the passing of Mr Saint James' wife, Trish, who sadly surrendered to a heart attack in May 1993, moments after Niamh Kavanagh proved victorious in the Eurovision Song Contest – her favourite night of the year.

'I know that Trish would have approved greatly of Azra along with our plans to take part in the competition,' Colin revealed. 'But we won't get to properly enjoy our new marriage because we won't have a spare minute between now and the heats in November when we will show the town and a certain councillor who the real victor is,' Mr Saint James asserted.

While waving her new wedding ring with carefree abandon, Azra added: 'This is my first time being introduced to this much-loved contest. It is the final one, but I promise that I will make it one to remember!'

The Meath Chronicle *wishes the pair a lifetime of happiness as well as all the luck in the world at the last ever Housewife of the Year competition. If the high praise heaped upon Azra in the pubs of Navan is anything to go by, she is going to be the one to beat!*

FIFTY-FOUR

Freddie sat alone in the meeting room of the Town Hall. He was a good ten minutes early, which was a first for him, but he wanted a little time to gather his thoughts before the other councillors arrived. He had been in Wexford for the past week with Mia, and little did he think that so much would be occurring back in Navan.

He had read the wedding announcement in *The Meath Chronicle* that morning about a dozen times. He had even drunk five strong coffees to focus his mind, but still the words on the page remained the same: his brother had married some foreigner and, together, they were entering the Calor Kosangas Housewife of the Year competition.

All because he'd taunted him in the shopping centre.

What have I done?

Though he'd considered it for a few moments after Mrs Brady informed him about this year being the final year of the competition, in reality, Freddie had never had any real intention of entering Mamie May into the contest. The thought of the woman being able to do anything other than say her name was laughable. But when she was dragging him to Jack Kiernan's to get new shoes for the children that Saturday, a moment of madness had taken him over. Like always when his brother was involved. As he'd barged his way through the throngs of silly women handing in their application forms – including his Finnish bit-on-the-side – he'd spotted his pathetic brother, whose limp was a pleasurable reminder of his embarrassment at the wife-carrying competition.

Unable to resist the opportunity to twist the knife further, he'd grabbed a pen and scribbled something on a sheet of paper at the stand; it hadn't even been an official application form – it was just for effect.

When will you ever grow up, Freddie?

On any other day he would rise to the challenge presented and compete. It wasn't like he would face any difficulty convincing Mamie May to enter – she would dance a highland jig on burning coals if he asked her to. The problem was that her skills as a housewife were on a par with Boris Yeltsin's ability to remain sober.

In comparison, the discreet enquiries he had just made revealed that this Azra woman ticked every box on the judge's list of criteria. According to Mrs Brady – who had just been up to his former home after suggesting that she collect Trish's belongings for St Vincent de Paul – Azra had treated her to some 'absolutely fabulous samples. Fabulous!' It wasn't just exotic Turkish dishes either – in the space of a few weeks, it seemed that his brother had ensured that Azra had become a dab hand at local fare as well. According to the town gossip, Azra's stew was 'worthy of poems and ballads'.

As Mrs Brady ransacked the dead woman's wardrobe on behalf of charity (*charity starts at home*, she thought as she placed a couple of bracelets in her handbag), she reported that, downstairs, Azra had been busy practising a selection of party pieces, including the most hypnotic dance that Mrs Brady had ever seen.

'Azra had a name for it – swirling, whirling dishes … something like that,' she informed Freddie, her nostrils flaring with the pride of being so well-informed and cultured. Should she perform that, complete with the traditional white costume and headgear, the seventy-two-year-old predicted that she couldn't see any outcome other than a top-of-the-podium placing for Azra Saint James.

Freddie was on the verge of flinging his folder at the wall in frustration when his fellow councillors sauntered in. He despised the sight of most of them; their bulging, insatiable bellies were indicative of the reason so many of them had entered local politics in the first place – to live the high life and milk the system for all it was worth. Of course, if Freddie were candid, that was the only reason he had also entered the game. Even still, he often made his feelings about them known. Once, he hurled the contents of the dustbin over two fossils who refused to compromise on the introduction of waste charges. On another occasion he had yanked Councillor Magee's ridiculous-looking toupee from his bald head after the eighty-two-year-old told the story about this dog swallowing his false teeth on Christmas Eve for the hundredth time.

'I placed them on the coffee table, and when I woke up they had vanished. It took us two days to realise what had happened – and I didn't get a chance to eat me Christmas dinner!' so the anodyne story went.

The other councillors could not get enough of the image of Magee going around the house with his big, gummy mouth, but if Freddie heard that stupid story one more time, he knew he would soon be standing in front of a judge pleading guilty to first-degree murder.

Most of them were bigoted, old-fashioned so-and-sos, Freddie thought, and he had no use for them.

Unless, he pondered, as he watched them take their seats and gobble up the biscuits in front of them, *I can use their Victorian outlook to my advantage.*

FIFTY-FIVE

Colin had been washing the dishes when his new wife rushed into the kitchen and announced the news. Upon hearing her words, he broke one of the plates in the basin, resulting in a messy laceration across his palm.

'What do you mean the heats have been cancelled? Who did you hear that from?' he gasped.

'I was having lunch with the ladies in Susie's Cookhouse – the first time I've ever been invited, by the way – when they told me the news. What are we to do?' Azra asked with great urgency. She was fearful that Colin might renege on their marriage if the heats didn't go ahead and she was determined not to lose her new standing in society that came as a direct result of said conjugal bliss – even if she found the wives' conversations quite dull and one-note. More selflessly, however, she also hoped to bring some pride and happiness back into this poor man's life; his form had undoubtedly transformed since entering the competition.

'Did they say anything further? I mean, why?'

'They say it was something to do with the councillors. They say it was an "inappropriate" thing for the women of Meath to do.'

'What?' Colin shouted, waving his blood-stained hands manically above his head. 'That's ridiculous! They've been entering for years! My mother was a national hero after her win!'

Desperate to get to the bottom of this bombshell, he went straight over to the phone and rang Raymond at *The Meath Chronicle*. Maybe he would be in a position to shed some light on what had just happened.

'Hello, Raymond? It's Colin Saint James here. Do you have a moment?'

It emerged that Raymond had more than a moment for his old schoolfriend. He explained the sudden cancellation of the competition in detail – he had been due to compère the event, so was privy to some insider knowledge.

'Basically, a bunch of councillors argued at last night's monthly meeting that the contest was vainglorious and against God's teaching of humility and subservience,' Raymond revealed. 'They felt that, quote, unquote, "Wives should tend to domestic matters quietly and efficiently without the need to go around tooting their horns."'

Whatever blood had not escaped from Colin's hand began to boil. 'Is there any chance they might reverse their decision? Surely there will be an uproar in the town? Don't our good ladies deserve a moment in the sun?'

Raymond's sympathetic voice responded, 'I doubt it – you know what that lot's like. Saying that, if any change of heart is to take place, it will have to occur before lunchtime tomorrow. That's when they intend on informing RTÉ television of their decision to abstain from the event.'

Much to Raymond's disappointment, Colin hung up without even saying 'thank you', 'goodbye' or 'let's get a drink sometime'.

'What are we going to do?' Colin wailed, his defeatist tone unbefitting of a person with his name.

Azra led him towards the kitchen table and sat down beside him. 'I am so angry!'

'I bet every penny in the Central Bank that my brother has something to do with this. I know that he became petrified that I – I mean *we* – were going to succeed on the night and this was his only way of preventing it. He's such a … such a … Oh, I can't even bring myself to stoop to his level!'

'Is there nothing that we can do to change minds of the councillors?'

'Azra, those old fogies are so stuck in the mud that not even a tsunami would be able to move them.'

'I can't believe that,' she replied.

'If only you knew them, Azra …'

She kissed him on his cheek and grabbed her coat before making her way towards the door.

'But I do know them, Colin. In fact, I know three of them *very* well.'

FIFTY-SIX

Azra relaxed in the sitting room of Councillor O'Malley, sipping on her third cup of tea of the evening. She was impressed by how he and his wife had decorated the space. Brown was a colour that appeared to be quite popular in Ireland. As she lounged on the chocolate armchair and rested her feet on the shaggy, tan carpet, Azra felt that what the couple lacked in moderation, they made up for in co-ordination.

'What excellent taste you have, Mrs O'Malley – I am getting lots of ideas for a big restoration – no, renovation – that Colin and I are planning on doing next year. I hope you won't mind me borrowing your style.'

'Of course not, Azra, although I am sure you are well equipped to turn that old house into a pal– Oh my word, I forgot to give you biscuits!' the horrified councillor's wife blurted out. She gave herself a playful slap on the wrist. 'How will you ever forgive such atrocious hospitality, Azra?'

'Would you believe, Mrs O'Malley, I have devoured so many biscuits today that I think I am about to explode like a bomb – which I really hope won't be the case because this rug in front of me is so beautiful.'

'That old thing, we are in two minds about whether to give it to the charity shop or just throw it in the skip,' fibbed Mrs O'Malley, who had no intention of doing anything of the sort with her prized piece of textile. 'And as for biscuits, can you ever have too many?'

With that, the woman hurried out to the kitchen, praying to the good Lord above that the children – or the two-legged mice as her husband referred to them – had not eaten the entire contents of the biscuit tin.

Seated directly opposite Azra, Councillor O'Malley stared into his cup of tea, wishing that he could disappear. His cockatoo, perched in a beautiful gold-ribbed cage in the corner of the room, was given the responsibility of breaking the awkward silence.

'Biscuit!'

'That is enough, Starburst,' his owner scolded.

'It seems you have quite the taste for exotic birds,' Azra whispered, before taking a loud, unrefined slurp from her tea.

'What are you doing here, Azra?'

'I thought that it was only fair that I called into your house seeing how often you have called into mine.'

'Sssh, be quiet! Why are you doing this? Haven't I been good to you? Didn't I bring you a burger and some chips from the Valley Café the last time I was over?'

'You brought them for yourself, you smelly pig!'

'Smelly pig!' Starburst repeated.

'Starburst!'

'And it took me days to get that smell of vinegar out of my bedroom.'

'Is it money you're after, Azra? Jesus, I thought that was why you married that deaf codger. Is he not looking after you?'

'I don't know what a codger is but if you are talking about Colin, don't worry about him, Councillor – it is your wife who you should be concerned about. I think forgetting to give her guests biscuits will be the most little of her troubles when she discovers that you are not spending your Tuesday and Thursday evenings watching the Meath footballers train.'

'Oh God, Azra, what do you want?' he asked, turning his gaze anxiously towards the kitchen. 'Say it before Annette returns.'

'I am going to ask you the same thing that I asked the two other councillors I just had tea with. Change your mind about the Housewife of the Year competition.'

'What?'

'The competition – let it happen.'

'Is that it? Mary, mother of God, I thought I was going to have a heart attack.'

'Heart attack!'

'Starburst, sssh! Yes, of course, no problem.'

'Excellent. Then our little secret can remain between you and me – or is it "you and I"? Colin keeps correcting me. You and me, I think.'

Councillor O'Malley took a large sip from his cup; tea had never tasted so good.

'While I have you,' he said in hushed tones, 'any chance of some "how's your father" one of these evenings? Annette has been having quite a lot of headaches lately.'

'How's your father? Well, mine has been dead for over thirty years, so he's not doing too well at all,' Azra remarked.

The councillor leaned forward. 'You know what I mean, you tease!'

(She didn't – English idioms would be the death of her, she was certain.)

'Sex!' he clarified. 'What do you think?'

Azra was about to respond when Mrs O'Malley returned with a sorry-looking plate of Ryvita crackers.

'I am so embarrassed, Azra – it seems the kids have beaten us to the biscuits.'

'Not to worry, Mrs O'Malley, these look perfect. After all, now that the Housewife of the Year competition is taking place once again, I had better be extremely careful about what I put into my mouth. Isn't that correct, Councillor?'

The councillor returned his gaze to his cup of tea. 'I suppose so, Azra.'

'How's your father?'

'Starburst!'

FIFTY-SEVEN

Freddie was finishing off a cigarette in the kitchen when he heard the phone ring. He had hoped that Mamie May would answer it, but then he remembered that she was putting Declan, the eldest child, to bed.

He's twelve, for God's sake – don't you think he's old enough to throw on his pyjamas himself by now?

His outrage at his wife's mollycoddling was ignored – as were most of his suggestions about how best to raise their three children. And for a good reason. Mamie May knew only too well that her husband had little interest in his flesh and blood – they were nothing but an absolute nuisance in his mind, and anything he recommended was only for his benefit. ('Why don't we send them to boarding school? It didn't do me any harm.')

Freddie often wondered if he should be more concerned about this contempt that he harboured for his wife and children. He had provided them with a roof over their heads – it wasn't a mansion, granted, but it was located along the Boyne Road, one of Navan's most salubrious addresses – but, other than that, his contribution to family life was virtually non-existent. For a time, after their first child had entered the world, Mamie May had encouraged him to read the child bedtime stories, a request that he informed her was on a par with having to go through forty days of Lent. When he discovered that she was seeking counsel from her mother and father, along with reading all the parenting books in the local library, he dreaded what ideas she was going to suggest. He soon rejoiced, however, when he overheard her on the phone telling a confidante that 'it is better for the children to have an absent father than one who's so cruel-hearted'.

Absence – that he could do.

And over the years, Freddie never gave Mamie May an iota

of hope that anything would improve – not just in his role as a partner but, more distressingly, as a father. What parent would, on hearing that their middle child had come down with a nasty bout of tonsillitis, rejoice on account of the silence the malady would bring about?

From Freddie's point of view, there were only downsides to having a wife who always fussed over her offspring. This included the way that he was often forced to do things like answering phones and doors, something he loathed doing, especially since the majority of his calls were of the tedious work variety. In many of these cases, he would put on a high-pitched child's voice and say, 'Daddy isn't here.' It had proven to be quite effective.

Tonight, however, he decided to use his own voice when the phone rang because he was in fighting form. After all, at the councillors' meeting last night he had managed to sabotage his brother's latest plan to get even with him and that felt bloody marvellous – even if the whole mess was initially his doing. As an added bonus, his efforts proved to be child's play thanks to some of his chauvinistic colleagues. Maybe they weren't such a bad lot after all. As he walked down the hallway to answer the phone, Freddie felt invincible.

'Hello?' he said, his voice full of verve. 'Councillor Alfred Saint James here. How may I be of assistance?'

He listened for a brief moment without uttering a word.

'I see,' he eventually said. 'Well, I think you're making a big mis– Hold on a second, you baldy bastard; don't think I don't know what those speckles of white on your moustache at the summer barbecue were. Talc, my arse! Would you like – Hello? Hello?'

Freddie stood for what could only be described as a dog's age, receiver still in his hand. He began chewing the inside of his cheeks, a habit he often did when he was anxious. Then, not knowing how else to calm his temper, he picked up the phone and flung it against the wall.

'Colin may have won this battle,' he shouted, leaving his wife and children stupefied upstairs, 'but he most certainly will not win the war.'

He marched to the top of the stairs and entered his son's bedroom where Mamie May was reading him some silly story by the Brothers Grimm – his favourite, apparently.

'Sorry to interrupt, Declan, but you will have to finish your little yarn yourself because your mother is busy tonight.'

'Doing what?' the child quizzed. This order was the most his father had said to him in years. He wondered whether he might even squeeze an 'I love you' out of the patriarch?

'Yes, doing what?' Mamie May added.

Freddie's cheeks flared red. 'You have just over three months to learn how to cook, dance and fucking string a sentence together!'

FIFTY-EIGHT

The night before the heats, Azra was exhausted and even though she longed for her bed and a night of uninterrupted sleep, she decided not to return to her side of the property. Instead, she stood outside Colin's bedroom and knocked.

'I'll just be a minute,' he shouted. 'I'm in the bathroom!'

Since their spontaneous wedding, Azra had slept in her own bedroom at night and, with her husband's blessing, continued her professional endeavours. However, since becoming one of just eighteen women to be shortlisted for the Meath heats of the Housewife of the Year competition, she had begun to cancel appointments with her ever-growing client list, not because she felt it was unfair to Colin – their arrangement was just that: an arrangement – but because the competition had stirred something within her.

Being surrounded by married women for the first time in her life, a status that had intrigued her for many years, she suddenly realised that these gals were equally as silly and two-faced as their male counterparts. Like so many of the men who had passed over her threshold down the years, her fellow competitors were also proving to be dab hands at presenting a version of themselves to the world that was completely at odds with their private personas. Having spent hours upon hours in their company thanks to photo calls, rehearsals and other social events in the lead-up to the big night, Azra had started to realise certain things – some of them profoundly simple yet startling.

Despite paying lip service to solidarity, compassion and humility, many of the women bitched behind each other's backs, interrupted and undermined, argued over whose children were the smartest, whose husbands were the best. There were even three who had confessed to Azra over drinks one night that they were having an affair – including the Chanel-wearing, pearl-clad Mia, the only Finnish wife to have made the cut. She had barely seen her husband in months, Mia had admitted, yet in the competition itself she was preparing to wax lyrical about her devotion to housewifery!

And what of herself? After all, Azra was hardly the personification of virtue, given her life choices, so who was she to pontificate? Had she not been instrumental in the break-up of numerous marriages? Had she not lied and cheated and compromised her values time and time again? With stars in her eyes, had she not been motivated by greed along with the thought of owning a Spoonmaker's Diamond one day?

In that moment of clarity, it dawned on her: *we are all as bad as each other. Why are these silly competitions always about being the best? Surely it would be more truthful to find the worst!*

As soon as her lofty expectations of the world had finally petered out, Azra realised that she had wasted so much time chasing things that she didn't have rather than appreciating the things she did have, like her darling Oliver. If it wasn't for the fact that her success in the heats meant everything to her new husband, someone she had discovered over their last few months together was a sweet and kind man, she would have written to the judges and told them that there were better ways of celebrating the success of women in the home than pitting them against each other.

Delighted with her newfound wisdom, five months after saying 'I do', she decided to fulfil her marital obligations and knocked on Colin's bedroom door. In that department, she was without equal! If only that skill could be judged in tomorrow's competition, she would win hands down!

FIFTY-NINE

Navan drivers heading in the direction of the picturesque town of Trim would have had great difficulty missing the Beechmount Hotel, one of the town's much-loved accommodation offerings. Not only had the large premises provided comfortable beds for its many guests over the years, it, along with the popular Hippodrome Nightclub, had also doubled as a successful venue for weddings, conferences and a myriad of other events. And on 20 November 1994 it held the heats for the last-ever Calor Kosangas Housewife of the Year competition.

News of the Meath heats' initial cancellation had reached every possible corner of the county – and had not been well received. The Royal County's inhabitants were known for being a feisty lot and there had been talk of pickets, strikes and tomato-throwing – one woman had even been prepared to streak across the Páirc Tailteann football pitch during one of the Sunday matches. Fortunately, such drastic action proved unnecessary following the abrupt U-turn.

To begin with, people had given credit for the change of heart to the beautiful Azra Saint James, who was said to have been instrumental in the reversal of fortunes. Eventually, however, those kind words were directed towards her brother-in-law, Councillor Alfred Saint James, who told anyone who would listen that it was he who had convinced those 'old fogies that the stone age was expecting them back any minute now'. At that stage, three of those aforementioned councillors wanted nothing further to do with the sorry mess and so allowed their comrade to take whatever glory was going.

Never ones to miss some positive press, the other councillors were not so quick to distance themselves from the resurrection of the heats, seeing as it was clear to them that they had underestimated the competition's popularity.

'I think one of us should make a speech on the night,' said Councillor Simpson during the final monthly meeting before the heats. 'I've no problem doing the honours, if everyone is agreeable?'

Not a single one of them was agreeable to forfeiting such a lucrative platform, however, and if one was to believe those wicked whispers spread around town following the monthly meeting, what followed was a hairy brawl between the men in the Town Hall with chairs and pictures being flung from one end of the room to the other. In the end, they decided it best that nobody do it.

Thankfully, by the time the day of the contest arrived, calm had been restored and everyone was full of excitement and anticipation. Attendees were so keen to look the part that the county's fashion retailers and dry cleaners thought that not only had all of their Christmases come at once but so had their birthdays and anniversaries. Not since that memorable night when Josie Byrne, the wealthy farmer and widower from Robinstown, invited the entire province to his only daughter's wedding had the hotel seen such a crowd. The large car park could scarcely keep up with demand, which did not seem to be much of a concern for drivers who happily left their motors on the side of the main road. Luckily, the traffic warden was off duty that night; his wife, Yvonne, was taking part in the competition, although few fancied her chances. She made the most of a recent successful insurance claim following the discovery of a rat's tail in a can of soup and had spent the best part of the past year 'recuperating' from the shock, drinking sangria and lounging by a pool in Marbella's exclusive Hotel Puente Romano. Her bloated face did have an enviable tan, though.

Yvonne was not the only contestant who was set to face something of a slog that evening. The week before, Nancy Cantwell had allowed her addiction to anti-anxiety medication to get the better of her, and in a rush to get yet another pill, she slipped on the kitchen floor and fell through the patio window. The pashmina she hastily purchased upon being discharged from A&E would cover the cuts on her arm, but the seven days of enforced cold turkey had led to some inconvenient shaking; this was sure to create carnage when she was charged with presenting her dinner.

Iris MacNamidhe was not considered to be much of a contender either. The staunch camogie fanatic had been in such a rhapsody following her local team's convincing victory the day before that the woman could now barely speak, let alone sing her intended party piece, 'Danny Boy'.

As for Noelle O'Shea – this lady was so besieged by involuntary spasms that it was a wonder she had even entered the contest in the first place. Few had forgotten her wedding day eighteen years earlier when, instead of saying 'I do', she quite randomly thumped her husband-to-be in the kisser. Raymond, who was due to officiate the evening's proceedings, made a mental note to remain a couple of metres away from that particular contestant.

Inside the hotel, these four ladies, along with a further fourteen contestants who had been shortlisted from hundreds of applications, packed themselves and their beautiful *gúnas* into the ground-floor bedrooms. Eye-catching geometric-print clothing in a rainbow of colours such as blue, orange, purple, turquoise and fluorescent pink were very much in vogue, and the ladies were confident that they could have stopped traffic. Tessie Burke and Gertie Weldon had purchased their outfits specially for the event, while the others had only worn theirs to a small handful of celebrations, such as confirmations or communions (they felt the sacredness of those auspicious occasions still lingered on their fabrics and would, therefore, stand them in good stead tonight). With seconds to go until the show kicked off, the contestants applied last-minute touches to their faces.

Outside in the foyer, and in the large function room where the event was due to be held, things were no less frenzied. With huge posters of the country's first winner of the overall competition, a certain Mrs Saint James, hanging proudly on the walls, local journalists roamed the venue, determined to capture every detail of this momentous event.

The participants were not alone in looking like they had just strolled off a Parisian catwalk; the hundreds of spectators who had gathered to cheer them on had also donned their Sunday best, including Mrs Brady, who was telling everyone who would listen about her thoughts as to what made the perfect housewife.

'Humility, compassion and kindness,' she opined, uncertain how to interpret the eye rolls her words then received.

Even the men were not scrubbed up too badly, especially the eighty-three-year-old bachelor, Henry Norman, who had misunderstood the nature of the event and thought it was some local matchmaking shindig. Still, everyone praised the pink carnation that he had placed in his breast pocket, as well as his never-say-never attitude.

'Isn't the atmosphere just electric?' the studly Roger Dunphy enthused to some of the lads from the Embassy Snooker Hall as he waited at the bar for his pint of Guinness and his wife's gin and tonic. 'I hope nothing goes wrong.'

SIXTY

'What is the best aspect of being a housewife?' Raymond quizzed the sixteenth contestant of the night, Frances Roberts, who was a little off-trend with her 1980s fitted shoulder pads and meringue-resembling gown. As soon as she heard the question, she smiled from ear to ear.

'Oh, that is a very easy one,' she answered without missing a beat. 'Feeding my husband and four boys!'

A loud hurrah followed from the crowd; there were very few people in Ireland who wouldn't give three cheers to the matriarch's culinary delights.

'There is nothing, absolutely nothing in this world that I prefer doing more than filling their bellies! Raymond, I could shove a field of spuds into their gobs all day long – you've no idea how much they love their mammy's cooking!'

Noticing some tears falling down her rosy cheeks, Raymond realised that the contestant was becoming a little overwhelmed by the occasion and decided it best to save her blushes and disregard the final two questions on his list.

'Wonderful answer, Mrs Roberts. I look forward to receiving my invitation for your Sunday roast sometime soon,' he joked as he began to escort her off stage. 'Who could say no to a good, hearty feed?'

'Nobody!' she gushed, returning to centre stage. 'Not my boys anyway.'

There was no way she could accept Raymond's assistance off stage – not when there was still so much about her hungry family to discuss. She grabbed the microphone from her interviewer and addressed her audience in the same manner in which Evita had ordered her beloved Argentinean peasants not to cry for her.

'Am I right, ladies? You know what I am talking about? That

feeling when you see five empty plates in front of you licked clean? That magical sensation when you hear the burps and the flatulence? The sight of five strapping lads crawling to the couch, nearly comatose from the sheer volume of food that they have just wolfed down? Food that you have spent hours and hours preparing?'

The culinarian started waving her hand frantically in front of her face in a fruitless attempt to prevent her emotions from taking over.

'Where are yis, lads?' she called out, the glare of the overhead lights almost blinding her.

'Here, Mammy, over here!' shouted her rugged yet jolly family.

And with that, the county's most enthusiastic over-feeding housewife disappeared into the crowd to be reunited with the men in her life. Nothing, not even a chance to stand in front of the revered Gay Byrne in some swanky venue in Dublin the following April, was more important than the bond between this mother and her hungry kin.

'It seems the family that grazes together stays together,' Raymond quipped.

As the Roberts were reunited in the back of the function room to a soundtrack of 'We love you, Mammy' and 'Let's go home and I'll put on some sausages', Colin was close to being diagnosed with epilepsy such was the wild nature of his restless movements. He stilled, however, as his wife walked onto the stage with incredible flair and confidence. As she had spent every waking hour over the past number of weeks practising all the requirements of the night's competition, he was fully confident that she would wow the judges. Mrs Brady had even revealed herself to be an ally – particularly teaching her a few idioms that continued to prove problematic for the Turk.

Nonetheless, Colin could not quieten the tornado of nerves

whirling within him. His brother stood arrogantly at the bar, downing yet another Jameson. But it was not the alcohol that was leaving a glint in his eye, Colin feared; it was because he had, most certainly, hatched some evil plan and was waiting for it to unfold.

Colin turned his gaze from his brother when he heard those gathered around him laugh hysterically; his wife had just made a joke, it seemed.

'It is true! Raymond – Turkish housewives are the best in the world! Later, during the cooking demonstration, you will see that I can beat an egg; after that, during our performances, you will see that I can also beat a drum; but the one thing that we Turks can't do is – beat the craic of the Irish!'

Like putty in her hands, the crowd roared approvingly at her performance – what an antidote to the cautious, fuddy-duddy ramblings that had been expressed earlier in the evening. Or Mrs Roberts' ode to gluttony.

'I hope I have pronounced that correctly – "craic"? Your mother has been giving me lots of classes, Raymond! I don't want her to give out to me!'

'It's only me who she gives out to, Azra,' he lamented.

When Azra's interview ended – 'A round of applause for Mrs Saint James everyone!' Raymond encouraged, the crowd heartily responding – Colin relaxed in his seat. There was only one further contestant left in this opening round, and that was the raspy, has-anyone-got-any-honey-and-lemon Iris MacNamidhe, so he could rest assured that his wife of just five short months had the edge over the others so far. Mamie May, who had been first up, had delivered rambling and indecipherable answers. Initially, he had felt sorry for her and wanted to jump on stage and assist her but, luckily for Azra and their quest for the top prize, that charitable instinct soon passed. Still, Colin knew that despite Mamie May's poor showing, he could take nothing for granted; with her partner being the most cunning and Machiavellian husband in town, anything was possible.

And, as the night played on, that prophecy proved all too accurate.

SIXTY-ONE

Following the conclusion of the first round, Raymond announced that only half of the housewives would make it through to the next stage of the competition, one which would require the three judges to sit and inspect the ladies' table settings and sample some of the food they had prepared a little earlier in the evening.

'Let's give the judges a couple of moments to tot up their scores – an extremely unenviable task, I am sure you will all agree. What a shame that we will have to say goodbye to nine of our great contestants. But there's always next ye–' he began to remind the crowd before stopping short, prompting a united sigh from the many lovers of the contest.

Taking advantage of the short break in proceedings, punters dashed to the bar to refuel. Children were bribed with Tayto crisps and bottles of red lemonade so long as they did not tell Mammy that Daddy had added a double whiskey to the Coke he had just ordered for himself. They were not permitted to say a word about Mammy sneaking out to the reception area to have a cheeky fag either.

'Aw, aren't they as good as gold, your lot,' was a line that was often said that night.

After the too-short intermission, Raymond ordered everyone to return to their seats as he had received the results from the judges.

'This contest is only getting started, there will be plenty of time to get a drink later in the evening,' he reassured concerned audience members as the shutters were brought down on the bar.

Colin had not had a drink all night, but he most certainly could have used something stronger than the ten cups of tea he had imbibed since entering the hotel – particularly now that Raymond had begun listing off the successful candidates. He closed his eyes as the names of the housewives were announced in a painfully slow fashion. Mrs McGuiver made it through, as did Mrs Wall and Mrs Lynch. Mrs Ylönen had also sailed through to the next round.

Still no Azra.

When Colin heard Mamie May's name amongst the list, he was conflicted. On the one hand, the residue of his earlier love for her continued to linger in the background of his heart so he still wanted her to do well; on the other, he had never forgiven her betrayal and thought that she should suffer for her actions. It was one thing to call off their engagement, but to do it so cruelly and calculatedly was inexcusable.

'Why couldn't she have just told me to my face?' he had asked himself time and time again over the years. It was a puzzle he had returned to almost every single day since the catastrophic event. But maybe being married to his wretched brother for so many years meant that she had paid her dues.

Mrs O'Shea, Mrs Norris and Mrs Higgins were next to pass muster. With his fingers, Colin counted the names, and realised that there was only one space remaining. His heart began to gallop.

Oh, God! Could we fall at the first hurdle? he queried, ill-prepared to face the humiliation that would inevitably follow. *How could she not get through? She was leaps and bounds ahead of everyone else.*

'And finally, Mrs Azra Saint James,' Raymond announced.

Not only did Colin's new and accomplished wife progress to the next round, but she also received the warmest applause of the evening so far.

That's my girl! he thought.

He turned towards his brother and saluted. If it were not for the fact that the younger of the two siblings had been brought up with such impeccable manners, at that moment he would have saluted Freddie with his middle finger alone.

SIXTY-TWO

When those blasted councillors reneged on their promise and decided to move forward with the competition, Freddie had needed to conjure up a plan. After observing his wife's efforts to make a lasagne (it ended up in the bin) and attempt a few jigs and reels (she broke several ornaments, including their prized Belleek china vase), he knew that no amount of training or rehearsals would suffice. So he decided to do what he did best in life.

Cheat.

He invited the two judges of the upcoming heats to a plush dinner in Dublin's Shelbourne Hotel. While he had already conceded that they were not going to be easily manipulated, at the very least he felt he could make his wife a contender for the title by celebrating her 'achievements' to the high heavens.

'Did you know that she volunteers at a local hospice?' was just one of the many untruths he uttered that evening. 'We have lost count of the number of times she has held the hands of patients on their deathbeds. You would need a calculator to add up the amount of tears she has wiped away from the eyes of grieving family and friends. A remarkable woman, indeed.'

Aware of Freddie's motives for arranging this meal, the pair of judges took full advantage, helping themselves to the most expensive items on the menu.

'I've yet to try lobster. What better time than the present?' one of them said.

While his comrade gorged on top-dollar shellfish, the other judge channelled his own inner fish and looked to drink the bar dry. While this initially irritated Freddie, he soon discovered that as the alcohol flowed, so, too, did the disclosure of information. And as the desserts were being prepared, the councillor finally managed to weasel a nugget of information from them that would aid his plan to scupper his brother's and new sister-in-law's intentions of walking away with the prize.

'You know that we will require a local judge to assist us,' the wine bibber slurred. 'Do you have recommendations?'

Freddie grinned. 'Would you believe, I know the perfect chap for the job.'

***

Neville Merriman had never married because, simply put, he was a bloody nightmare. There were very few people who could tolerate being in his company for more than a 'hello' and a swift 'goodbye'. Even Mrs Brady recoiled when she spotted him walking down the street. Everything had to be exactly the way the arrogant so-and-so liked it, which, even for the most fastidious of folk, was ridiculously excessive.

Nobody would dream of having tea with him in the Pepper Pot or the Ardboyne Hotel, because no matter how much love and attention went into the preparation of the tea, it was never good enough. Sometimes, it was too cold – others, too hot. The sugar was either too sweet or not sweet enough. Even if the waitress drained a Holstein Friesian in front of him, Neville Merriman would argue that the milk was sour.

The kicker, however, was that his lodgings, nestled in the middle of a small woodland on the Athboy Road, were, to put it mildly, rough around the edges. For those who knew his stuffy personality, it would have been understandable if they presumed that his cutlery and delft were positioned in a manner similar to the way art was mounted in the Louvre; or that his wardrobe showcased seven three-piece suits, one for every day of the week, all of which were the same navy shade. But it was nothing of the sort. It was a hostile environment into which neither Edmund Hillary nor Tenzing Norgay would have dared venture. Piles of dirty plates kissed the ceiling, bins mounted high in the corner, shoes and dirty clothes lay strewn across the floor. Neville Merriman was the textbook definition of a walking contradiction. In public, he was an insufferable fusspot; in private, he was no better than an unruly and unhygienic teenager.

In truth, he was an incredibly lonely and unhappy bachelor, whose only source of comfort was knowing that others were having as bad a day as he was – and if they weren't, he would readily attempt to rectify that. If life had decided that he should be down in the dumps – in his case, quite literally – then, in his mind, everyone else should be too.

Not that anyone should be playing violins on his behalf. Another characteristic that had long since been attributed to Neville Merriman – one that particularly appealed to Freddie – was that he was an out-and-out xenophobe. Oh, how he loathed anyone who was not from his motherland! Those local waitresses may have thought they were the recipient of unfair abuse, but they had no idea how a person who was not Irish felt when confronted with Merriman's caustic gaze. According to Neville Merriman, they were akin to those pesky bumblebees who deserved a good swatting.

This is why Councillor Alfred Saint James recommended him as the ideal local person to join the two official judges and oversee the Navan heats of the Housewife of the Year competition. 'He will be the perfect person to officiate over the dining section of the competition,' the councillor informed the two judges as he assisted them into taxis outside the Shelbourne Hotel. 'The reputation he boasts in the town for his attention to detail is second to none!'

SIXTY-THREE

During *another* short, ten-minute interval, assistants placed nine modestly sized tables on the stage. The semi-finalists had just five minutes to display their tableware; once the time elapsed, their culinary presentations were then scrupulously inspected by everyone's least-favourite person, Neville Merriman. The frequency with which he shook his head as he went from table to table suggested that the housewives were not scoring too highly.

'The stupid, cantankerous old f–'

'Sssh, Desmond!' one non-participating wife whispered to her irate husband.

When Neville caught sight of Azra on the middle of the stage, his stomach appeared to turn. 'The audacity,' he mumbled, holding his clipboard up to his face so that he could pinch his nostrils together without being noticed (he had exemplary social etiquette, after all). 'If it wasn't bad enough having a Finnish contestant … This takes the biscuit!'

Neville concluded that the best way to deal with this outlander was to humiliate her in front of the hundreds of people present; that should send a strong message to foreigners that they ought to stay put on their own turf. (That thousands upon thousands of his Irish brothers and sisters were, at that moment, boarding ferries and planes to England, America and Australia to seek employment didn't alter his viewpoint one iota.)

'So, Contestant Number Four,' he exclaimed with a generous dollop of condescension, 'can you tell me why yours is the only table that is circular rather than square or rectangular? Are you intentionally trying to be difficult?'

'Well, Judge, there is an excellent reason for this,' Azra confidently replied. 'In Turkey, where I originally come from, our tables are round because no matter where you sit, the person is equal to the others around them. Even though we have just met, Mr Merriman, I can tell from the, how shall I put it, warm and kind way you have addressed me that you are one person who is a fan of equality.'

'Naturally,' he replied, remembering that time he hurled a large rock through the window of a young Asian family who had moved to the town to start a new life.

'I noticed,' he continued, 'that you have opted for water in those earthenware containers as your chosen refreshment. Don't you think, given the occasion, a Sauvignon Blanc or Merlot would have been more appropriate?'

Azra coolly looked to the other contestants' presentations, then smiled. 'I see that the other ladies who are sharing this stage with me are happy to agree with you, Mr Merriman, and I can fully appreciate why – who would wag their finger at a glass of wine to accompany their evening meal?'

'You, obviously.'

'Indeed. Well, I decided to provide my imaginary guests with water because one more tradition that we have in my home country is to drink plenty of it before our meals to make our bellies big and full so that we eat less food! It is a way to avoid obesity, we believe – something that is currently proving to be an extremely big problem across the world, don't you think, yes? "Your health is wealth" is an expression that you are familiar with, I'm sure? Well, I agree and wanted to make a mirror reflection of that in tonight's presentation.'

Along with another morsel of her rather delicious food, Neville Merriman also swallowed a 'damn' and continued examining Azra's beautifully presented table, which included, amongst many other delightful touches, embroidered napkins and placemats – not that he had any intention of admitting as much. If he were not such a horrid racist, he would have given full marks for her magnificent floral arrangement of seasonal wildflowers. But, like Mrs Ylönen from Helsinki, she was not from Ireland, so she deserved no encouragement – a fact that had not gone unnoticed by Azra as she had a clear view of the scoresheet on which he had given her a disgraceful zero. Even Mrs Wall, whose table caught fire thanks to a lopsided candelabrum, had received one point.

There is only one solution to this, Azra concluded. If this odious creature wasn't going to thwart her husband's designs at retribution, she was left with no other choice but to quietly rearrange the dessert the weasel was about to sample. She had prepared two versions of *kaymakli kayisi*, a traditional delicacy where dried apricots were stuffed with buffalo cream. According to tried-and-tested recipes, the dessert was then expected to be rolled in ground pistachios, but each contestant had received notification that Neville Merriman suffered from a severe allergy to nuts, and under no circumstance could they be used in any of the food they served to him. Initially, Azra had no issue embracing such restrictions and had, instead, used mint chocolate as an alternative topping. Now that the pompous bigot stood in her way, however, she had no other option but to force him to eat from the nut-laden batch that she had made for the other two judges. Deftly, she bunched three of the sweets together on a fork – the naughty, nutty one squashed discreetly in the middle – and presented it to Neville Merriman.

Minutes later, when the universally despised local judge fell to the stage floor, clutching his throat and gasping for air, nobody in the function room moved a muscle to help. It was left to Neville Merriman alone to retrieve his epinephrine from his pocket and inject it into his person. Secretly, many of those looking on were disappointed that he had come armed with his medication – he was most certainly not someone who would have been missed in the town.

As the invalid slowly struggled to his feet and assured everyone present that he was in fine fettle once again, a faint groan reverberated throughout the space.

'I think, under the circumstances,' the champagne-loving judge announced, 'it would be best to step down from the panel. Surely you should go to the hospital, even if it's just as a precaution?'

Merriman tried to stand tall, though his face was still red and looked a touch bloated. 'I don't think that is necessary,' he stuttered. 'I am feeling one hundred per-'

'Get off the stage, you prick!' someone heckled.

This was a sentiment that was echoed throughout the crowd if the round of applause that followed Neville Merriman staggering off the stage was to be believed.

And just like that, Azra avoided elimination.

Men and their nuts – that will always be their downfall, she thought as she helped herself to some of the leftover dessert.

SIXTY-FOUR

Following his sister-in-law's impressive sleight of hand, a furious Freddie fled the hotel, attempting to get as far away from his imminent defeat as possible. His incompetent wife was limping through the various stages thanks to the favour the two judges owed him from their boys'-night-on-the-town shindig, but that indebtedness would soon run out. Now that Azra had gotten the better of his racist trump card, there was no way that he and Mamie May would emerge triumphant.

You only have yourself to blame.

As he navigated his way through the car park, he whacked a handful of side mirrors from their rightful places; only for the fact that there was an assembly of scorned housewives standing nearby, he would have gladly inserted his boot through some of the windows.

He stormed through the town and because of his foggy and frenetic mind, Freddie soon found himself within a stone's throw of the one place he wished to avoid: the family home.

Owing to several storms over the decades, the blasted oak tree no longer stood as tall or as straight as it once did, but how it continued to taunt him, and once again he berated himself for failing in his youthful attempts to maintain his crown within the clan.

Ill-prepared to be subjected to further horrific memories and reminders of his inadequacies, he turned on his heels, but his rage, combined with the fading light, led him to crash straight into Seamus Leech, a well-respected technician and owner of an electric shop on Canon Row.

The technician apologised, as he was also eager to be elsewhere. 'I hope I haven't missed the housewife thing-a-ma-jig. My cousin Delilah is taking a punt, and I promised I would cheer her on.'

'She didn't even make it out of the gate, I'm afraid,' Freddie replied without looking at him.

'Oh dear – although that hardly surprises me. Delilah has more interest in being captain of the ladies' golf cl–'

'Do you think I am interested, Seamus?'

'No,' he blushed. 'Here, I suppose your sister-in-law is competing?' the nuisance continued. 'I'm just after calling up to her for a bit of jiggery-pokery, but there was no answer. Or maybe, now that she's a married woman, her days of being a prostitute are behind her?'

Freddie couldn't believe what he had just heard.

'Sorry, what did you call her?'

'God, Freddie – I didn't mean to offend. I suppose I shouldn't have spoken so crudely. She is your family, after all. I've had a few whiskeys tonight – my filter isn't what it should be, I suppose.'

Freddie tried to make sense of the bombshell that Seamus had just dropped. Had his deaf and pathetic brother really married the town whore? Yes, he had heard a few rumblings about a prostitute knocking about the town, but he'd assumed it was, like always, just idle gossip or boys-being-boys' bravado. Little had he realised that the woman currently wowing the judges in the Beechmount Hotel had been wowing the rest of the town under the sheets for the past year.

'I don't suppose you have any hard evidence of this, my friend?' Freddie questioned. 'You know, something more substantial than hearsay.'

'I hear the floozy has a sneaky Polaroid camera somewhere in her room,' Seamus informed him. 'She takes photographs of everyone who visits her. I suppose it's her way of insuring herself, in fairness to her.'

'You couldn't fault her for that,' Freddie replied as he draped his arm around his new best friend. 'Now, I wonder whether or not you know where she keeps the incriminating snaps.'

'I actually don't, Freddie. Look, I have to get going ...'

'You're not going anywhere, pal, unless you want me to tell the entire town of your perverted ways.'

Swallowing a gulp, Seamus walked with Freddie up the driveway towards the councillor's childhood home, reminding himself to stay away from the whiskey in future.

***

It had been many years since Freddie Saint James last broke into someone else's property, but as he smashed the downstairs bathroom window, that fantastic adrenaline rush he had enjoyed so much as a teenager immediately returned. Seeing as there were the remaining cooking presentations and party pieces to get through, along with a raffle, he calculated that he had about an hour to find the incriminating evidence, rush back to the hotel and make the big reveal. If it weren't for the fact that the clock was against him, he would have relished causing such destruction across the many rooms.

While Seamus looked for something to drink in the kitchen below to calm his nerves, Freddie scoured every inch of Azra's love nest. Based on the fact that her belongings were strewn across her bedroom, he suspected that his brother had yet to make an honest woman out of her and that her days of sexually satisfying the horny male contingency of Meath had not been fully suspended. This realisation gave him hope, as it meant that she probably hadn't yet discarded the much-needed, compromising evidence.

He forced open the drawers and wardrobes and rifled through the contents within. He then pulled the duvet from the bed and examined the pillows, but the elusive photographs were not to be found. He patted the curtains. He searched for any lumps underneath the carpet and rugs. He rummaged through a small collection of books on a shelf. He upturned chairs, tore cushions apart. He rifled through a large but mostly empty jewellery box and make-up case that sat on top of the vanity table, but his efforts did not have the desired results. Instead, all he'd achieved was having a brown powder explode all over his good suit, suggesting that there were certain belongings owned by women that should remain untouched.

Enraged, he decided to continue his search in the other areas of the house – she must have hidden them somewhere nearby.

The bloody gall of her!

However, as he raced towards the bedroom door, his mania blinded him to the mess that he had just created, and he tripped on a stilettoed boot, leading him to wallop his forehead against the door, knocking him out cold. For the best part of twenty seconds, the intruder remained sprawled on the ground, blood gushing out of a nasty wound on his forehead.

When he regained consciousness, it took him a moment or two to work out what had just happened, and once he overcame his frustrations and, indeed, embarrassment, he decided to continue the hunt. Nothing, not even a clumsy mishap, was going to prevent him from besting his sibling.

Just as he was about to get to his feet, he looked up and noticed a large brown envelope attached to the bottom of the bed frame. A quick examination revealed the bounty he was longing for: the envelope was stuffed with photographs. X-rated photographs.

Let's get this show on the road!

Freddie spent the next thirty minutes dragging Seamus Leech to his store on Canon Row and forcing the technical wiz to place as many photographs as time allowed onto a series of slides. (As a way of thanking him for his support, the photograph of Seamus was torn up and flushed down the toilet.)

The master plan was to hijack the projector screen that he had noticed being used earlier in the night to project the sponsor's logo onto the stage and then use it to reveal the debauched material for the entire town of Navan to see. Along with Azra's red cheeks, there would be a few fellows with black eyes in the morning, he wagered.

'If this doesn't dismantle my brother's designs on gold, nothing will.'

SIXTY–FIVE

Azra knew she had real competition in Ursula Higgins, and if it weren't for the fact that her new husband was so desperate for her to succeed, she would gladly have tipped the contest in the good-natured housewife's favour.

Earlier, Mrs Higgins informed the audience that she had been married for twenty-five years to Michael, and they lived with their three children in a large, detached house on the outskirts of Oldcastle. The family had never wanted for anything in life. There was always money to pay the bills and to go on a two-week holiday to sun-drenched Italy each summer. There were always birthday cakes and presents when required. There was always heat in the house and petrol in the car.

However, there was a big difference between what the world did and did not see. What she hadn't told Raymond and the rest of the county was that rather than being the dutiful and content wife that many assumed, Ursula's spirit was on life support. This was mostly caused by the routine and the monotony that had been firmly established in the homestead.

Every morning, she would rise an hour before the rest of the house and bake fresh brown bread for the family's breakfast. The jam, which the family later spread across it, was also made by her two hands. While other families had to make do with some sugar-laden, concentrated drink, the Higgins family enjoyed washing down their poached eggs and bacon with delicious orange juice, freshly squeezed every morning. That was saying nothing of the mouth-watering fare she would prepare for lunch and supper. All told, Ursula could have opened a restaurant such were her talents in and around the kitchen.

Every evening when her husband returned from work at the County Council's Motor Tax Office, she would greet him at the front door and hand him his slippers. The obedient wife would then follow him into the sitting room where she would present him with a stress-releasing rum and ice, his only drink of the day.

'You're the best catch I ever caught,' he would say as he took a sip and gave her a gentle slap on her bottom.

'You're welcome, honey,' she would reply robotically. 'I hope no one got the better of you today.'

For this Housewife of the Year contestant, every day someone got the better of her, and it was not her dull husband or her demanding children. It was Ursula herself. She still lacked the confidence needed to pursue the one dream she had always harboured: to be a magician.

Every Saturday evening when her husband brought the three children to see their grandmother in the nursing home in Kells, Ursula would pour an enormous glass of Chardonnay and watch *The Paul Daniels Magic Show*. (Earlier that summer, she'd cried for over a week when news broke that the series, like the Housewife of the Year competition, was coming to an end.) She would have happily cut short her life by twenty-odd years if it meant having a television show with her own assistant, like the lovely Debbie McGee – even if it were for just one night.

Years earlier, she had purchased a magic set from a catalogue that came through the door and every time her husband went to work she would practise, using her babies and toddlers as her assistants. She was never one to toot her own horn, but she knew she was good. Very good, in fact.

When she finally told her husband of her secret one night as they read their respective books in bed, she was left crestfallen at his dismissive, condescending reaction. It wasn't even what he did or didn't say; it was more the look he had given her – the same one he gave his children when they asked if they could have additional pocket money.

You are silly was how she translated the arched eyebrows. Taking his reaction to heart, Ursula returned the magic set to the attic and left it to gather dust.

Deep down, Ursula did not blame her husband for putting the kibosh on her dreams; she blamed herself. She had read enough self-help literature to know that people's happiness should not depend on the permission of others – no matter what your relationship was with that person. At the age of forty-three, the woman was old enough to seize the day, as it were.

Except she didn't; the fear and self-loathing which crippled her were far too powerful.

'I may as well throw it out,' she reluctantly decided one morning. And so, when her husband had left for work, and the children had been dropped off at school, with a heavy heart she hauled the massive set down from the attic and lifted it out into the garden where she had filled a barrel with pieces of wood, ready to be lit. She struck a match and within seconds, a lively fire had formed. Battling a heavy heart, Ursula lifted the set, but as she was about to hurl its entire contents into the flames, just like magic, she heard the phone ring inside the house. Worried that it might be something important (did she forget to give her children their lunch boxes?), she returned inside.

It turned out that it was something important: it was her husband reporting that the upcoming Housewife of the Year competition was set to be the last one. Just like the previous years, he once again pleaded with her to take part. Yes, Mr Higgins was happy for the country to know of his wife's talents – with the proviso that they were domestic in nature. Unlike his earlier attempts, this year Ursula gave a surprisingly enthusiastic 'I'll do it' down the phone.

This was her final chance, she had realised. At long last, Ursula was going to have her moment in the spotlight and show the entire county that this housewife had more than one trick up her sleeve; she had about one hundred!

Naturally, she had informed her husband that her party piece was going to be an inoffensive rendition of 'Peggy Gordon' and not an assortment of well-rehearsed stunts that involved hats and rabbits, levitation and, to finish, the sawing of her assistant in half!

Everything had gone to plan so far for Ursula in the competition. As expected, she had breezed through the heats (who could say no to homemade rhubarb crumble and a finely tuned soliloquy about how much she doted on her family?). Now, she was waiting backstage for her big moment to arrive. And this was when everything fell apart at the seams.

Firstly, Ursula's rabbit had gorged itself on one of the less-talented contestant's undercooked efforts, meaning its bowel movements suddenly became quite animated and showed no signs of quitting. Secondly, she realised that one of the other contestants had mistakenly taken her trick knife for the dinner presentation and now she hadn't anything to ram down her throat. Then, worst of all, she discovered that her friend and assistant, Delilah Dunne – who had been eliminated in the previous round – had stormed out of the hotel in tears, meaning she had no one to saw in half!

With just minutes to go until she was due on stage, Ursula was desperate. She scoured the corridors and reception area, but it quickly transpired that not even the great Paul Daniels himself could have sourced somebody as everyone was either inside the function room watching or preparing to be watched.

Except for a bloodied Councillor Alfred Saint James who suddenly dashed into the hotel, looking suitably vexed. She begged him for assistance.

'Why on earth would I help you, and you being the direct competition of my wife?' he barked, brushing past her.

'I just want to perform magic for once in my life. You've no idea how much it means to me.'

And to her delight – and surprise – her words seemed to resonate, as the councillor stopped in his tracks.

'If I scratch your back, will you scratch mine?'

SIXTY-SIX

When Ursula had initially begged Freddie to be her assistant, greed had gotten the better of him. Like so often in his life, the man simply did not know when to stop. Now, not only was he able to name and shame the promiscuous Azra and get her booted out of the competition (and, inevitably, the country), he could also see to it that his dumb wife became the winner after all!

This night is turning out far better than I could have ever imagined!

Ursula received her instructions. In return for getting her much-needed assistant and achieving her goal of being a magician for once in her sad little life, she was then going to withdraw from the competition for 'personal reasons'. With Ursula out of the running, and Azra disqualified after her alternative lifestyle choices were revealed, Freddie was sure that the path would be clear for his useless wife to achieve gold and glory.

'I can do what you ask, absolutely no problem. Let's have a quick rehearsal, okay?' Ursula asked as she led her new assistant into a small room backstage before locking him inside her coffin. She was far too modest to have designs on the title – she just wanted a shot at being a magician, nothing more, nothing less.

'Thank the entire county for their support then humbly withdraw,' he shouted at her from within as he wiggled around, trying to get comfortable.

On hearing those words, panic set in for Ursula.

'The entire county?'

She struggled to breathe. What if everyone's reaction was similar to her husband's? What if they, too, arched their eyebrows as she pranced around the stage or, worse again, what if they hurled rotten tomatoes at her and booed her off the stage? Oh, the ignominy!

'I can't do this,' she repeated to herself over and over again. She felt her cheeks redden; her breath became even more laboured. 'I can't do it. I am sorry, councillor, I can't do any of it.'

And with that she performed her first magic trick outside of her home – vanishing into thin air. It was quite some time before someone came to Freddie's rescue. By then, it was almost too late.

Almost.

SIXTY-SEVEN

Before her name was even announced, Colin deduced that the other contestant joining Azra in the final two would be his former sweetheart, Mamie May. He had come to this conclusion because he knew the judges wouldn't frown upon the fact that her diabolical attempts at 'Ballaí Luimnigh' would have been more suited to a Baby Infants' Christmas recital, just as they hadn't frowned upon her effort at making a Danish apple pudding, even though it had left them reaching for the dustbin. That the woman had barely been audible in her first interview had not mattered a jot, either. She was Councillor Saint James' wife and, regardless of the fact that the judges were official representatives of the competition and expected to be impartial, he was positive that his brother had, as always, found some underhand way of getting them on his side.

Not that Mamie May was far behind most of the other competitors; plenty of them had suffered as many limitations. Other than Azra, the only one who had in any way cut the mustard was the elegant and charismatic Ursula Higgins – who could really and truly cut the mustard, as she had demonstrated in her excellent dinner presentation section. But much to everyone's surprise, she had failed to turn up for her performance piece, which had resulted in her elimination.

Colin was struck by how dejected Mamie May had looked upon hearing of her success in reaching the final two. He had not expected her to follow Azra's lead and fist pump the air, but he had expected a smile of some sort to appear on her soft, ageing face. Instead, she looked forlorn. The Mamie May he had known in school had been full of resilience and bounce. No matter how often people picked on her or ostracised her from group activities, she would always inhale deeply and sally forth. She had possessed the most incredible ability to compartmentalise the difficulties she faced, which she would then dispatch into the ether as if they never existed.

As Colin continued to applaud the success of the two finalists, his memory returned to that incident with the biscuits in Third Class. Having just received four lashes from the principal for devouring the not-even-God-can-touch-them biscuits, Mamie May hadn't gotten angry at tonight's host, Raymond Brady, for tricking her; she had taken full responsibility herself and struggled on. Which is why, all these years later, Colin felt hugely saddened to see that her admirable fortitude had abandoned her.

Not only was the Mamie May in front of him a shadow of her former self; she was a completely different person.

Or so he thought.

SIXTY-EIGHT

Mamie May knew what she had to do from the moment her husband informed her that she was entering the county heats of the Housewife of the Year competition. She had spent seventeen years searching for atonement, and now, at long last, the right moment had arrived.

Since she'd agreed to enter the event, Freddie had barely even referenced it. And why would he? Nobody knew better than her husband how limited she was around the house.

Except that she wasn't. Far from it.

What he didn't realise was that his wife could, in fact, cook. As it happened, she was also accomplished at cleaning and sewing and singing and dancing. The many years spent in a loveless marriage had afforded Mamie May ample time to develop a host of skills that had eluded her in her early years. Freddie had simply never become aware of her domestic effectiveness because she refused to play the role of doting housewife when she wasn't one. She had quickly grown to detest him after their marriage and, as the months and years went by, this hatred had only grown stronger.

Although her hatred for Freddie was nowhere near as strong as the hatred she reserved for herself.

Creating a horrific home environment for Freddie had not been enough to satiate her need for revenge. After all, he had mostly dined out over the years, or purchased new clothes rather than ask her to repair old things. Based on the amount of time he spent away from the home, she was also certain that he was having more affairs than JFK, so her refusal to engage in lovemaking, which had solely been limited to matters of procreation, had not mattered to him in the slightest.

She had tried to redeem herself years earlier, planning to swing the wife-carrying competition by falling from Freddie's shoulders or tripping him up before the finish line, but Freddie had ensured that the prize came home with them by whacking Colin on the head – with her own leg! So when he'd revealed that he wanted her to enter this competition so as to further humiliate his only sibling and her former sweetheart, outwardly, she appeared reluctant; inwardly, she jumped at the chance.

On the night, she would be the most incompetent housewife imaginable – although she suspected that no matter how subpar her performance was, her husband would, more than likely, ensure that she still made the finals.

But even if that were the case, there would be nothing he could do to stop her from speaking the truth, something that she should have done many years earlier.

***

'Mamie May, first of all, may I congratulate you on your success in reaching the final two of tonight's heats?' Raymond said, although his dubious tone hinted that he knew only too well why this substandard housewife had proven so popular with the judges. 'You must be delighted.'

'I most certainly am,' she replied, adamant that what was to follow would not be repaired by her husband's political influence. In fact, she hadn't seen him in the auditorium in quite some time; maybe, at long last, he and his destructive compulsions had had the decency to disappear. Somehow, she doubted that.

'They say that charity starts at home,' Raymond continued. 'We have seen tonight that – how shall I put it – you are a dab hand at ensuring that your husband and children are loved and nourished. So what else do you do to give back to the community? Seeing as you are the wife of a councillor, I'm sure that you have a long and varied answer to this. Although, hopefully, not too long.'

Mamie May leaned towards the microphone. 'Well, if I'm

allowed to be honest, I'd say that the best thing I've ever done is what I'm about to do now – I'm withdrawing from the competition tonight.'

Understandably, her announcement produced a slew of gasps, sighs, and a 'What did she just say?' or two.

Raymond scratched his head, struggling to understand what he had just heard. 'Why on earth would you do such a thing, Mamie May? Especially seeing as you are so close to representing Meath in the national finals.' As her words sank in, he became greatly concerned that a controversial ending like this to the competition might somehow result in the organiser withholding his pay cheque. (He and his boyfriend had already paid a deposit for a month's safari in Kenya at Christmas and woe betide anyone who stood in the way of him befriending a tower of giraffes.) 'Do you not want to meet Gay Byrne, Mamie May? Would it not be great to meet Uncle Gaybo?' he pleaded.

Mamie May snatched the microphone from Raymond and addressed the audience. 'The only thing that I want is to say sorry to someone here tonight,' she began. 'Someone who I hurt very badly many moons ago when I, foolishly, married his brother instead. I can't change what I've done, and I wouldn't want to – I've been blessed with the most extraordinary children and I wouldn't want to change that for the world – but I'd like to take this opportunity to acknowledge what I've done and the hurt that I caused.'

The many audience members who had, prior to this, quite understandably grown tired of the night's seemingly endless itinerary suddenly had their interest piqued again.

'You see, the title of this competition is all wrong – it's not just the house that makes the wife, but the husband as well. It's a joint effort. I don't think you have to be your man, Einstein, to conclude that Alfred and I aren't in a happy marriage – we never were and never will be.'

She noticed how frantically her heart was now beating – and considered it a pleasant surprise, in some ways, given that it had not stirred much in many years.

'So it seems only fair to me that the winner should be the lovely Azra – and her even lovelier husband, Colin.'

A long, awkward silence descended. The entire county knew only too well what a rogue Councillor Alfred Saint James was; however, not in their wildest dreams did they expect his wife to renounce him in front of hundreds of his constituents.

'Mamie May, if you pull out at this stage of the competition ...' Raymond didn't know what to say next. 'I just hope we won't have to start the whole shebang over again.' He turned to the judges. 'We won't, sure we won't?'

Mamie May cut in. 'No, you won't, Raymond. Even though most people here think that I'm thick, I'm not and I've combed the rule book, cover to cover, and it says that as long as Azra completes all the stages of tonight's heats, she can be declared the rightful winner.'

The lights being used were almost blinding her but, even so, Mamie May could make out that Colin was walking towards the exit, tripping over handbags and umbrellas as he went. It seemed clear from his demeanour that her actions had not had the desired effect. He appeared angry and not in any way interested in forgiving her, as she had hoped he would. But what else could she do to rectify all these years of hurt and betrayal, she wondered, despair filling her heart.

'Colin, wait!' she shouted. 'I know how I'll make it up to you once and for all.'

What she did next might not have been necessary if she had only realised that the man from whom she wanted forgiveness more than anything in the world had not been rushing out of the function room in a rage. He was actually making his way to the stage to give her a hug – albeit taking the long way around, as a child who had clearly over-indulged on fizzy drinks was throwing up all across the centre aisle. Contrary to what Mamie May had thought, her act of contrition had touched him. She had finally acknowledged the heartbreak she had caused, something that he would have expected from the old Mamie May who, it now emerged, had not wholly disappeared.

But so many of the world's most historic events had occurred as a consequence of misunderstandings and misinterpretations, and this one was no different.

Mamie May handed the microphone back to Raymond and dashed to the area behind the stage where the nine tables from earlier in the event stood, all of which were still perfectly set with beautiful centrepieces, floral arrangements and fine china.

And cutlery.

She grabbed the nearest knife she could find and returned to the stage.

'Colin, I'm really and truly sorry for all that I did to you. I love you and always will.'

She stretched her leg out in front of her.

'It won't forgive what I did, but this is to say sorry for the cheating at the wife-carrying competition. If it wasn't for Freddie kicking you with this leg ...'

Screams of horror echoed throughout the entire hotel as Mamie May raised the knife and stabbed herself in the thigh. As she collapsed to the ground, an army of attendees dashed to her rescue.

'Nobody came to *my* rescue,' Neville Merriman was heard to mutter in the back of the room.

The well-meaning helpers were quickly pushed aside by Colin, who ignored the sharp pain in his ankle and was by his true love's side in a split second.

'Mamie May,' he roared, his heart smashed to absolute smithereens. 'What have you done?'

It had come as an incredible surprise to Mamie May that the stabbing of her leg had not hurt in the slightest. The night when she had seen her nephew's school production of *Hamlet* flashed in her memory.

'Jesus, they really overdid their reactions to the knifings,' she retrospectively critiqued, now that she had first-hand experience of the deed.

It was when she heard Ursula Higgins – who had made a sudden reappearance – that Mamie May realised her spontaneous attempts for redemption had failed.

'My magic knife!' Ursula exclaimed. 'It's fake! She hasn't stabbed herself at all.'

As sighs and endless oh-thank-heavens-for-thats followed, the young boy with the upset stomach approached Ursula and tugged on her beautiful mauve dress.

'Were you going to do magic tricks for your party piece?' the child asked, wiping his mouth.

He turned to his friend. 'Barry, she does magic!'

Barry then turned to his friend. 'Ruth, she does magic!'

Before Ursula knew it, a gang of hyper children had surrounded her.

'Yes, lady, show us what you can do!'

Buoyed by their earnest requests, Ursula retrieved the bloodless knife and took centre stage. What came after was so incredible that in its report the following week, *The Meath Chronicle* claimed that 'her rabbit trick was so intricate and sophisticated, the audience was left pulling its own *hare* out'.

Even Mamie May and Colin, standing together by the side of the stage, revelled in the exciting spectacle – the perfect antidote to the earlier drama.

This merriment was not to last for long, however.

SIXTY-NINE

It wasn't Freddie's forehead alone that enjoyed a bloody status – after the relentless pounding he had engaged in while trying to escape the coffin, his fists were in a similar state. The actual box itself wasn't fashioned from sturdy materials; its prisoner could easily have smashed his way out of it if only he had more room to take a proper swing at it. He had tried kicking it and kneeing it, but it didn't have the desired effect. In fact, it didn't have any effect, other than further frustrating him.

He had given up yelling, knowing that such attempts were futile – how could his raspy, cigarette-damaged voice compete with the microphone-enhanced tomfoolery that was at play within the function room? Oh, how he rued the day he sabotaged his simple yet bulletproof plan by agreeing to play the role of that weasel's sidekick.

Bit of an own goal, don't you think? Not even Mamie May would have been such a half-witted imbecile! he chastised himself as an image of his mother loomed above the coffin. *You never knew how to quit while you were ahead, did you?*

Yes, his hard-won, explosive slides remained in his pocket, but they weren't going to have any effect loitering in between his wallet and house keys, were they?

'Oh, come on!' he roared, eyes closed. 'Get me out of this fuc–'

And, just like that, the lid opened and Ursula, his captor, beamed down upon him.

'We're on!'

'Yeah, good luck with that,' he replied, hoisting himself out of the contraption. 'I have something important to attend to.'

'No problem, Councillor – I know a few children who would only be delighted to help out!'

Before he disappeared out of view altogether, he turned to Ursula and forced a smile.

'Take your time with your magic, will you? I have a few things to set up, and I'll need a few minutes.'

Ursula was only halfway through her rapturously received performance at this point, and from the first hint of applause, she had taken up residence on Cloud Nine and had no intention of upping sticks anytime soon.

'You can count on me, Councillor,' she replied, before carrying the coffin onto the stage. 'I am in no rush at all.'

SEVENTY

'So, Azra, tell us how you make a happy home?'

Azra stood on the stage, aware that she would be announced as the overall winner of the heats as soon as she completed this second interview. She had arrived on stage nearly a full hour later than anticipated – thanks to Mamie May's botched attempt at martyrdom and Mrs Higgins' rather lovely display of wizardry. With the prize in the bag, so to speak, she decided that she would take this opportunity to enjoy watching the sweat pour from her former clients in the audience. She suspected, quite rightly, that they were petrified at the thought of what she might say.

But discretion was part and parcel of being a prized concubine, and even though she now realised how false marriage could often be – and would certainly enjoy some of the smug couples in the audience getting a shock – she wasn't going to betray her code now. That didn't mean she couldn't have a little fun watching the men squirm, particularly seeing as the pressure was off.

'How long do you have, Raymond?'

'Not long.'

'I see. Well, your mother taught me an expression, "an apple a day, keeps the doctor away". I have said that right?'

'You certainly have.'

'My version is, "a massage a day, keeps the doctor away!"'

A few dry coughs echoed through the hall.

'Tell us then, Azra,' the compère pressed, trying to stifle a yawn, 'what altruistic activities have you partaken in?'

'I was a concubine, Raymond, and I operated a one-woman harem from my beloved Oliver's house for over a year,' was the response she would have secretly delighted in giving. Her actual response was: 'Without going into specifics, let's say that I have always felt it my duty to service the community.'

'You can say that again!'

The entire auditorium turned towards the voice that had come from somewhere towards the back of the room.

'Is that what prostitutes call it these days? "Servicing"?'

A blast of fireworks paled in comparison to the explosions throughout the room that followed this accusation.

'What's all this talk of prostitutes?'

'Who's a hoor?'

'Disgusting talk!'

A cocksure Freddie swaggered down the aisle and, as the bedlam was gaining momentum, stopped next to his brother, who was sitting beside Mamie May in the front row. He placed a hand on his shoulder.

'You have always had difficulties with your hearing, Colin, so in case you missed what I said, I thought I'd bring along some visuals.'

Freddie – who had earlier given the guy who was overseeing the projector a few bob to vanish – displayed a series of shocking images onto the wall behind Azra on stage with the help of a remote control.

'I hope the judges score Azra highly for her fantastic work ethic,' Freddie continued.

Owing to his sexual orientation, Raymond was one of the very few men present who was genuinely shocked by the councillor's revelation. He looked towards Azra, who remained centre stage, before turning to the two remaining judges to see if they had any thoughts about how best to proceed with the situation: they had not; they were too busy attempting to lift their jaws off the floor.

'There are many people here tonight who have started their own enterprises,' Freddie continued, storming the stage and taking the microphone from Raymond's grip, 'and I am sure that they could write books detailing how difficult it is getting a business off the ground.'

He placed his arm around Azra.

'For this lady here – and I don't want to sound like a boastful brother-in-law when I say this – she has never faced any teething problems. I should not be revealing this information, I suppose – the tax man will be soon knocking on her door!'

Freddie grabbed a chair from the edge of the stage and sat down; he had more to discuss and thought it best to take the weight off his tired feet.

'From the start, without having to print a single poster or pamphlet, it appears that Azra was inundated with customers,' he explained, pointing towards the montage on the screen behind them. 'If you look at the images currently showing on the wall, you might even recognise some of the faces – or naked bodies.'

'Gerry!'

'Martin, you bastard!'

'This is the thanks I get for allowing your blasted mother to move in with us, Austin?'

One by one, images of Azra and her many clients in various stages of undress flashed across the wall. Mrs Brady was just short of having a heart attack at the sight of her husband on the screen. (At home that night, it would be Mr Brady who'd wish he'd had a heart attack – it would certainly have been more pleasant than what his scorned wife subjected him to!)

How Freddie relished every single moment of the fallout that was spreading throughout the room, even if several of the chairs being hurled at Azra had made contact with him.

'Don't forget to vote for me in the upcoming elections, guys! A vote for Alfred Saint James is a vote for common decency!'

Yes, along with losing a few votes, he would probably acquire a few bruises to go along with the gash on his forehead, but they would fade away; the scene that was unfolding in front of him would not. He'd cherish it forever.

Punching.

Slapping.

Hair-pulling.

Kicking.

Head-locking.

Spitting.

Shouting.

Crying.

The two cameramen from RTÉ television salivated at the mouth. They were filming once-in-a-lifetime footage that had the potential to be seen around the world. How they prayed that they wouldn't run out of tape!

As the carnage continued, Azra's instinct was to slip out before the angry mob booked her a one-way flight to the pearly gates. She had been in enough precarious positions over the years to know when it was best to make an early exit. But as she studied the conceited grin on Freddie's face, something stirred within her.

Defiance.

So, rather than exiting stage right, she decided upon a better solution. She sat on a chair, crossed her legs – a position that so few present were used to seeing – and gave her new relation the finger!

'I assume you'll be joining us for Christmas this year, Councillor?'

Elsewhere, quick-thinking staff emerged from behind the bar with not just whiskey to calm nerves but also buckets of ice to soothe black eyes. One of the technicians attempted to diffuse the situation by blaring a little Debussy from the speakers; however, it had the opposite effect, and the dramatic notes only encouraged more violence. Even the elderly members of the audience got involved – their frail hands might not have been strong enough to land heavy blows, but their walking sticks certainly could.

Terrence Walsh, the hotel's manager, took to the stage and pleaded for order. 'Ladies and gentleman, I am sure you will agree that we have all experienced a pleasant time here tonight – and it would be such a shame if sordid revelations sullied it at the last moment. Maybe we could all make our way towards the exit and resolve any personal difficulties in private – and not here in my lovely hotel.'

As expected, his few words did not have the desired effect, so minutes later, Mr Walsh wisely decided to involve the local Garda station. (So long as Garda Maguire, whose face was currently gracing the screen, was not on duty, they would be sure to assist.)

The manager wasn't the only person present who tried to restore calm in the auditorium.

'If you'll excuse me,' Colin said to the people sitting around him, many demanding answers. Even though the damage had already been done, he hoped to limit it by putting an end to the X-rated show-and-tell currently provoking the attendees. His aim was to get to the back of the aisle to where the projector stood and turn off the contraption that was currently revealing the secrets of many of the town's more lascivious residents. Within metres of his target, his eyes noticed that a lead, which was connected to the projector, was plugged into a socket on the back wall. All he had to do was yank it out.

En route, he passed an elevated platform where an elderly nun in a wheelchair sat. Given her nondescript facial expression, Colin wondered if the startling confessions had gone over her head or, having lived through civil wars and world wars, she was merely indifferent to the revelations. Before he could give any more thought to the matter, a maddened wife stormed in his direction and gave him an almighty push.

'You should be ashamed of yourself, Colin! And here we all were, feeling sorry for you.'

Whether it was her civic-duty convictions or the eight bottles of Ritz she had consumed that evening, the force of the woman's actions was so great that Colin went crash bang into the wheelchair-bound sister behind him, resulting in the bride of Christ crashing into the crowd with a loud thud.

All around, everyone had jumped to their feet and in addition to insults and chairs, they were now hurling anything they could get their hands on – tables, glasses, bottles, even pictures pulled from the walls. But it wasn't just disloyal, philandering husbands who were at the receiving end of punches and boxes; now that it was a free-for-all, many took advantage of this once-in-a-lifetime opportunity to settle a few scores, and they gladly released their inner barbarians. Sheila Durkin, who had not complimented Goretti Newman's new handbag that evening, got a wallop to the back of her head. Wayne Ford tripped Mandy Davis, a woman who had refused to be his date to the Debs fifteen years earlier. Fittingly, Wendy Smith received a pinch on the arm from Julia Oates, seeing as the new mother had recently pinched her baby's exotic name, Rocco.

As the chaos continued, Colin hurried towards the socket on all fours. His adrenaline resulted in him being immune to the various kicks and knocks he suffered along the way. A couple of metres shy of his target, a random, child-free pram crossed his path, stealing valuable seconds from his mission. He got up, and while his head told him to push the pram away, his body, ablaze with excitement, tried to hurdle it. As such, as he powered forward, he toppled over the pram and became ensnared in the lead, somehow managing to tear it partly from the projector, freezing the image above the stage rather than switching it off entirely.

And the face that remained fixed to the screen? Azra's glazier, who had been the unwitting recipient of Colin's baked Alaska.

Father Cutbirth.

SEVENTY-ONE

The function room was destroyed. The fire that had started when the projector was finally hurled against the sound system had been extinguished by one of the night's guests, local firefighter Barry Nolan (his wife was one of the few women who felt any pride for their husbands that evening). The contents of the bar had either been consumed or flung around the function room. The stained carpet was fit for the scrapheap; the broken windows were fit for nothing.

Navan had let itself down in front of the national broadcaster and while they had enough footage to produce a film worthy of the Oscars, one of the quick-thinking members of the Chamber of Commerce had taken advantage of the madness and propelled the two cameras out the window.

What happens in Navan stays in Navan.

The now-crooked posters of the original Mrs Saint James overlooked the carnage as a lone Colin sat amongst the rubble. He was convinced that he could detect a look of disgust in her eyes; not even a bomb would have been so inconsiderate to the venue.

You always knew Freddie was a rotten scoundrel, Mummy. But I always wondered if you'd perhaps been a little kinder ...

Azra returned from the ladies' and sat beside him in silence, allowing him to continue gathering his thoughts. He'd a lot to process.

'I am surprised that I don't feel more contempt for my brother,' he finally said, although his mumbling words suggested that he was speaking for his own benefit. 'I'm not angry that, once again, he was the catalyst for my public humiliation, it's more ... I am just realising that I've been ever so foolish over the decades, allowing my brother to dictate each sentence of my life's story.'

His thoughts turned to Mamie May. Despite her best attempts at atoning this evening, it did not change the fact that she had not turned out to be the woman that, at one point, he had hoped she would be. From an early age, Colin had always known that she was easily led, but in 1977 she had also proven herself to be the one thing that could not be justified or condoned.

'Disloyal.'

'Sorry?' Azra asked, her husband's random words now leading her to wonder if he had been too hasty in refusing a medical examination.

Still, Colin continued in his head, *was it not, in fact, better that I discovered her heart was not fully mine before committing to each other for life? Granted, there might have been a more sensitive means of breaking off an engagement rather than eloping to Dublin with my older sibling, but, in life, I have learned that there is no ideal way of revealing the truth …*

'As many Navan couples would currently attest!'

Azra didn't quite understand why he was laughing and muttering to himself but decided that she should get him home as quickly as possible.

'I'm just going to get my belongings backstage,' she said. 'Don't go anywhere.'

Alone again, Colin now realised that he should have allowed that life-altering moment in 1977 to fuel and inspire him. Instead, he had dedicated his life to hiding away from that heartbreak or getting revenge.

Why?

All of those many years he had spent doubled over his desk, doing homework and receiving top scores in his class, they had all been wasted. Thanks to his parents' sizeable coffers, he could have achieved anything in life. He could have been a scientist, an astronaut, even better – a world-class baker! But, instead, he had chosen to spend his years either licking his wounds or planning to inflict new ones on his brother. Now, as he sat amongst ruins, he finally realised that his greatest enemy all his life had been himself. As he watched Azra return, he was struck by how stunning she was – almost for the first time.

Colin, you are married to a prostitute for heaven's sake but rather than making up for years of near-celibacy, you politely refused her advances last night and demanded that she get an early night before the competition. Regardless of what all those As in your school copybooks might suggest, you are not the brightest pupil in the classroom, are you?

He still had time to remedy his wrongdoings.

'I think it's time we went home, Mrs Saint James,' he said to Azra, offering her his hand.

'Definitely time we went home, Mr Saint James,' she replied.

'If I might be so bold as to enquire, does last night's offer still stand?'

She smiled, but before she could answer, the door of the function room opened.

It was Mamie May.

'You're still here; I thought I might have missed you.'

She approached the pair and, as she stopped in front of them, removed a small box from her handbag.

'I have something that belongs to Azra.'

She opened the box and within it proudly sat the Saint James' heirloom.

'But I thought ...' Colin spluttered. The last thing he foresaw happening this evening was a reunion with the stunning ring he thought his brother had squandered in some seedy poker game on the night of his wedding years ago.

'Yes, he did gamble away a ring but not this one. I know I can be dumb at times, but not dumb enough to leave such a prized possession in his care. "I'll get it cleaned," says he! No, the ring that the Spanish sailor won off him back in the seventies was a fake – and not even a good one. I was shocked that I even got away with it, to be honest! They must have been drunk as skunks!'

A smile crept across Colin's face.

Mamie May shrugged. 'Anyway, it doesn't belong to me anymore – it belongs to you,' she continued, handing it to Azra. 'You probably never thought that one day you'd receive a beautiful pear-shaped rock like that, did you?'

This time, it was Azra who was compelled to smile.

'Let's meet for coffee tomorrow and I'll tell you an interesting story.'

EPILOGUE

2019

Even if Colin had had a crystal ball at the time, he wouldn't have been able to predict the changes Ireland experienced in the years following the colourful Meath heats in the Beechmount Hotel.

In the final-ever nationwide Housewife of the Year competition in 1995, Meath's eventual representative, Ursula Higgins, was pipped to the post by an enchanting Philomena Delaney, but the magician received an unexpected runners-up prize when she was subsequently approached by a talent-spotting producer and asked to make a pilot for her own magic show.

Colin was tickled pink at the thought of his late wife annoying everyone in heaven following the news of Ireland's unstoppable success in the Eurovision Song Contest, winning for a record-breaking seventh time in 1996 thanks to the angelic voice of Eimear Quinn.

Most interestingly of all, the traditions of marriage were dramatically reimagined in the years following the Housewife competition. Divorce finally became an option for unhappily espoused couples in the country thanks to a referendum. First in the queue? Mamie May.

More recently, the country took to the polls and voted to amend the constitution to allow for same-sex marriage. One of the highlights of Colin's life was acting as best man for his dear friend Raymond (the wedding took place on the ninetieth birthday of the groom's mother, thereby affording him an opportunity to steal Mrs Brady's thunder for a change).

On a personal level, after all the chaos of the Housewife of the Year competition, things had become quite pleasant for Colin – despite the couple becoming social pariahs thanks to the revelations about Azra's profession. Being outcasts afforded them the opportunity to really get to know each other and he was extremely pleased to learn that Azra made a wonderful wife, and he, in turn, did his utmost to be a wonderful husband.

Azra also had plenty of time to perfect her many recipes and, together, the duo spent endless hours in the kitchen, cooking and baking. Colin quickly pronounced that her talents were not just limited to the bedroom – a claim that he could now proudly vouch for himself.

It wasn't just at home where Colin worked up a sweat, as another satisfying aspect of his life post-Housewife fiasco was that he enjoyed long walks along the ramparts every few days with Mamie May, weather permitting. They both knew that their relationship would never be anything other than friendship, but that suited them both well enough. They just wanted to catch up on all those years apart. Every time they parted ways, Colin would remind her of her silliness during the night of the heats by humming the Bryan Adams song 'Cuts like a Knife', much to Mamie May's mock annoyance. She thanked her lucky stars hourly that said weapon was of the magic variety and had not done the damage she had intended to cause in her moment of madness. There were more successful ways of getting the point across than stabbing yourself in the leg in front of the entire county, she often reminded herself.

Luckily, stories have shelf lives and, over time, as the population of Navan multiplied, with new arrivals descending upon the town daily thanks to its close proximity to Dublin, Colin and Azra were slowly welcomed back into the fold – although the former concubine was rarely left alone with any randy married men.

Instead of occupying the entire house by themselves, they decided that they wanted the splendid property to be enjoyed by others. They sold Azra's side to a young Dublin family who were friendly and considerate and, unlike Azra's stint in the property, there was not a hint of anything untoward taking place – unless the husband's insistence on hanging his home county's flag from the bedroom window during the All-Ireland Football Championships could be counted.

With the money received from the sale of Oliver's side of the house, the irrepressible duo opened their own bakery on Navan's Market Square, which celebrated all things Irish and Turkish. As a tribute to the square's newly erected stone sculpture, the Bull of Navan, they decided to call their bakery the Istanbull Bakery.

***

It was while checking over the Istanbull's healthy accounts, one late afternoon in 2019, that Colin thought he heard a knock on the door. His neighbours were on their annual holiday to Connemara, and the rest of the town was likely glued to the television screens, watching the Meath team battle it out in an All-Ireland match, so he wondered who it might be – if it was anyone; his hearing had been known to confuse the poor fellow on more than one occasion. He opened the door and found the last person he expected to see on the other side.

Freddie.

Without so much as a smile, the ex-councillor grunted 'Finally', and shortly thereafter barged straight past Colin, making his way into the kitchen.

'I'll make myself scarce,' Azra suggested, taking a pot of pilaf off the boil.

The two brothers had not been in the same space since that ill-fated night almost twenty-five years earlier, although Colin had taken great pleasure at Freddie's embarrassing defeat in the local elections that soon followed the heats.

Freddie's uninvited presence in the house displeased Colin greatly. Yes, he had made his peace with their relationship, but that didn't mean he wanted to spend any time with his brother, shooting the breeze as it were.

'Something smells nice,' Freddie commented as a way of breaking the ice.

'Azra is making dinner.'

'I thought it was you who was the chef. Mummy would be so disappointed.'

'Indeed.'

An awkward silence monopolised the room. Colin could see that something was troubling his brother. Being the dutiful host, he turned on the kettle and started to prepare some tea as Freddie sat down at the kitchen table. He had no buns or cakes left to offer as he had made a couple of 'Have a Great Holiday' goodie bags for the children next door. But even if he had brought home the entire contents of the Istanbull Bakery, he probably would not have given his brother anything. Yes, he was the bigger man these days, but only just.

The younger sibling delighted in the fact that the only sound in the kitchen was the whistle of the kettle – he suspected Freddie had something to reveal but hump him if he expected Colin to do the work for him.

After a seemingly endless period of time, the kettle boiled, and Colin made the tea. He laid two cups and the pot on the table in front of his unexpected guest and went to the fridge to retrieve some milk.

'I don't know if you take sugar or not,' Colin mentioned, realising that there were very few things about his brother that he actually did know.

'I couldn't care less about sugar, Colin. I need your help.'

Freddie slumped back in the chair and closed his eyes. Colin noticed how yellow-ish and weak he looked – a far cry from the man who had terrorised him for most of his life.

'What seems to be the problem?' Colin quizzed, although he kept his tone neutral; he was enjoying this far too much to ruin it by revealing any concern.

'I have just come from the hospital.'

'I see.'

Silence, once again.

'Do you have anything stronger than flippin' tea? We're not two nuns, are we?'

Colin fished a near-empty bottle of brandy out from one of the cupboards. It was covered in flour; its purpose in the house was for culinary reasons alone.

'Don't worry about a glass,' Freddie grunted and snatched the bottle from him. He took a large mouthful and, courage found, he looked directly into his only sibling's eyes.

'I saw a specialist this morning, who told me that my kidneys are no longer functioning properly.'

'I see,' Colin replied.

Freddie polished off the contents of the bottle. Noticing that his brother could do with a refill, Colin asked if he could get him something else. 'I don't have any more alcohol here, but I could see if the neighbours next door have anything – I have a spare key.'

'I don't want their fucking drink, Colin – I want your kidney. If not, I will not last the year.'

And there it was, the moment Colin had craved for so long.

Power over his brother.

Following the Housewife of the Year competition, Colin had genuinely thought that it was something that he did not need in his life, but to see Freddie squirm like this was just as gratifying as he had always imagined it would be.

Any remnants of hurt or anger finally faded away. Despite what Alfred Saint James had thought, he was fallible after all and not the indestructible force that he claimed. This bombshell would surely teach him a dollop of humility at long last, he reasoned.

Colin's mind turned then to Mamie May's children, his nephews and niece, and he wondered how they might take this information. They were adults themselves now, of course – and Colin knew that they had never had a close relationship with their father – but it would still be something of a shock he imagined. And what of himself? How did he feel at the thought of not having his brother in the world, even one who had caused him so much heartbreak over the years?

'Actually, on second thoughts, maybe pop in next door and grab something off them,' Freddie said, the suspense proving too much for him.

Still processing the news and subsequent request, Colin reached for the set of keys on the windowsill that his neighbours had given him for safekeeping. He made his way out through the pantry and, as he walked the few steps towards their back door, he mulled over the request and realised that no matter how much he would love to refuse, such an act was not in his nature. Besides, Freddie had already broken his heart; he may as well swipe a kidney, too.

He entered his neighbours' kitchen, which had once been the Saint James' main kitchen. He bent down in front of one of the many cupboards and opened it. He knew that within stood a healthy supply of beer and other alcoholic beverages that would be much appreciated by his brother. He didn't want to abuse their trust, however, and so retrieved just two, but as he reached in to lift them out, his hand brushed against a tattered sheet of paper. Colin would not have thought anything of it only for the fact that the handwriting that was scrawled across it looked familiar. It couldn't be, could it?

He placed the bottles on the floor in front of him and retrieved the page from the cupboard. He sat down on a chair nearby and started reading what was on it. He'd been right; the handwriting was his mother's. It read:

I hate that evil child with every fibre of my body. My husband suggested cutting down that oak tree in the garden the other day – as if its absence could erase from my memory the part it played in that dreadful act when I was pregnant with my darling Colin. People keep stopping me in the street, praising me for my success at the Housewife of the Year competition. If only they knew what an unhappy home we actually keep.

Even though the clear majority of what was on the sheet was incoherent ramblings, for the first time in sixty years Colin finally discovered the likely reason behind his hearing difficulties. It had not been down to his mother's apparent drinking splurges, as he'd been told time and time again by Freddie – a story he'd always been sceptical of – but because his older sibling had tried to kill him while he innocently lay in the womb.

He read and re-read what his late mother had written, and the cycle was only interrupted when he heard his impatient brother next door, cursing and blinding, most likely because he was being denied his alcohol.

Moments later, Colin returned to his own kitchen, empty-handed.

'Where's the drink?'

Colin shook his head and led a confused Freddie down the hallway and out through the front door. As they stood on the threshold, Colin's gaze fell upon the oak tree that stood halfway down the driveway. He didn't know why he felt compelled to do so, but he thought that he would attempt to prise Freddie's version of the actual story out of him. Maybe the combination of his weak physical state along with the alcohol he had just imbibed would loosen his tongue.

'Mummy told me about the tree before she died,' Colin lied.

'You are not going to bring that up now, are you?'

'How do you remember it, Freddie? I would be interested in hearing your version.'

'For God's sake, Colin. Why are you so selfish? Today is about me, not about the time that alcoholic tripped on her shoelaces in front of the tree because she was as drunk as a skunk! Yes, you became partially deaf as a result, but at least you didn't die, did you? Unlike me, if you don't give me your kidney.'

'Why did you attach a wire to the tree, Freddie?' Colin asked, trying to keep his emotions in check; after all, it was not every day that you discovered that your wretched brother was even worse than you could possibly have imagined.

Realising that the cat was out of the proverbial bag, Freddie tried to downplay the gravity of the situation.

'Fake news, as they say! Alternative facts!'

Colin did not appear amused.

'It was a joke! For God's sake, Colin – build a bridge and get over it! I was only a child; I didn't understand what I was doing, not really.'

'And stealing Mamie May? The wife-carrying competition? The Housewife of the Year competition? You weren't a child then, were you?'

Freddie turned away from Colin, his shoulders slumped. 'I was … jealous, I suppose. Threatened.'

'I see.'

Colin looked at the tree. Today was a day of firsts: for the first time, his brother had asked him for a favour. For the first time, he discovered why he had been rendered partially deaf. For the first time, Colin felt truly emancipated.

'To give you a reply about your kidney situation, Freddie.'

'Yes?' Freddie said, facing his brother again. His bloodshot eyes were full of hope and spite.

'I'll think about it.'

With that, Colin slammed the door shut in his brother's face.

ACKNOWLEDGEMENTS

I would like to thank:

My parents, Máire and Seán, for the never-ending devotion shown to me and my siblings over the years.

My mentor, Alexander Fitzgerald, and his darling mother, Ethna, for welcoming me into their beautiful home in Marbella, where I wrote the first draft of this book.

My agent and dear friend, Lorraine Brennan, and all the staff at LB Management. We did it, my loves!

Jill Guest and the Turkish Tourist Board for hosting me in the magical city of Istanbul on behalf of *Woman's Way* – a press trip commissioned by one of the kindest magazine editors in Ireland, Áine Toner.

The archive team in RTÉ, Patriece Dwyer from Calor Gas, and Mia Ylönen from Finland for helping me research the Calor Kosangas Housewife of the Year competition and the wife-carrying competition.

My second family, *Ros na Rún - míle buíochas as ucht bhur tacaíocht uilig.*

Máire Ní Mháille for inviting me into her beautiful home in Connemara – a location from where the edits for this book were attempted.

My friends who I forced to read various incarnations of this manuscript – Alexander, Lorraine, Vanessa Keogh, Eamonn Norris, Gayle Norman, Stephen Wall and my brother, Déaglán.

My boyfriend, Gabriele Bianchi, and our cat, Prince, for keeping me company as I tackled new drafts.

My best friend, Betty – just for being awesome.

Standún Department Store, Blackbird Books, Sinéad Burke, Gillian McCarthy, Christina Edge, Louise Ferriter, Gina Trench and Tirgearr Publishing for their support with my first book, *Sister Agatha*.

The incredible team at Mercier Press – Patrick O'Donoghue, Deirdre Roberts, Aileen Ferris, Alice Coleman and, in particular, my editor, Noel O'Regan, and the editorial project manager, Wendy Logue, whose magnificent insights are evident everywhere throughout this final manuscript. Also my proofreader, Bobby Francis.

Last, but by no means least, the brothel that operated in the apartment next to me in Dublin back in 2016. Yes, you and your clients kept me up all night, but at least you provided me with insider knowledge for this book! Wherever you are now, ladies, I do hope that you are safe.

Míle buíochas.

ABOUT THE AUTHOR

Hailing from Navan, Domhnall O'Donoghue works as an actor and journalist, dividing his time between Dublin, Venice and Galway, where he films TG4's award-winning series *Ros na Rún*. Domhnall has written for the majority of Ireland's leading newspapers and magazines, including the *Irish Independent*, *The Irish Times* and *Irish Tatler Man*. He also writes a monthly column in *Woman's Way*, the country's biggest-selling weekly magazine. His first novel, *Sister Agatha: the World's Oldest Serial Killer*, was published in 2016.